# THE PROMISE

*Also by Alison Bruce*

Cambridge Blue
The Siren
The Calling
The Silence
The Backs

# THE PROMISE

Alison Bruce

Constable • London

CONSTABLE

First published in 2016 by Constable

A CIP catalogue record for this book
is available from the British Library.

ISBN: 978-1-47211-226-2 (hardback)
ISBN: 978-1-47211-232-3 (ebook)
ISBN: 978-1-47212-261-2 (trade paperback)

Typeset in Times by TW Typesetting, Plymouth, Devon
Printed and bound by CPI Group (UK) Ltd, Croydon, CR0 4YY
Papers used by Constable are from well-managed forests and other responsible sources.

MIX
Paper from
responsible sources
FSC
www.fsc.org   FSC® C104740

Constable
is an imprint of
Little, Brown Book Group
Carmelite House
50 Victoria Embankment
London EC4Y 0DZ

An Hachette UK Company
www.hachette.co.uk

www.littlebrown.co.uk

*This book is dedicated, with much love,*
*to Stella*
*my wonderful sister and equally wonderful friend.*

# PROLOGUE

The document archive reminded PC Sue Gully of the final scene in *Raiders of the Lost Ark*, the one where the all-important crate was slipped in amongst so many others that it disappeared.

This building was modest by comparison, but the effect was the same and her ark was in here somewhere. Or so she hoped. The shelves were stacked with document boxes, some containing details of a single case, others packed with many small files of other logs and registers, each filled with hundreds of names.

Much of the newer information had been digitalized but the project to go from the mid-1990s backwards had stalled, so the luxury of accessing the information from the desktop didn't exist. She was on her own. Literally.

Her hair was two shades darker brunette now and had grown just long enough to tie back into a ponytail; she tightened it, blew her fringe from her eyes, then lifted the next box from the shelf, stacking the library trolley and only wheeling it away when it was fully laden. She used a small square table in the corner furthest from the door, the kind with metal legs that schools use for exams and dinner break. It faced a wall covered in health and safety advice posters.

The surroundings were uninspiring but, if she'd learnt one thing from the death of her friend, it was the importance of moving forwards with the meaningful things in life. Searching amongst these boxes for the answers to a very personal cold case had ceased to be a 'one day I will' kind of plan, and she didn't need any further inspiration than that. So far she'd spent about four months of her spare time amongst the faint smells of printer ink, paper and whiffs of sawdust that reminded her of rodent cages and mouse droppings, reading until the dust aggravated her eyes and left her fingertips feeling greasy and grey. Not knowing a criminal's name didn't help of course; she had to follow every possibility, jumping between files and ruling out long-shots. She moved on to the second file of the second box and hesitated. A very familiar name jumped out to greet her: 'Goodhew'.

She ran her index finger across it. Everything this box held was from 1992, too long ago surely to have any connection to Gary. How old would he have been back then? Eleven? Twelve? She would have moved on to the next page immediately but her gaze was faster than her hands and had already picked out the address in Park Terrace, Gary's house.

It seemed a strange phenomenon; looking for one thing and invariably coming across another. There ought to be a scientific term for it; there probably was. In this case she'd found a name which seemed to be in both the wrong time and the wrong place.

She'd already followed a paper trail to get to this box, skipping from witness statements to charge sheets before finding her next option was to check unsolved cases from the spring of 1985 onwards. The cases in this box weren't closed, but dormant, still theoretically capable of bursting into life, and a distraction wasn't what she needed right now. She'd set her mind against diversions of any kind but, if there was to be an unexpected tangent, it was fitting that the name 'Goodhew' was stamped across it.

She cleared the surface of the table, leaving just the one bundle of papers in front of her. The pages were secured with green tie-tags wound through an inch-thick sheaf of hole-punched pages with the form where she'd spotted Goodhew's name the uppermost sheet. The information on it was minimal; surname, address, case number and the document date. Next to category it read 'B & E'. Most of the page was taken up with a black box headed 'OUTCOME'. The black ballpoint ink had yellowed but not faded and read: 'Merged with case

CAM-GOODHEWJ-920716037'. It had been signed off with a squiggle of initials.

She didn't recognize the form and it gave no clue as to whether this Goodhew had been the victim or suspect. If knowing Gary was any indication, it could go either way.

She turned the page and began to read. The breaking and entry had occurred at Gary's house. The report had been made by a Joseph Goodhew. She checked the date of birth. Yes, Gary's grandfather.

She looked up from the papers and whispered the name to herself, 'Joseph Goodhew.' It sounded odd. 'Joe Goodhew.' Yes, that worked better. It also seemed odd that she'd never heard it before, particularly from Goodhew's grandmother. Gully's gaze dropped back to the page.

She read a few more paragraphs then stiffened.

The name she stared at now was far more familiar: 'DC Marks'. Her fingers had already lifted the corner of the page, poised to turn to the next but, instead, she lifted the whole document, raising it so that it filled her field of vision. DC Marks. Her boss's name was at the epicentre of her focus. The questions followed quickly, filling her thoughts. How had she never known that there was some kind of history between Marks and the Goodhew family? Why had Goodhew's grandmother never mentioned it? Was it so incidental that it had been long forgotten? Well, the answer to that question had to be 'no', especially since this page was directing her to another case entirely. She let the papers drop onto the table-top and worked her way through the indexing system until she located CAM-GOODHEWJ-920716037.

She pulled it from the shelving, opened the lid and immediately realized that the box and its contents belonged to a murder investigation. Joseph Goodhew's murder.

By then she only had a single question. Did Gary even know?

She sank down until she was sitting on the cold concrete. She held the top handful of pages on her lap but didn't begin to read them until the queasy feeling in her gut began to subside.

Instinct told her he had no idea.

At first the sound of Parkside Pool had felt too intense – arrhythmic and booming – and Gully had consequently found it too difficult to gather

her thoughts. But after several weeks the sounds had separated; she could now easily pick out the slap of the water and the words hidden in the echo-drenched shouts. There were other bonuses too – the temperature in the public gallery had been set to 'balmy June', and, more importantly, this ritual of meeting Goodhew after he swam helped her believe that he would return to work sometime soon. It was too easy to dwell on the moment that she'd seen her colleague, Kelly Wilkes, fall to her death from a rusting fire escape. Goodhew had been elsewhere, answering a different call, and she would never forget the moment when she heard that he lay seriously injured, possibly paralysed. She couldn't have done anything to save Kelly – neither of them could – but she instinctively knew that they both carried an illogical guilt.

Before his injury Goodhew had always swum and seeing him regain his fitness felt like a step towards normality. He'd gradually built up to his usual one hundred lengths per day and now his speed was almost back too. Not quite, but close.

She'd been certain that he'd swim again, even before she'd heard any news on his recovery. She'd moved desks and sat by a window that offered a better view of Parker's Piece, and often glanced towards his house. She could have phoned but didn't. By late autumn she had fallen into the habit of checking for him amongst the pedestrians crossing Parker's Piece; then, one Tuesday, she spotted him walking slowly from his home to the pool. Goodhew was close to six foot and lean, but from her window she could see that he'd lost weight and that his short hair had grown a little longer. After that first time he appeared more frequently, either first thing in the morning or in the early afternoon. He never seemed to carry a bag or towel but she always watched him until he disappeared inside the entrance, and sometimes she caught sight of him returning home, walking more quickly, often with his jumper or jacket in hand. She'd noted the timings and continued to check some more until he fell into a routine and she decided that she was ready to 'bump' into him.

'Gary?'

She'd caught him by surprise. His green eyes had double-blinked and he'd forced a smile.

'Sue, how are you?'

4

Despite always having found it so convenient to live close to Parkside she could now tell that he valued his privacy more; she realized then that she had never seen him glance at the station and he turned his back on it as they spoke. After a few minutes they fell into a polite but heavy silence.

'I'm about to swim,' he said finally, and took a step backwards in the direction of the pool, then another.

'You're OK then?'

He nodded and had clearly wanted her to do the same. She'd nodded, then he turned to walk away.

'Will you meet me afterwards, Gary?' she'd blurted. 'Let me know how it's going?'

He'd turned back to face her and she saw him frown, perhaps trying to think of an excuse. It had never occurred to her that this would turn into one of those *I-liked-you-when-I-worked-with-you* conversations. 'Coffee, if you like.'

She'd been tempted to come back at him with a comment about his obvious enthusiasm, but his expression remained as unreadable as it had been when they'd first met. 'It's not really a coincidence you're out here, is it?' he asked.

'No, not at all.' She'd scowled as she'd felt her cheeks redden. 'I've made it my personal mission to remind you to get back to work.' She said it firmly, forcing her words out in a fake bossy tone when her private fear was that he really wouldn't return.

He was quiet for a few seconds more, but it became easy after that.

The post-swim coffee had become a regular event and today, as with the other days in the last few weeks, she'd turned up just a few minutes before he finished his lengths. It had been a while since she'd felt it necessary to reassure herself of his progress by keeping stats; his lengths were smooth and fast. The rhythm had returned and so had the tone to his arms and shoulders.

The seating area ran in ascending rows down the long side of the pool, and faced out across Parker's Piece. They sat side by side looking in the general direction of Hobb's Pavilion and Goodhew's flat.

'Woman in the red coat.'

Goodhew tilted his head and picked her out, pushing a pram from the corner nearest the bus station and hurrying towards the centre. 'No,' he said, 'that one, the guy with the ear muffs.' Goodhew had picked a youngish man in a sombre grey mac, black trousers and turquoise ear muffs. No doubt the ear muffs were a Christmas present.

'Mine's going to win, it's one of those 4x4 performance buggies.'

It was their version of Pooh Sticks, picking two random strangers and guessing who would be the first to pass the lamppost where the paths crossed, which was known locally as Reality Checkpoint.

'Didn't you win last week?'

She shrugged. 'So?'

'So I should've chosen first; challenger breaks and all that?'

'Bad loser. You never pick anyone pushing a pram.' The buggy was yards from winning when she suddenly stopped to check inside the pram.

Goodhew grinned. 'And that's why. Coffee's on you.'

'I don't think so.' At the last moment the woman straightened and continued on, cutting in front of Mr Earmuff with just a couple of yards to spare.

'Pooh Checkpoint champion again.'

Gully grinned too and she nudged his elbow with her own. 'And biscuits?'

He brought back the drinks and this time they looked out across Parker's Piece in silence, and it occurred to Gully that they had got to know one another pretty well by not ever saying a whole lot. It seemed to her that the best way to understand some people was by exception; by learning who they weren't, what they wouldn't do and the events that made them turn away.

Neither of them had turned away from Kelly's fall, but they weren't turning to each other either. Whenever they were together she saw the shadow that Kelly's death had cast caught up in his expression. She sensed he could see the same in her too. Neither of them commented, but both of them knew. The *you-need-to-talk-about-it* brigade were undoubtedly correct; there'd be a price to pay for failing to put it into words. Tough shit. She wasn't taking that route, she'd keep her grieving to herself and some of it would pass; the moment Kelly died never would. And it would be wrong if it did, so she accepted that as more than fair.

'Sue?'

She turned. 'What?'

'Did you hear a single word?'

'What did you say?'

'Just your name several times. What were you thinking just then?'

'Absolutely nothing. But here's a question for you, Gary, what do you do when you're too incapacitated to poke your nose where it doesn't belong. Like now, when you're not on a case?'

'I don't think about anything either.'

'Such a liar,' she muttered, her words lost as the public address system rumbled through an announcement. She had so much she needed to tell him, but first, she needed to see him return to work.

# PART ONE

# ONE

The house they rented was small, but still they'd been lucky to end up with it. Cambridge's property market meant racing to secure anything worth living in. *Worth living in.* In relation to their house the phrase was certainly dubious. It had too much damp in the bathroom, too much mileage in the kitchen and far too much of the 1980s in every other room. But it was this or a rented flat over a shop in Cherry Hinton. Hannah liked the idea of the flat, convenient for the shops and the bus route into town.

She'd never stopped to consider why Cherry Hinton was absolutely out of the question.

Instead he talked her round to the idea of this rundown post-war end of terrace in Barnwell Road. The convenience of his mother living five minutes away had swung it; Hannah loved the thought that babysitting would be pretty much on tap. And Kyle had loved the simple fact that there would be an upstairs. One floor good, two floors better had sprung to mind. He didn't share the thought with Hannah, she was the reason the second floor appealed so much. Or maybe spreading themselves over two separate floors was their relationship's best chance of survival.

Right this minute the plan seem to be failing.

'Your mum's happy to have Harry tonight,' she told him.

Despite starting out with good intentions of spending time with her, so far he had done little apart from watch the slightly hypnotic pattern of the rolling news. She was animated, where he felt lethargic. 'I don't think we should wake him now, Hannah, I'll stay with him. You go.'

He caught the tiniest widening of her eyes, the softening of her mouth. 'You don't mind?' she asked.

'No, it's fine.'

A knowing look flashed across her face. She'd expected him not to come, already arranged company, he guessed.

He went through the pretence. 'You can't go on your own.'

'No,' she agreed, then frowned. He could have counted down, 3 − 2 − 1, to the moment when her eyebrows shot up with the pretence of a sudden idea. 'I'll ask Trudi, see if she's busy.' She reached for the bag she'd left on the floor beside the settee, took her mobile and texted. Reply came within the minute. Her voice had a smug edge. 'Perfect.'

At that moment he felt relaxed enough to see her as others might − and as others probably would tonight, as she and Trudi held court at Lola Lo, or the Revolution bar, or wherever it was they were headed. She was twenty-three but could pass for eighteen, lithe and longing with pouty lips and eyes made up so large she reminded him of a computer-generated avatar. She used pop videos and perfume ads as style guides. Underneath all that she was pretty, almost certainly too pretty for him, but he had trouble seeing her that way now. He had to work on that, Harry was only twenty months old; they had time.

'Be good.' He reached the remote and killed the muted screen. 'I'll be fine.'

Her expression darkened in an instant. 'Why wouldn't you be? Come with me if it's a problem.'

'It isn't.'

'Well it doesn't seem like it, Kyle.'

'Because I said "I'll be fine"?'

She moved in front of him, standing on the spot but adjusting and readjusting her weight. He knew the pattern, often it would be the same. She wanted him, then didn't, but when she didn't, she couldn't stand it if he didn't mind. And how different was he?

She drew him in and repulsed him in equal measure. Right now she could go to hell, take her too-short dress and flaunt her overly tanned legs in the winter streets. This minute he really didn't care but, the minute she left, he knew he'd think about little else.

'You're probably feeling guilty for going . . .'

'Feel guilty? Why should I?' she snapped.

'You shouldn't,' he replied gently, 'you really shouldn't.'

She gave no response apart from a growl of frustration, and an angry retreat upstairs where the floorboards creaked and the wardrobe doors banged until, finally, she was ready to leave.

She stood in the doorway for several seconds before she spoke. 'I won't be too late.'

But he had a book in his hands by then and barely glanced up. 'I think I'll go out tomorrow.'

Her expression hardened again and a final response was to slam the front door. Above him he heard the first notes of Harry's waking cry.

# TWO

Harry had gone back to sleep quickly, draped across Kyle's shoulder and only stirring when Kyle needed to use his supporting hand to turn the page. It only took a few minutes before Kyle laid the book to one side. He could see himself in Harry. Their baby photos looked alike too, his son had the same dark hair and broad forehead. They'd both inherited dark brown eyes from his father and the stubborn expression that filled them from his mother. He hoped his son would grow up a little taller, a little less gawky and a whole lot happier. He pressed his nose to the side of his son's head and closed his eyes. There was no pretence now, no self-conscious acting out and no hiding the truth. Harry reminded him of nothing bad whatsoever.

'Harry,' he whispered. He just liked to hear himself saying his son's name. The thought of having a child, being a dad, had been frightening and alien. The reality had been momentous.

'You saved me, Harry.' He rubbed the little boy's back. 'You and Auntie Leah. But mostly you.' It would have been easy to spend the whole evening like this. 'Mummy misses out, doesn't she?' It was weird the way he found it so natural to speak to his sleeping child who, even awake, barely understood a word he said. How was that different to talking to himself in an empty room? It just was.

How was making love to Hannah so difficult when she hadn't changed? The answer was the same; it just was.

14

He knew the change had been his own, but not in any way that should have affected them. But here he was, stuck with a woman he couldn't talk to. A woman he no longer wanted, but couldn't let go. There had to be a name for a relationship like this, the clinging, biting death roll that had them trapped and was dragging them down.

Harry lifted his head and turned so that his other cheek rested on Kyle's shoulder. Harry's face glowed and he smelt of baby sweat. Harry didn't deserve to have his family broken up. 'Do you want Daddy to fix it then?' Kyle stroked the feathery hair at the nape of his son's neck. 'How can I fix it, eh? I'll think of something, don't worry.'

Harry dribbled until the shoulder of Kyle's shirt became damp. Kyle transferred him back to his cot, then went to his own room for a fresh T-shirt.

He owned one drawer of clothes and about eighteen inches of hanging space. The drawer was wide and he kept his T-shirts folded and stacked in two piles at the right-hand end. He grabbed the nearest, pulled it partly over his head before he realized exactly what he'd just seen.

Or what he hadn't, to be precise.

He smoothed down the fabric, straightening the T-shirt as he continued to stare at the folded clothes. He was aware that his palms suddenly felt clammy and he wiped them on his jeans before sliding the drawer wider and lifting the T-shirts out of it one at a time. He squeezed each in turn in case the envelope had somehow become lost inside one of the garments.

It was unlikely, but he needed to be sure.

He told himself to stay calm, but he already felt the tell-tale tightening of his throat and nausea in his gut. 'What the fuck?' he muttered and felt the sweat as it began to break out across the back of his neck. He grabbed the second pile of shirts, his hands moved clumsily and, within seconds, he found himself ripping the drawer from its runners and turning the contents out onto the bed. He shook each item, then tossed it unfolded back into the empty drawer. Once he was done he dumped it onto the floor and pulled out the next. This one only held towels and took a matter of seconds.

The other two drawers belonged to Hannah and he could see the contents of the first through the gaps in the cabinet's frame. Underwear. Plenty of it. He tipped that straight onto the carpet and kicked through the pile of knickers and bras. There was no possibility of an envelope going unseen in that lot. But he kicked through the items anyway. Then grabbed up the empty drawer and swung it against the wall. The base fell out, the other four sides collapsed into a buckled trapezium. Exhausted.

He immediately turned back and dragged out the final drawer. This one contained papers and what looked like the items that had no other home; he'd never even opened it before. He fought back the desire to throw this one too and instead he sat next to it on the bed. He slowed his breathing, forcing himself to become calmer and letting his thoughts settle enough to allow him to concentrate. He lifted an inch-thick pile of typewritten letters out first. His hands didn't shake, but they'd become uncoordinated enough for the corner of the top sheet to evade the first couple of attempts at lifting it. At first he only checked between the sheets, not at the paperwork itself. It only took a glance to see that the pages were mainly utility bills and random articles printed from websites.

He just needed the envelope.

He began to find a rhythm, a comfortable speed that kept the pages flicking by without fumbling or dropping them.

About halfway through the first pile he paused, then read the facing page more slowly. The first word that had jumped out at him had been 'judgement'. He knew the two words that usually preceded that. 'County' and 'Court'. This letter was the threat of proceedings, but it was dated last October. Four months ago. Surely it would have gone to court by now unless it had been paid. The creditor name didn't ring a bell.

£853.26, plus court costs if it had reached that point.

He spread the next few pages out across the duvet, trying to understand what she'd bought for that amount. He looked through more sheets and found other unpaid bills and bounced payments. But still no envelope.

Downstairs the front door clicked shut. His watch told him it was a couple of minutes after 1 a.m. He didn't trust it though; it felt as if she had only just left. He must have moved fast then because nothing else registered with him until he found himself in the downstairs hallway. She still stood within touching distance of the door, and he was leaning over her, his right palm pressed against the panel above the catch as though he thought she might try to leave.

'What are you doing, Kyle?' She didn't look frightened, just angry, and shoved past him. He didn't try to stop her, but followed close behind as she headed for the lounge.

He had no idea whether she would try to ignore him or spin it round and make it his fault.

'Don't you dare, Hannah,' he muttered out loud.

She spun round to face him. 'Dare what?' Her eyes narrowed. 'I went out with Trudi. What do you think? You accusing me of something, Kyle?'

'Yeah, I am. But not whatever you think. You are a stupid, selfish bitch, Hannah.'

'Because of what? A night out? For fuck's sake. Your head is so rammed up your own arse you don't even know me. Or how I feel. Or what it's like for me.'

His hand shot out and grabbed her wrist. 'I know what you've done.'

There was a moment then when he didn't pull at her and she didn't pull away; the challenge, the face-off. She smirked, but he saw it for exactly what it was, defensive and deliberately antagonistic.

He wrapped his other arm behind her back and propelled her towards the stairs. She squirmed, pushing back against him. It made him stop and hold her still. 'You need to see what I've found, Hannah. We are going upstairs. Now.'

She stopped fighting him then, shot a glance towards the landing, then shook him away before beginning to mount the steps. He stayed close behind, ready to push her along at the first sign of a wobble from those stupid platform shoes of hers.

£64.99, unless they were yet another pair. And that dress, a bargain at £49.99. The heating? The water bill, the council tax and the household insurance? Not worth a fucking penny.

She gasped when she saw the room. He waited for her to accuse him of *having no right* in some way or another, but realization swiftly pushed away all her indignation.

'Like I said, I know what you've done. But do you understand, Hannah? Do you understand what it will cause?' He wasn't shouting now, just calm and patient, and maybe it was that unfamiliar ground that held her still and silent. She seemed to watch his lips as he spoke. 'I saw a child pick up a gun. A four-year-old boy. And *he* didn't know, didn't know which part was the muzzle and which was the trigger. He played with it because it seemed interesting. That's you, Hannah. I need to know exactly what you've done, all of it.'

Her lips barely moved. 'It was while you were away,' her voice was little more than a whisper. 'I missed you and I started doing things, buying things to cheer myself up. And it was OK because you had good money coming in.' Then she stopped and shrugged, as though she'd said enough to explain it all away.

He waited. 'Go on,' he said finally.

'That's it. Harry was born and you were injured. I had so much to deal with and even when you came back home you weren't yourself. You were here but I still felt like I did when you were away. I was lonely, Kyle.' Tears welled in her eyes. She didn't try to move towards him so he didn't have to push her away.

'So you kept spending?'

'I started spending again. I'm not irresponsible . . .'

'You're thick and self-centred. Now tell me the rest.'

She blinked away the tears but her eyes were damp enough for the outer corners to shine inkily. 'That's it.'

'No, you've spent what we haven't got. We live in a cheap rental because we don't have the money to live anywhere else. I earn what I can and we had only just enough to pay the bills.'

'Hardly.'

'And the answer to that is to spend more? How much debt do we have, Hannah?'

'I don't know.' She flicked her hand as though the whole problem could be batted away like a stray crumb. 'I really don't know. There's a little bit of catching up to do.'

He shook his head, 'Look at the room, there are official letters every-where. Do you really think I would believe that we're *just a bit behind*? It's staring me in the face, Hannah. Our bills have not been paid, there are threats of court action.' He jabbed a finger in the direction of the paperwork, then pointed it back towards her face. 'I'm asking you just to respect me enough to tell me the truth. How much do you owe?'

'I don't know. Thousands maybe. I stopped looking at the letters and you were impossible to talk to.'

'So talk to me now, Hannah. Tell me what you did next.'

'I didn't do anything.'

'You went through my drawer. You found an envelope. What did you do with it?'

'Nothing,' she said, but the colour had slipped from her cheeks as soon as he'd mentioned it. 'Stop looking at me like that, Ky. We needed the money. He paid you last time.'

'So it's gone? The envelope's gone? And everything that's in it? And that little kid with the gun just shot himself right in the face. Did you post it?'

She nodded.

'When?'

'Only yesterday.'

It made sense; he thought he had checked on it every day, there was no way that it could have been gone for long.

There was only two years' difference in their ages but, as he looked at her, he couldn't see his child's mother. She was just another kid playing at being grown up, dressed like a teenage wannabe and thinking it was all-so-very-simple.

He used to think like that. Briefly.

Before Lila. He could hear his own pulse, suddenly, filling his ears with the relentless pump-pump-pump.

He hadn't known the girl's name at first, but much later, when he came home on leave, he began trawling the Internet again. Ostensibly just casual hours drifting between sites, but always gravitating towards local news and missing persons. The missing persons' pages had sent him burrowing through endless appeals by desperate relatives, and so many pixelated or blurred photographs that he began to doubt that he'd recognize her again. How long had he spent looking at her real face anyway? One minute, maybe two, probably less.

He'd read the accounts that accompanied each and the cynic in his head argued that the missing people who had run, had run for a reason, that some of their *loved ones* exaggerated their own pain, and were putting up a show filled with the type of comments that they were expected to make. And knowing that this particular runaway was also dead changed nothing for him; she could have been just as glad to run but just ended up unluckier than most. He could clearly remember how he'd been back then – unfeeling, naive, ignorant – and he just didn't relate to it any more. He'd always loved his family but, beyond that, he'd had detachment. He knew too well that, once someone was dead, nothing would bring them back. He doubted that he'd understood anything beyond that.

He certainly hadn't realized that finding a body gave him a responsibility, a debt due to the bereaved.

Back then his ability to care deeply had stretched about a hundred metres in any direction, he hadn't understood the people who occupied the opposite emotional pole, where everything from rescuing dying hedgehogs to donating to refugees in the remotest corner of Africa became their problem.

Then came Harry and his world had flipped on its axis. Now everything mattered.

And, a few days after Harry's birth, he'd found Lila's photo – he'd spotted her face staring out from the rows of other faces of the lost. Suddenly he'd been unable to kid himself that he could remain immune to it all. He'd clicked on the image and the thumbnail that had looked clear enlarged to a fuzzier square. He'd narrowed his eyes, attempting to manually refocus her face.

Lila Rasnikov. It was the first time he'd seen what she'd looked like when she'd been alive. The first time he'd read her name. The first time he'd seen the words from her family telling the world how much she was missed.

He'd returned to the webpage too many times, until sometimes he'd wake in the night, open his eyes and see her face emblazoned in the nothingness of the blackened room. When his leave had ended, the image went back with him, reappearing whenever his mind was idle or forgetting to focus elsewhere.

In the daytime he'd thought of Harry and Hannah, he'd carried them

20

on patrol, tucked safely in a better corner of his brain, acting as his talisman. Gradually, though, the images blurred and he'd wake with Hannah's features filling the gaps in his memory of Lila.

Finally he'd printed Lila's photo and kept the 2 by 3.5 cm rectangle of printer paper tucked away so that he could remind himself that Lila had nothing whatsoever to do with Hannah. His Hannah.

'You're shaking.' Her voice brought him back.

His arms were wrapped around her and his face pressed into her hair. He didn't remember grabbing hold of her or how long they'd been standing there like that.

'Is this about her again?'

He nodded wordlessly. He could have tried to explain to Hannah, tell her how he only saw Lila's face when they made love, how he felt Lila standing beside the bed and looking down on them. He no longer had the right to lose himself with Hannah. He'd tried since he'd been back, but his mind no longer separated the two women and they were not the sentiments that Hannah would or could understand. Ever. It would turn into another fight, fuelled by Hannah's illogical insecurities, twisting in on themselves until he knew just what he knew right now; to keep quiet and try to work it out without her.

'I lied about the money, Hannah.' He glanced away as he spoke, focusing on his words and hoping that was what she would also do. 'I said he'd paid because I didn't want you to think I'd cocked up.'

'He paid *nothing*?'

'He said if he found me, he'd kill me. He said that if the police found her body, he would kill my family too.'

'So you just gave up?' She seemed close to laughing. 'That's bullshit. He has no way of finding out who we are. Don't think you can control me or even scare me, Kyle.'

'You have no idea what you're doing, Hannah. I'm sorry I ever got involved.'

'Well, I know how *that* feels.' Kyle couldn't quite decipher the expression that flashed across her face then. 'I have the balls for this, Kyle, even if you don't.'

'There's no point trying to wind me up. Not this time.'

He knew they were on the threshold of a full-on slanging match. He

21

turned away from her. 'Believe what you want, I'm taking Harry to Mum's.'

'Good luck with that.'

'You're not safe, Hannah.'

He knew she wouldn't drop it in a hurry, he just let her rant without interruption. 'You lie to me about money and now complain because I've lied to you? And you pretend to give a damn? You'll be sorry when I'm sorted out and you're on your own.'

He nodded slowly, even though he knew she was mistaken.

# THREE

*What do I know?*

It had been a casual question at first, then it became a way of passing hours when Kyle had wanted to ignore the people who spoke just too quietly for him to hear.

At first, the quiet murmur of the voices had been a comfort, the lulling sound of normality, like listening to road noise. He remembered when he'd lived here, at home. This house lay within yards of Barnwell Road. He could lie in bed with the curtains drawn and know what time it was by the sound of the traffic on the road. Once in a while there'd be the siren of an emergency vehicle – even that never broke the rhythm of early morning commuters and taxis – and the sound of planes from the airport.

Now he lay flat on his back and stared up, the dusty peaks of 1980s Artex blurred. This ceiling had been over him since childhood, until he swapped it, and swapped it again. He borrowed it now, he'd slipped into his old room, moved boxes on the floor and flopped back, waiting until the sounds from outside became familiar again.

*What do I know?*

Two things. Too much, and not enough.

It brought nothing in the way of comfort, but it cleared his head enough for the problem and him to be alone.

He circled it. He imagined it contained in a small square box, half the size of a brick. Nondescript. Inanimate. It looked as though he'd be able to just wrap his hand over it, grip it, maybe crush it. Certainly bin it.

Opening the box and dealing with what lay inside wouldn't work now. He knew better. He'd already been naive, he'd walked into the problem with seemingly open eyes only to discover he'd seen just one well-lit corner of a very dark room.

*What do I know?*

That the problem had dwarfed him and now the solution needed to be of that same scale. Harry was in the car seat next to the bed. Kyle listened for a few seconds to the relaxed and rhythmic pattern of Harry's breathing. It was a sleep unaffected by the adult world, by anger, a twenty-month-old could do that. In fact, everything about Harry was still unchecked and Kyle envied him.

His mother would hear him when he woke and Kyle could picture her blunt disapproval when she found Harry here. Always the bluntness, the hard exterior.

Like the medic, Captain Murray. 'Don't try to move.' It hadn't been the words, but his mum's *shut-the-fuck-up-and-do-as-I-say* tone that he'd understood. He'd stared up then as well, at the light blanched sky and listened to the familiar traffic of that unfamiliar place. Low-geared vehicles whining, bouncing on the rutted tracks. Shouting that carried almost a mile. Static. Crackle. An engine revving in the mid-distance and again the quick *pop, pop, pop* of a few rounds fired somewhere to his left.

He didn't pretend he wasn't there, instead he told himself to accept it, to be there and be unafraid and let it be what it would be. He'd silently told Harry he loved him and had imagined that the message would somehow cross continents and take root in his newborn son's mind. He closed his eyes and waited for Morphine Murray to come back to collect whatever remained of him by then.

He thought of that peacefulness now. He guessed it had been shock rather than any great insight into facing death. Or maybe, it was the release that came from not attempting to control the outcome.

He stared up in the field hospital, on the transport home and from his bed in the ward. He still stared up even when he had a choice, when it became medically safe to move his head.

24

His mum had come to visit and had brought along his sister, Leah. She had hung back, and he could see her in the edge of his vision, her skinny thirteen-year-old frame half in, half out of the curtained area around his bed. She'd waited until their mum had gone for coffee.

'Are you ignoring me, or what?' she'd asked.

'I'm not ignoring you.'

'You haven't looked over once.'

He turned his head just enough then and managed a smile; after all, none of it was her fault. 'Sorry Lee. I didn't want visitors. I wanted to see you all when I came back home.'

'We won't look any better in Cambridge, you know.'

'Damn.'

'I'm serious, Kyle. It's still us, wherever we are.'

'I know,' he'd sighed. 'Afghanistan . . .' His voice trailed away for a few moments. '. . . we all see things from a safe distance here and we think we know what they're like. I didn't have a clue. I had to learn to be a different person. I'm being discharged and I want to leave most of that behind.' *If I can.* 'I don't want home to be tainted with this. You understand, right?'

'You are full of shit sometimes, you know *that*, right?'

It wasn't in Leah's nature to give up and she'd been right, of course; sometimes she knew him better than he knew himself. What she hadn't been able to see, then or now, were his limitations. His injuries had been treatable, but he still wasn't so sure about the rest.

Right then he hadn't been ready for them, his family. He'd asked his mother to phone Hannah, to tell her not to come. He knew that she and Harry brought out two different sets of feelings; waves of less manageable emotions. He certainly hadn't wanted to see Harry when he couldn't hold him. Hadn't wanted Harry to become frightened in the unfamiliar surroundings of a hospital ward.

And he hadn't wanted to see Hannah when the feel of her skin and tautness of the body reminded him.

*Reminded him.*

Just the thought of seeing her had smothered his thoughts.

How could he tell her that, in the time he'd been away, his view of his old life had changed? Everything belonging to Cambridge had joined together under the heading of 'home'. And from then on he found it impossible to think of Cambridge without thinking of his two biggest mistakes: Hannah and Lila.

The cause of his problem.

He knew Harry was always fine when he was here.

Kyle pictured Leah sitting on the floor with him, passing him his beloved Duplo blocks. It was a familiar sight; Hannah across the room somewhere, probably watching Harry, but not close to him as Leah would always be. Kyle still found it hard to see Hannah as maternal, not because she wasn't, but because of his own visions. Sometimes when he woke he caught sight of her in the half-light and he wasn't sure whose face he saw. He studied the back of the bedroom door, he needed to find a way to integrate, to feel part of his own world, but this small room felt safer. And he needed space to think.

Kyle had never read much or watched documentaries, but somewhere he'd heard that for every man who killed there were a hundred fighting the urge. It had never explained about the urges of men who had already killed. Just to realize that he couldn't ever be part of the hundred had left him on an uncharted course.

He had no desire to kill again, but he'd had no desire to kill the first time either. Maybe a first-time killer might feel the drive for it, be sucked along by some fictionalized TV version of a righteous kill, one where the victim didn't linger and there were no repercussions. A second kill was something else and he could only wonder at the type of mind that relished it and fantasized about doing it again.

The disparate thoughts were muddying his thinking. Sometimes he needed to remind himself to stay in check. To focus on just one thing. The *problem* was all that mattered.

He imagined himself walking a slow circle around the box containing it.

*What do I know?*

Harry matters. Leah matters.

Hannah and his mother mattered. But Hannah mattered far less than he'd thought. His mother coped, she always did.

Harry and Leah then.

26

He whispered the words to himself, 'What do I know? What do I know?' The Artex stared back, grey and uncommunicative. Kyle drew a long slow breath, it caught in his throat and, without warning, he was perilously close to tears. How had he ever thought it wouldn't come back to hurt him? How could he let them suffer for what he had triggered? Just the thought was enough for him to glimpse the void that his life would become if anything happened to them.

He should have gone to the police back then.

It was too late now.

He rose from the bed; this room held comfort, not safety. Harry slept on while Kyle slipped downstairs.

# FOUR

Leah curled onto her side and faced the party wall that they shared with Solomon Levinson and his wife. Leah often woke when Solomon or his wife visited the bathroom. Sometimes she'd hear a double bump from their headboard as it rattled against the wall when one of them climbed out of bed, and three minutes or so later the double bump again as they returned. And, if Solomon had woken Valda, or vice versa, then the whole thing would go again. Usually there would be a couple of hours' peace before her school alarm, but today was Saturday and she hadn't been woken by Solomon or Valda but by the creak and scrape of someone rising from one of her mum's kitchen chairs. This wasn't the kind of house where a restless person could pace the floor and make subtle footfalls or gentle creaks. Nothing was private here.

Her bedroom had been emulsioned in a shade of mint green; it had dried more turquoise and she preferred it that way. Street lamps and moonlight kept it toned down to grey but now she could pick out a film of colour and she tried to work out whether extra light was also filtering up the stairs and through her doorway.

She rolled over slowly and quietly.

The person downstairs wasn't moving now but she could still sense someone; it felt to her that a sleeping person gave out a different energy

28

to one who was awake, and she didn't believe that her mum was the only other person in the house right now.

People often ignored what surrounded them but Leah was sure that sometimes she could walk into a room, any room, and sense what hung in the air. When her history teacher had finally broken down in tears she had been the only one of her classmates who hadn't seemed surprised. Or when her mum was struggling to cope after dad had gone. Or when Kyle's expression became empty and her brother disappeared into his own distorted version of the world, leaving him as a part-functioning shell.

She heard a teaspoon stirring in a mug.

And it had to be Kyle down there now.

She couldn't hear anyone with him. Kyle without Harry or Kyle with a sleeping Harry, but no Hannah; she didn't know what that meant. Another fight maybe. He began to pace and it felt as though another hour passed before there came another break in his restlessness. Leah had almost fallen asleep by then, warm under her duvet and letting the threat of Saturday morning chores push her deeper.

She stirred as the third and fourth steps from the top of the staircase creaked. She slipped out of bed and was halfway across the room when he reached the doorway. She took one look at his face and, even though the light was weak, she felt her stomach tighten with apprehension; Kyle looked . . . *wrong.* She'd seen this expression too many times now and that had been the only word that fitted when she'd tried to explain to her friends. *Possessed, vacant* and *strange* had all been contenders, but *wrong* said it better.

'Leah, I've fucked it all up.' His voice sounded hoarse. 'I can't think.' He closed her door and stood with his back pressed to it.

'What's happened?'

'It's just a mess.' He thumped the back of his head against the wall a couple of times. 'I can't make Hannah see. She won't listen. She just keeps pushing for what she wants. That's all she does, push people. It's all a mess.' He stopped speaking aloud but she could tell that the words were still running on inside his mind.

'Kyle,' Leah hissed, 'tell me.'

With no warning Kyle grabbed her, hugging her clumsily. He buried his face in her hair. 'I can't. I don't know how to fix it yet. Harry's here, he's in my room. Me and Harry are moving back in. I'll square it with Mum later.'

'She won't like it.'

He shook his head. 'She'll be fine.'

'She'll want rent.'

He blinked, screwing his eyes tight until she'd stopped adding further objections. 'I'm going out now, I need to clear my head.'

That startled her. 'Where?'

'I don't know . . . I just need some space.'

'We need to know where you are.'

'No, you don't. I just need to be able to think. I'll be back, Leah.'

'When?'

'Leah,' there was a warning tone in his voice as he said her name, 'I don't know, OK? I just will.'

She had no idea whether he was talking hours, or days, or worse still whether he really didn't know.

'And what about Harry?'

'I want him to stay here. Hannah too, maybe.'

Leah didn't know whether he had intended it, but Kyle hugged her a little tighter then. 'Mum hasn't agreed it or anything, I left her a note. It's on the kitchen table.'

'Yeah Kyle, we did that at school – it's called cliché.'

'Whatever.' Then he pulled back and studied her face for a moment. 'You're a smart-arse, Leah. But that's the reason I'm telling you and not telling anybody else. You can keep it all in your head, just like you always have. There's not much to remember. Hannah has blown our cash, all of it.'

'On what?' Leah snorted. 'Ugg boots and hair extensions?'

'All in all it doesn't matter.' He sounded indifferent to it too.

'What? You're not mad at her?'

'I'm livid. But I can't go back and undo it. The money has gone, and not on paying for us to have somewhere to live.' Kyle had grabbed hold of Leah's hand and now he squeezed it every second or two as he spoke, as if that pumping would improve her listening skills. 'Look, don't start focusing on the bits that are irrelevant. We have to get out of that house. Harry is here now, he's asleep, and this is where he needs to stay. In fact, Hannah can do whatever she likes, but Harry must be here with you and Mum.'

'There's no way she should go anywhere without Harry, unless it's a nightclub.'

'Leah!' He gave her hand an extra squeeze, and this time it felt almost playful. 'You know I'm serious though, don't you? I love you and Harry, and I know you love Harry too. I know you will always do your best to look after him. So listen, there'll be no need for you to go there to babysit, to walk round with him in that pram, I've never liked you walking up the main road like that . . .'

'Kyle, it's fine.'

'No, it's not.'

She could see by his expression that there was no room for negotiation. 'I'm not making myself clear, I didn't want you to be scared so I wasn't spelling it out. That's me being shit.' His hands stopped moving and suddenly he was still, 'You and Harry must stay away from our house and you *must not* take him out by yourself. It's dangerous.'

'How?'

'It just is. I know it is.'

'Kyle, stop. You will scare me if you keep talking like that. It's freaky enough that you've turned up in the middle of the night. Just do whatever it is and get back here as fast as you can.'

'Sure thing.' He drew her in tighter then and hugged her close to his chest; it could have been comforting if her ear hadn't been pressed against his ribs. If she hadn't heard the speed and intensity that pumped his heart. She lifted Harry in his car seat into her room, tucked his blanket in tighter around his legs then settled quietly back onto her own bed with her head on the pillow, the duvet up around her ears and tears making a creeping patch of wet across the bedding.

They were losing him again.

Why couldn't he see that Hannah would never move in here? That Harry couldn't stay here without her, and that Leah and her mum would babysit more without Kyle at home to pin Hannah down? And whether Kyle had just walked out for a couple of hours or longer, he still didn't understand that he couldn't do that without leaving them to pick up the pieces.

Leah waited for almost an hour after the front door clicked shut behind him. Finally she padded across the landing and lay on the bed, in the vacant space beside her mother. 'Mum? Mum, I need to talk to you.'

# FIVE

Ratty trailed his way towards the market. He had enough in his pocket for a final portion of chips from Gardenia in Rose Crescent. Most places served him now but he only had to go back a few years and he could list the ones that turned him away, the ones who didn't want him tainting their shop or their customers. The staff at Gardenia had never done that; they'd looked him in the eye and been as polite as they'd been to the previous customer. He knew they probably didn't care who they served, but he preferred to think of them as people who had shown him respect and, for that, they had earned the last of his change.

He waited, loitering inside the doorway for a few minutes as he let the arse-end of the Saturday-night drinkers stagger by. Ratty's senses were heightened. It was the point of the night when blood alcohol rose and common sense fell away; once the two crossed over then it became too late to reason with these people.

He watched until last the group of men had jostled their way towards Trinity Street and he slipped onto the pavement with his open bag of chips. He kept the bag close; the night would be a cold one but he was more interested in keeping his chips hot than using them to warm himself. He hated the chill that invaded after a blast of heat far more than he hated the consistent cold itself. Besides, he would be let into the shelter tonight, he'd just wait until the others there had settled and there would be no risk of catching the wrong man's eye.

He emerged onto Market Hill and turned immediately right, flanking the first row of market stalls. There was little to see at night, shutters on some, tarpaulins on others. But they were more than empty wood and metal frames, they were rows to walk through and snippets of today left in the cobbles. Shabby, but human in a good way.

He ate the chips, pacing himself, so that they would last until he had wound his way back and forth through all the rows. He reached the final turn and plodded down the gap between the final two rows. Turning corners. That's what this last year had been about. He couldn't always walk through the market like this, of course, but the sky was clear and the moon almost full. Some gaps between stalls fell into absolute darkness; where the moonlight caught the others he could read the signage and see the shiny blackness of the damp trails of rainwater that ran beneath between the cobbles.

Ratty and his chips walked round the market like this once or twice every week now. He still shunned company, but had at least pulled himself back far enough from the oblivion of absolute addiction and most days he was muddled by nothing more serious than booze and weed.

He turned the next corner. He was approaching the fountain, a Gothic and slightly off-centre centrepiece to the square. The water didn't run and they'd filled it with a flower bed. He cast his mind back . . . by years. When he'd been about eighteen and hung out with some of the first-year students from Anglia Polytechnic, as it had been then. He thought he'd been one of them, but now, as he looked back, he realized that they had always had a brighter future than his own. There used to be a man here then, Professor Hobson everyone called him. It was years later before Ratty realized that it probably wasn't his name but a reference to the spot where he sat.

Hobson was one of the old names that still touched the city. There were many others of course, like Coleridge, Sayle and Perne, whose names appeared dotted around the city, on house fronts and signposts. But Ratty had warmed to Hobson. None of the other notables touched the city in quite the same way as Thomas Hobson and his eponymous conduit, which had provided a water system for the whole city. Sections of it had been filled in over the years but Ratty thought of the streams as still running underground; buried tentacles reaching out from here to Parker's Piece and St Andrew's Street.

*Their* Prof. Hobson was rumoured to live in public toilets in the centre of the market place. Certainly, nobody knew anyone who had seen him anywhere else and popular belief held that he was a man with a brilliant mind, a man who had walked away from an amazing career in academia. Students would ask his advice, partly in jest, often with the quiet hope that he really did hold the secret to an easy first. Better that than following him into a life on the streets.

Ratty stopped, chips still in hand, and stared at the black hulk of a monument. *Hobson's Choice.* Back then he thought it meant that there was no choice at all, but finally, when he had stood here almost a year ago, he had understood that Hobson's words 'this one or none' meant something quite different; no one was forcing him to sort out his life, there was in fact a choice, sort out this life or have none.

And so, for the first time in many years, he had seen a way forward. Hobson, deliverer of mail and hirer of horses, had reached out and touched him too. Ratty didn't expect great things, too much had gone too far for that. A tiny bit of peace for the last fifteen or so years of his life would do him fine.

The chips were almost cold now, a sign that he had spent too long in one spot. He tilted the bag towards the moonlight, hoping to find a couple more thick ones amongst the fatty crumbs. They'd gone, and he tipped the last scraps onto the ground for birds, or rats, or anything desperate enough to want them.

He looked up from the chips but still didn't see the blow that swung in towards his right temple. After all his years of suspicion and attempts at self-preservation he had sensed nothing.

Nothing.

He took one step backwards. The pain and then darkness chased through his head. He collapsed to the ground, his cheek in the gutter until the final blow came. For several seconds he heard nothing then, suddenly, the noise was harsh, like a log splitting.

And everything he knew was over.

# SIX

Dr Addis rose stiffly from crouching next to the body, the hem of his trouser leg damp from touching the ground. He suddenly felt middle-aged and crumpled next to DS Kincaide. He pushed his glasses back to the bridge of his nose. 'I'd put the time of death close to midnight.'

The doctor wasn't sure if Kincaide was even listening; the detective stared over Addis's shoulder, scowling into the middle distance and holding the pose as if he was waiting for cameras to flash. Everything about Kincaide could be relied upon to look polished, gelled and manicured, and to possess a sheen of newness. Addis guessed that Kincaide's attention was fixed on the woman who'd found the body; she continued to sob quietly. Addis turned to look and saw that she was being comforted by two other stallholders, one each side, and all three women huddled with hot drinks and consoling touches.

'I can see her next,' Addis offered.

'Whatever you think,' Kincaide dragged his attention back to Addis. 'It's the noise, it's distracting me.'

Addis opened his mouth to make the obvious observations about people's varying responses to shock, but was cut short.

'Yes, I can see she's in shock, Malcolm, but she needs to take it a bit further away out of earshot.'

He raised his voice as he said the last three words and one of the women shot a filthy look back in their direction.

'You were enthusiastic and charming when I first met you.' Addis smiled slightly, making light of the comment, even though he meant it. It seemed that once Kincaide had learnt to get out of the wrong side of the bed, he'd just carried on doing it. 'And I'm not surprised she's shocked.' That prompted them both to look back in the direction of the body.

'He looks like a local rough sleeper, one I've seen in the cells a couple of times.' Addis narrowed his eyes and tried to recall the face before the damage. 'Ratty, I think.'

Kincaide nodded. 'Yeah, that's him. Like Stephen Hawking.'

'I'm sorry?'

'Everyone knows he's lurking around Cambridge but we only remember when he starts spouting about something or other.'

'Still charming, after all,' Addis replied drily. 'Are we done here?'

'There's a chip wrapper on the ground and grease on his hands. The nearest chip shop closes around 11.30, before midnight seems more likely.'

'I've taken his temperature, my estimate's based on some rough calculations, it'll probably be narrowed down a little more, but I wouldn't be surprised if the window ended up being as wide as 10 p.m. to 2 a.m. It's the way these things can go when there are so many variables; rate of blood loss, air and ground temperature and core body temperature.'

The police side of the investigation had little to do with Addis but, even so, the sudden activity behind Kincaide's frequently doubting expression raised his curiosity. 'What are you thinking?'

'Find out what time the "guests" turned up at the night shelter and there's the first list of the most likely.'

Ratty's death had not been caused by accident but by design, by someone who'd hit him in the right place in order to incapacitate him, and who had then continued with an attack aimed at nothing short of killing him.

'Do you think there's that much animosity there? They have the odd scrap but that,' Addis pointed at the body, 'wasn't the work of someone heavily under the influence of alcohol or drugs.'

'In your opinion?'

'In my opinion, not everyone who's homeless is under the influence

37

of either,' Addis conceded, 'and I'm not a detective, but I think you may need to look a little wider than the night shelter.'

'Don't worry, we'll cover it all.' Kincaide couldn't help a smugness slipping into his voice.

Addis wondered, and not for the first time, what had turned Kincaide into such a self-absorbed prick. It had certainly been a turnaround from Addis's first encounter with him. The newer, more cynical Kincaide had emerged through the last few years, or perhaps he'd always been there, but previously he'd been well disguised.

'I'm guessing your friend Goodhew will be back soon.'

Addis spotted Kincaide's jaw tighten and his eyes harden just a shade. It killed the smugness too, and amused Addis for all the minutes that it took him to sign off on the death certificate and complete the basic documentation required for the police reports. By the time they were done, his minor victory over Kincaide had given way to the observation that he really knew nothing about what made Kincaide tick.

Mrs Cartwright had stopped crying, but he made his way over to her in any case. 'I'm Dr Addis.'

She nodded gratefully. 'I'm OK really. Just shocked I suppose.' She was under the awning of a stand selling sweatshirts bearing Cambridge University logos. The stall next to that one sold jacket potatoes straight from a cast-iron oven. It was already throwing out heat and there didn't seem to be anywhere else on the market where she would have been better sheltered. She'd been given two tartan travel rugs, one draped around her shoulders and the other across her lap, tucked under her thighs on either side. She still shivered uncontrollably. 'Please don't offer me another hot drink.'

'You should go home. Being here won't be helping.'

'The police will want to talk to me.'

'As long as someone has your details you'll be free to go.' It wasn't his job to tell her that but he knew it was the case.

She nodded but he could tell that she had no intention of moving. 'He must have suffered a lot. He was dead already though. I couldn't have helped him.'

Although it was a statement he could hear the question lurking behind it; the worry, however unlikely, that she had missed an opportunity, or somehow failed to avert this final outcome.

Addis tested his weight on a box next to her then sat gently on the corner of it. 'I really don't think he lived for a long time after the attack. I'm sorry you had to find him, but he would have been dead long before then.'

She began talking about the market then, about how long she'd been there, about the other stallholders and the usual pattern of sales. Reconfirming to herself, as much as to him, all the details of the average day. He doubted that she was even paying much attention to her own words, just giving in to the need to fit the morning's events into the bigger picture of routine life. He let her talk but also let his own attention wander back towards Kincaide, and realized that his own response to the detective's abrasiveness had been less than professional.

Addis spoke to Kincaide again before he left. 'I apologize if you felt I overstepped with my comments.'

Kincaide managed a thin smile. 'Everyone likes to have an opinion, I understand that.' There was no warmth in Kincaide's expression. 'We'll bear your thoughts in mind, doctor.' He held out his hand and shook Addis's. Kincaide's grip was overly hard but very brief.

Right then Addis could have congratulated Kincaide on his promotion to DS but even professionalism had its limits. Instead he walked back towards his Volvo wondering why Marks had sanctioned Kincaide's progress.

# SEVEN

Walking to work had been Gully's New Year's resolution. She had not promised herself that she would do it every day, and maybe that was why it was February and she hadn't yet given up. The challenge she had actually set herself was to achieve it at least one hundred times across the year; twice a week didn't sound too difficult.

This morning she had woken to a bright and cloudless sky. It was a faded blue, the way it often was in winter, but it was 7 a.m. and she had no doubt that the walk would be against the bitter cold. She'd decided to do it anyway; she always allowed forty minutes, thirty for the walk and ten to re-acclimatize to the indoors before the start of her shift at eight. She therefore counted a mug of coffee and two Jaffa Cakes as a legitimate part of her morning fitness routine.

People walked as a hobby. She set her coffee down on her desk and was still puzzling that one when her radio interrupted.

It was Kincaide.

'We're moving a body from Market Hill right now. I could do with an extra pair of hands, the traders will want to be up and running.'

Gully nodded to herself and muttered, 'They'll be lucky to open up before lunch, won't they?' She didn't expect a reply.

She took a couple of quick sips before leaving the half-full mug on her desk and heading out. By the time Kincaide spoke again she was halfway down the first flight of stars. 'We won't keep them longer than necessary, looks like a homeless person.'

'Male or female?'

'Male I'm guessing, they usually are.'

Homeless people? Or just the dead ones? 'You must know if the body is male or female.'

He didn't respond at all that time but as soon as she arrived at the market she repeated the question.

'Male, all right?' He sighed. 'At this point, there's nothing you really need be aware of. We have people on site now, I sent a couple of officers and Addis to sign off on the death cert. I just need another couple of officers to stand on the outskirts of market stalls, to deflect the beaky locals. I don't mean to sound rude, Sue, but I really don't think there's much that you need to know at this point.'

Preparing herself for a long morning, Gully pulled a face as she walked away.

Gully spent most of the first hour facing the bench and the rubbish bin at one end of the Guildhall. Somewhere behind her, screened off by the congestion of people and vehicles and half-set-up stalls, was the body. By 9 a.m. it had become fairly obvious to her that *whoever* had died of a *whatever* involved facts that were more suspicious than hypothermia, alcohol or choking on their own vomit.

'Male aged thirty to fifty' was the most that she'd gleaned via her radio. She shifted her weight from foot to foot in an attempt to get the circulation going again and began to use the movement as a way of sneaking the occasional peek at progress being made around the body.

'That one is my stall.' The woman was short with tightly curled grey hair and a Barbour jacket fastened up to neck. She had pointed towards a narrow stand with the blue-and-white striped canopy; there was no sign that hinted at what it usually sold. 'I came to see if you'd like a hot drink?'

'Thank you, but I'll wait until I get back to the station.'

'Should I just give up on today then?'

'I really don't know anything. But they won't hang around longer than they need to.'

The woman shrugged then nodded. 'That's fair enough.'

'What do you sell?'

'Candles and soap mostly. I'm always here for the Sunday market, I suppose I fit in better here. I certainly sell more on a Sunday, but I do like it midweek too.' She tipped her head towards the body. 'Mary from the bread stall found him, poor sod.'

'Was Mary the one who phoned in then?'

'No. Tariq did, he's at the other end on the right-hand side, he came over when she started shouting.'

'Have either of them spoken to anyone, a police officer I mean?'

'I don't know, I sat with Mary for a few minutes, she was really shaken. Kept crying. A doctor had a chat with her but I don't know about any of your people. Once she calmed down she cleared off pretty quickly.'

'Perhaps not then?'

The woman stared down at a damp patch on the ground that had, until recently, been a puddle. 'She just kept saying that there hadn't been much blood. She said, if she had seen blood she would have known that it was a body. She just kept staring at it, thought it was a model, some kind of prank maybe. I suppose the light isn't great at that time in the morning.'

'At what time?'

'It would have been before six, maybe 5.30, I don't know.'

Gully nodded. That tied in with the time the call had been placed.

'I think what upset her most,' the woman continued, 'was that she poked his head with her foot. She said that it was so misshapen that it didn't look like a head at all.' She shrugged then looked back at Gully, 'Of course, once you know what something is, it's easy to see what it's not. The idea now that it could've been papier mâché or an old mannequin seems ridiculous.'

Gully took out her notebook, 'I'll need to take your full name, and hers, and your contact information.'

'Louise Polly. Mary Cartwright. I'm Louise, obviously.' She started to speak again and Gully immediately caught another tone in her voice. 'We could tell you who he was if we'd ever bothered to ask his name, and I suspect I will feel ashamed of myself for that. It's not that you don't feel sympathy, you just don't want to be too inviting . . .'

'Did you see the body too?'

'No, no. When Louise explained I knew who she meant.'

'So he was a familiar face around the market then?' Gully felt it was to her own shame that she hadn't asked that question in the first place. 'Can you describe him?'

'He just looked like a homeless man,' Louise shook her head in apology, her speech had picked up in pace over the last couple of minutes. Mild shock could do that, sometimes people jumped from unnatural calmness to jittery within minutes. 'Bad skin, bad teeth,' she continued. 'The sort of person you pity from a distance. And I can tell you what he wore, in fact I never saw him in anything else. I suppose that might have been all he had.' Louise paused at that point and took a breath. 'He wore Doc Marten's and one of those dustman coats.'

'A donkey jacket?'

'Yes, I was at school with a boy named Drew, he wore one of those with "Killing Joke" written on the back. Sorry, not relevant.'

And not exactly the most subtle comment either, Gully noted. She looked away from Louise Polly and saw Kincaide step into view from behind one of the stalls. 'Stay here, I'll be back in a moment.'

Kincaide would have seen the body by now. He would know.

'Did you recognize him?' she asked as soon as she was close enough for him to hear her without her needing to raise her voice. 'Is it Ratty?'

'Goodhew's chum?' he muttered thoughtfully, and turned to look across at the open rear doors of a private ambulance. Gully realized that the body now lay inside the vehicle and would probably be leaving the scene within the next couple of minutes. 'You must know him better than I do, you ought to have a look.'

Gully nodded and followed him across to the driver.

'She needs to see the body,' he told the man, then gestured for her to go ahead. The body lay bagged and on the trolley, she found the light, then pulled the door closed behind her – neither of them needed spectators.

In those few seconds walking behind Kincaide she'd developed a theory. Kincaide knew Ratty almost as well as she did. He would have known whether this was him, unless of course the body was too seriously disfigured. And, even then, he could have made a reasonable judgement. He hadn't even offered her his amazingly prolific opinion.

It added up to one thing only: what was in this body bag was a mess and she'd been sent in here to puke or cry or both.

Her fingers trembled as she gripped the tab on the zip.

She pulled it down just enough to expose a tuft of blood-matted hair. She took a breath then opened the next eighteen inches in one determined move.

It was him. But instincts had told her that already.

She asked herself why she'd really come in here. To prove to herself that she could face whatever Kincaide threw at her? Or to prove what a complete shit he really was? The bloodied hair was on one side of Ratty's head, his skull misshapen.

She concentrated on his face, forcing herself to study where his eyes had been mutilated until she'd overcome the need to recoil. She would be stronger than Kincaide thought she was.

She studied the eye area carefully, moving closer as the curiosity overcame the revulsion. The eyes were still there but they'd been punctured and their entrails lapped onto his face.

Her basic knowledge of Shakespeare served up the phrase 'vile jelly'.

She was careful not to touch but drew closer until his eye sockets were just inches from her own. There appeared to be no damage to the upper lids, or, as far as she could see, the lower lids either. There was plenty of dirt and blood across his face but through it no signs of other facial injuries.

She could see how the eye damage had been inflicted; the fingers of one hand had parted the lids, another hand had slit the eyeball. One assailant or two, but definitely two hands involved. And no sign of a struggle, so he'd been dead by then.

She straightened, still staring at his eyes. The mutilation wasn't a spontaneous act or a violent outburst gone too far. Ratty hadn't been stabbed first, but beaten to death. The assailant had deliberately picked one method to kill but planned to finish like this. What *did* it mean?

She reclosed the body bag, then left the ambulance, gently shutting the door as she stepped onto the market square. Kincaide still stood with the driver, they'd been laughing about something. They'd moved up to the railings that surrounded the entrance to the old public toilets. Each held a takeaway drink carton. Their voices carried as though they were closer. '. . . and that was on the stag night!' Kincaide concluded.

It was obviously a punch line because they both laughed. She wondered if it was the first time she'd ever heard Kincaide laugh. She strode towards them. Kincaide saw her and continued to look amused. She realized how paranoid it sounded to think he was laughing at her more than at that joke now. Paranoid, but true.

She was still about ten feet away when she spoke. 'You knew it was him, didn't you?'

The driver nudged Kincaide. *Yes, the joke was on her all right.*

'Are you telling me you have a positive identification, Sue?'

She waited until she was just couple of feet in front of him and then spoke quietly so that there was little chance of anyone hearing. 'Treat him with a bit more respect, Michael. He deserves that at least.'

'If he'd wanted to do something with his life, Sue, he would have done. You'll see, it'll have been a fight over nothing. One of his mates probably and they'll end up inside and living in better conditions than they've got out here. That's a bigger crime.'

'I'm heading back to Parkside,' she said and turned away.

She'd only taken a few steps when she felt Kincaide's hand on her arm, he tugged it and she stopped and turned to face him, 'What?'

'I want you here.'

'Don't do that, Michael.' She turned away and kept walking towards her car. 'I'm not staying. I've just identified a body, I have paperwork.'

She waited until she'd driven away from Market Hill, then called Goodhew. He cut the call off while it was ringing then sent back a text a few minutes after that. 'Busy, will phone, one hour-ish.' She pulled up outside his flat, but looked at his message again then decided not to knock. 'Time for you to come back, Gary,' she muttered.

It was only when she returned to her desk and found the unopened box of Jaffa Cakes planted in the centre of her mouse mat that she knew why Goodhew wasn't answering his phone. She grabbed her pad of Post-it Notes and took them to Goodhew's old desk, hopefully still his desk. She wrote on the top square and slapped it onto the midpoint of his monitor. 'About time. Your turn to make coffee.'

# EIGHT

Goodhew sat across from DI Marks. He ran his gaze across the desk and onto the rest of the room. He'd been away for six months, give or take, and everything looked roughly as he remembered it, but it was the finer detail he wouldn't have been able to describe, the position of picture hooks, the dented wastepaper basket, the coaster from Malta; all these things that he'd forgotten and now remembered with complete clarity. Marks wore glasses now, oval lenses with wire frames. Marks was looking anywhere apart from at Goodhew.

'Sir? I'd like to come back to work as soon as possible.'

'You've been signed off for another three weeks yet.' Marks strummed his fingers on his desktop. Goodhew had forgotten that Marks did that, too. 'Come clean with me, Gary.'

Gary nodded slowly. 'I've heard that there's been a murder, a dead body found at the market. It *is* Ratty, isn't it, sir?'

'No one should be passing you confidential information when you're not at work.'

'They didn't, sir.' Goodhew leant back in his chair and placed his palms flat on his thighs; he wasn't hiding anything now. 'I listen to police transmissions. I know it isn't within the rules . . .'

'The law, Gary, not the rules.'

'OK, law then. I listen in because I don't want to lose sight of everything here, I hoped that I would want to come back but I didn't know I was ready for it until I heard about Ratty.'

'Well, I do want you back, but not on some emotive whim.'

Goodhew chose not to comment. Marks would follow his own judgement and trying to persuade him could just as easily backfire.

'Tell me Gary, how much have you learnt over the years about Ratty's personal life?'

'Not much.' He shook his head. 'Actually, there's nothing.' He wished he could conjure up a few scraps of conversation that would convince his boss that he was the right person to follow it up. 'He told me once that he saw plenty of trouble happening but never got involved. He said, "I don't let it seep over me."'

'Maybe this time was different? Tell me what you think, what you've thought in the half-hour between hearing his name and turning up in my office.'

'That's easy.' Goodhew smiled ruefully. 'Ratty never wanted to stick his neck out and yet, once or twice, he passed on information. He helped me when he could easily not have bothered. I respected him for that.'

'So working on this investigation feels like the right thing to do?'

'I don't have any doubts. None. And that's the first time I have felt like this.' Goodhew looked across the desk at his boss. DI Marks was notoriously difficult to read but Goodhew guessed that the main hesitation from his boss stemmed from his own unannounced and spontaneous arrival today. Maybe Marks saw it as a sign of impulsiveness but, in his own opinion, he had been as honest as he could've been. And now he had nothing else to say.

Marks pressed his index finger to the gap between his eyebrows, then slowly turned his hand until the finger pointed straight at Goodhew. 'I have concerns, reservations that relate to your welfare. However, that is my own opinion and not the opinion shared in any official documentation that I have been shown. If things aren't right, talk to me.'

He waited for Goodhew's agreement, then he stood and shook his hand. 'Welcome back, Gary.'

# NINE

Marks moved straight across the tiled floor towards the table where Ratty's body lay. He obviously wasn't in the mood to spend any unnecessary time on conversation, but then Strickland never was either.

They stood silently as Strickland's assistant reordered the implements on the tray, the only sound the quiet clinking and scuffing of metal on metal. She finished and waited for him to nod before stepping aside. It was only then that they moved closer and Goodhew had his first clear view of Ratty.

Goodhew took several controlled breaths as he ran his gaze over the length of the body. Ratty was taller than Goodhew had imagined, logically there were other observations that should have come first: old scars, new injuries, the tattoos, Ratty's face . . .

'How tall is he?' he asked.

Strickland flicked an impatient glance in his direction but answered anyway, 'One-six-nine centimetres.'

'A touch under five eight,' Goodhew relayed to Marks, saving him the trouble of converting. 'He always seemed about three inches shorter than that.'

'It is him, though.'

'I know. It was just an observation, sir. Death usually makes people look smaller.'

'And,' Strickland cut in, 'this one had a tough death to go with his tough life. There's plenty here to keep us occupied.' He picked a scalpel from the tray, held it like a fountain pen and drew a circle in the air above Ratty's face. 'A few points of interest here.' The discolouration of the head injuries stood out against the marbled whiteness of the skin, but there was more. The dirt had embedded itself into the wounds with a heavy gritty blackness that clung to the patches of congealed blood. Gelatinous smears marked the eye sockets.

Strickland turned to the other end of the table. 'Usual routine.'

They'd be inspecting Ratty's face once Strickland had worked his way up the body. Goodhew dragged his attention back to Ratty's feet; he knew what he thought he'd just seen, but Strickland would have him removed from the room before he'd allow him to ask questions out of turn.

Marks stared at Ratty's face for a few seconds longer. 'Gary, it's late to say this now, but you don't need to stay,' he muttered.

'It's fine.'

'It's different when it's someone you know,' Marks pointed out.

Goodhew already knew that and he wasn't about to leave. 'Thank you but I'd rather stay.'

Marks nodded to Strickland, after which neither he nor Gary spoke. Strickland's assistant had stayed in the room and she remained silent too, stepping forwards only when her boss gave an instruction. For the next hour Strickland spoke slowly and clearly as a digital camera recorded each step of the autopsy. His voice adopted a single monotonous tone.

When Strickland reached Ratty's upper torso, Goodhew moved with Marks to gain a clearer view of the chest cavity and head. They stood level with Ratty's elbow and faced Strickland across the table. Now Goodhew was close enough to study Ratty's face properly. He'd never seen an injury like it, and yet there was no mistaking it; Ratty's eyelids were partially concave and, from behind them, blood-streaked fluid and membrane had leaked. Goodhew forgot to stay silent. 'He has been stabbed in the eyes, right?'

Strickland scowled at him, then nodded. 'It would appear so.'

He wondered how deep the implement had gone. 'Was that what killed him?'

'Slow up, Gary,' Marks muttered.

'We can't jump ahead,' Strickland added.

After that Goodhew accumulated questions in his mind, waiting for the moment when talking was allowed. Finally Strickland straightened, then returned his tweezers to the metal tray and straightened the other implements too. Goodhew's gaze wandered around the room; stainless steel, white, clinical and reflecting nothing. Strickland was the same. Goodhew had no idea what he would say until he spoke.

Strickland began, 'The victim died primarily from the head injury. The wounds to the eyes were inflicted post-mortem. The weapon used on them would have been reasonably sharp, possibly a tool such as a screwdriver or a bradawl. I should imagine that the blow which disabled the victim was substantial, but you must also bear in mind that you have a man here who, despite his age, was relatively frail . . . We don't know how old he was, do we?'

Marks shook his head.

'Quite,' Strickland continued. 'He may look older to you, but I'm estimating somewhere between thirty and forty. Drug abuse, heavy drinking, sleeping rough, you know the score, gentlemen. He would not have been a particularly difficult person to disable. I really cannot offer many pointers on who has inflicted this damage. It's a single hard blow to the right temporal, but almost anyone with the strength to swing a bat could have done it.'

Strickland paused and stepped back to study Ratty's head from a few feet away. 'He was struck at an angle with the attacker slightly behind the victim and the weapon in the assailant's right hand, but, beyond that, there's not enough to even indicate the attacker's height.

'The first blow was sufficient to render him unconscious and, if not fatal, may have proved so without medical attention. He was then hit multiple times, with the subsequent blows falling on a similar area as the initial one, but causing wider damage to the right side sphenoid and parietal bones.'

'He would have been on the ground by then, so was the same weapon used each time he was hit?' Goodhew asked.

'Look at this.' Strickland leant in close to Ratty's face and touched the hairline. He pointed to a narrow bruise that ran horizontally across the right temple and into the hair above Ratty's ear. 'This kind of bruise is caused by an object with a hard and straight leading edge. Up to a point you can see similar style bruising from the toe of certain shoes and boots, but the difference is that footwear would be narrower and frequently curved at the front, and therefore the bruise would be shorter, more intense in the centre and tapering at either end. This is more heavily bruised at one end,' he clenched an imaginary implement and swung his hand slowly through the air in front of him towards the outstretched palm of the other hand. 'This injury is consistent with the hard long edge of, say, a metal bar with a square cross-section, a chunk of two-by-two or something similar. At this point I'm speculating, but my guess is that he was hit with something that was swung at his head followed by stabbing blows made by the end of the same object. There is an abundance of debris in the wound but you know the score, it's a waiting game. And in this particular case we'll be sending you the analysis by the box load.'

Goodhew turned to Strickland. 'About the eyes? Have you seen this before?'

Strickland forced the corners of his mouth downwards and nodded slowly for far more seconds than necessary. 'Broadly, yes. Accidental eye damage isn't uncommon, especially when there are severe facial injuries. Road accidents, for example. And when there's alcohol involved . . . glass in the face can make a mess . . . but this? It's interesting.'

His gaze settled on Ratty's face, his expression rapt.

'This particular mutilation caused matching damage to each eye; imagine the eyeball as a sac of fluid, it has been punctured, causing it to deflate. The back of the eye is still attached. What you're seeing here are the parts of the eyeball that have escaped between the upper and lower eyelids.'

'I don't understand,' Goodhew muttered.

Strickland frowned at him, 'There's fluid in the eye—' he began.

Goodhew clarified himself. 'I don't understand the motive for doing this.'

Strickland shrugged. 'I don't understand plenty of things. They still happen.' He laughed; little more than a humourless grunt. 'And you won't accuse us of any shortage of information this time.'

'So you said; by the box load.'

Marks blew out a long slow breath. 'We need to identify him, what can you tell us about the tattoos?'

'I realize you need to identify him,' Strickland bristled. He didn't like to be rushed and while he wasn't irritated yet, Goodhew could tell it was on its way.

Goodhew dragged his attention from Ratty's face. Plenty of his questions related to the tattoos. Ratty had several faded and blurred blue ones, little better than the ones teenagers sometimes gave each other. The most prominent of those was a small dagger on his forearm, blurred and inexpertly drawn. Ivy curled around it, although it could just as easily have been brambles or a failed attempt at a serpent, any detail virtually obliterated by time.

The tattoo on Ratty's neck interested Goodhew the most; a swallow which at first glance had nothing more unique about it than a piece of clip art, downloaded and pasted into position. But it looked newer than the other tattoos and next to it in tiny letters were the initials 'AR'.

Goodhew showed Marks. 'Ratty's?'

'How often do tattooists sign their work?' Marks replied.

Only Strickland failed to notice that it had been a rhetorical question. 'I've seen it on a few large or distinctive pieces; but it would be a delusional tattooist who thought that this bit of painting by numbers merited any recognition.' Strickland pointed to the left upper arm. 'Have you taken a good look at this one?'

Goodhew knew the tattoo he meant, a mottle collage of old-school roses, a mermaid and a couple of scrolls spreading across the width of his bicep. The inks varied in intensity and definition and Goodhew doubted it could all have been the work of one person, and was sure that the first and last were years apart in age. Goodhew recognized this tattoo but this was the first time he'd ever seen it up close.

Strickland took multiple photographs, general shots at first, then focusing on small sections at a time. 'See this?'

Goodhew and Marks both leant closer, but neither could see what he meant.

Strickland pointed to the mermaid's tail, indicating an inch-wide area. Goodhew could see some faint marks behind the pattern of scales. 'Writing?'

'It looks that way. This ink is all old though so it might prove irrelevant. I'll make sure you have all the images, we'll do what we can to enhance what's there.'

Marks nodded. 'If necessary I'll send someone over to take some more shots.'

It was enough to raise Strickland's professional hackles. 'I doubt you'll be able to improve on what we send.' He glared. 'Up to you of course, he's not going anywhere.'

'Send them through then as soon as you can. How soon can we have the initial report?'

'This department is very efficient.' Strickland glared and managed to look like an irritated Garfield. 'You will have to trust me when I say that your department will receive it as soon as I have completed it.'

Marks blanked Strickland's attempted at posturing. 'Thank you, doctor,' he nodded, 'I'm glad you appreciate the urgency.'

# TEN

They had walked as far as Addenbrooke's concourse when Marks told Goodhew that they both needed a coffee.

He turned to Goodhew as they queued. 'Bloody Strickland, never steps out of line but always manages to irritate the hell out of me.' And after they'd paid and found a quiet table, he continued the conversation as though there had been no break. 'Why couldn't he retire before me? I dream of cases that don't involve Strickland. I do not enjoy unnecessary irritation, Gary.'

'I have noticed.'

'I'm sure you have.' Marks stirred his coffee. 'You knew Ratty as well as anyone else at Parkside, what do you know of his background?'

'He talked to me a few times. If I had questions he would object but often answer anyway. I don't remember ever asking him anything personal. And he could be very unreliable as a witness. When anything came up concerning Cambridge, he liked to think he'd heard it first.'

'Delusional sometimes?'

'Yes. Smart though, smarter than a lot are in that situation, and I had wondered whether he'd been one of those people who'd once had a more conventional life and lost it because he couldn't cope. What I don't understand, sir, is why we never pinned down his real identity when he was arrested before.'

Marks flashed his palms upwards. 'I have no idea. It'll be a case of someone cutting corners or a lack of time and resources, probably coupled with Ratty being assessed as low risk. Officers can have good intentions to follow things up but time moves on and they drift.'

Goodhew couldn't decide whether Marks was alluding to a particular case or officer. He certainly didn't plan to backtrack over his own paperwork from months ago if that was what Marks was getting at.

'That's guesswork by the way. Something else for you to find out.' Marks picked up his mug and sipped his coffee. Goodhew said nothing, he sensed that Marks was about to add to the comment. 'Lack of thoroughness back then isn't a reason for there to be any corners cut now though. There mustn't be any implication of a disregard for procedures. And I must say, Gary, I am amazed you know so little about Ratty. I think of you as someone who collects information.'

Goodhew felt the focus of the conversation heading his way. He had made a deliberate decision not to hunt for details of Ratty's former life. He'd taken Ratty at face value and delving into his personal life would have seemed like a betrayal. In the light of Ratty's death that now seemed illogical. He studied Marks's expression but it gave away nothing. 'What do you want me to do?' he queried.

Marks raised his hand from the table in a stop sign. 'I need to ask this first. Ratty's the reason you came back today, I know that, but I can't let you work on this case if I feel that anything you know, or you've done, may have contributed to Ratty's death.'

'Of course there isn't.'

'And what have you been up to while you've been away?'

'Nothing.'

'Gary, you knew about Ratty's death within minutes of him being identified.'

'Which I already explained.' Goodhew took a slow sip of his coffee before continuing. 'I came back for the right reasons. I don't always behave as I should – that is, I haven't in the past, and I realize that it has caused you problems but when I heard about Ratty I wanted to make sure . . .' he took a breath just in time.

Marks nodded slowly. 'You wanted to make sure that his death was investigated properly? Don't you think it matters to anyone else?'

'Mostly, yes I do,' he conceded, 'but not to everyone.' He held

Marks's gaze until he was sure that the correct unspoken message had passed between them. It was an almost invisible softening of his boss's expression that told him it had.

'Put it this way,' Goodhew said, 'I am signed off for another three weeks. By coming back I am extra manpower, a resource that you didn't know you had. Let me find out what I can about him. It would only help the investigation, wouldn't it?'

Marks pressed his lips tight for a few seconds, then nodded reluctantly. 'It would, and there are worse cases for you to come back to,' he admitted.

'It's important to me, sir, it will nag at me if I don't.'

'There's already too much on your conscience and you let it cloud your decisions. You'll see that one day. Do you know I have less than a month before I retire?'

Goodhew knew Marks was due to leave but it had crept up on him, and he was startled that it was now so close. 'That soon? I didn't realize.' Goodhew drained his cup.

'Having you here for a few weeks before I leave may work well for both of us. And I had the concern that if you stayed away too long, coming back might have become a problem. So, dig, Gary. Get out as soon as you can, speak to anyone who knew him. Find out as much as possible and keep me informed.'

There was no one else closer than two tables away but Goodhew still lowered his voice, 'Sir, that business with the eyes? Have you ever come across it before?'

'I haven't actually,' Marks replied. 'It seems very . . . pointless, I suppose. I've attended accidents where there were severe facial injuries, a body disturbed in a cemetery, and I've even seen examples of eyes being attacked on a living victim, in a torture situation or for the purpose of disabling somebody. I imagine when a victim realizes that he's been blinded in one eye then there's the terror of thinking that the same can happen to the other . . . well, warped as it is, there's a reason to that.'

'This must be something to do with the psychology of the killer.'

'That, and not taking anything away. Removing an eye after death might indicate a trophy-type motivation, but leaving it in place? It smacks of a trademark, a signature, call it what you will.'

'I can't imagine that the person who carried this out has only killed the once.'

'I agree,' he said, but then shook his head. 'There's nothing like this locally though. At least, not since I've been here. And an unsolved case like this? It would have been notorious if it had happened anywhere in the country. I would have heard. It's the lack of precedent that makes this so important.'

'I understand,' Goodhew replied. He'd understood within moments of seeing Ratty's body, he'd understood Marks's impatience and he understood what he now needed to do. It was all too clear that this person would kill again.

'It will take an hour to organize a briefing, see what you can find out about him by then.'

# ELEVEN

A single shade of grey covered the sky from horizon to horizon, the streets seemed dull, the open spaces bleak and they were driving back from an autopsy of a murder victim known to Goodhew. He knew the last thing he should be doing was smiling, but he couldn't deny the surge of excitement that had hit him as they'd left Addenbrooke's; thoughts, instincts, energy suddenly seemed to realign. It didn't matter about the downsides that would inevitably follow; right this second the glad-to-be-back feeling was close to euphoric.

They stepped from Marks's car, Goodhew turned to Parkside. For an incredibly ugly building it looked highly appealing. He inhaled deeply and managed to avoid anyone else until he was alone in the corridor leading to Sergeant Sheen's desk, and it was then he finally acknowledged that he felt more alive now than at any point in the previous six months.

He sobered quickly as Sheen stepped from his doorway. 'I heard you were back, Goodhew. 'Bout time.' Goodhew followed, just about keeping up with the shorter, older officer as Sheen hurried back to his desk. Sergeant Sheen was a wiry man, kept thin with mental exertion.

His desk the centre point of his small but formidable empire of local knowledge. He passed on information and kept databases up to date but, between his big red file and his brain, the truths, half-truths and urban myths of Cambridge would, one day, retire with him.

'How are you?' Goodhew asked.

'Well, I discovered how easy it was to keep my files in order without you.' Sheen kicked a stack of copies of the *Cambridge News* lying on the floor beside his desk. 'I go through them every week, that lot's from New Year onwards and there's bugger all going on. All we've had since you've been away is a suspect package in the Grand Arcade, a couple of protests and plenty of business as usual.' He pulled his chair round to the side of his desk and watched while Goodhew cleared a pile of boxes from the guest chair. 'You've got the look of someone who's had too much time on his hands. So what were you doing, conserving your energy until something worthwhile came up? Probably were.'

His distinct Suffolk accent rolled easily through sentences and he often answered his own questions.

'I was sorry to hear about Ratty though. Nasty one, by all accounts.'

'What do you know about him?'

'I've been thinking about that ever since I heard.' Sheen reached across the desk and pulled a thin folder towards him. 'It's just a print-out of incidents called in by the public related to rough sleepers and homeless people.'

'The ones that didn't require further action?'

'Yes, going back to New Year's Day, and it's yours to keep. Nothing springs to mind but, who knows, you may find Ratty in there. He liked to keep a low profile.'

'Any idea of his real name?'

'No. And, you know what, if anyone else had come in asking you'd be the person I'd be sending them to see. He'd talk to Sue Gully but only to find out where you were. You knew more about him than anyone else in here.'

'Which wasn't much. And you knew him before I started. He was cautioned once or twice . . .'

Sheen gave a snort of amusement. 'Oh, yes, I'd almost forgotten the infamous singing incident.'

And that was enough for Goodhew to remember it too, '"Unchained Melody" at 3 a.m. on Four Lamps Corner?'

'See, that's a few years ago, before the Lorna Spence murder. He set fire to a rubbish bin one night too – I think that would have been the first time we crossed paths.'

'But still no name for him.'

'He gave us someone else's details and by the time we tried to follow it up he'd got himself a serious drug problem and it all fell by the wayside.' Sheen clicked his fingers. 'I know who you should talk to.' He swivelled in his chair and leaned back to read the fronts of the files on the shelf overhead. 'Do you know Sam?'

'Male or female?'

'Female. Mid-twenties. Blondish hair to about here,' he marked an imaginary line level with his jaw. 'It's matted, like dreadlocks.'

'She used to busk with a penny whistle, then came back last summer with her dog?'

'That's the one. The dog's a bad-tempered border terrier, called Mooch,' he nodded. He reached up, pulled out a file marked 'Useful Info #11', then handed Goodhew a blurred photo which looked like a still taken from a security camera. 'That's Sam.'

'Yes, I recognize her. What's the connection between her and Ratty?'

'I saw them together a couple of times. Ratty was out there,' Sheen pointed in the direction of Parker's Piece, 'holding on to the dog for her. Not much to go on, but worth a try. The night shelter might know where she is.'

'Thanks.' Goodhew was almost at the door when Sheen spoke.

'Good to have you back. I'd prefer an interesting few months before I retire and things always seem to happen when you're in the thick of it.'

'You're off as well?'

'Six months after Marks. It's time for our batch to drop off the end of the conveyor belt.'

Goodhew shook his head and smiled, 'That's cheerful,' but was surprised to see the older man looking serious.

'Is it true about his eyes?' Sheen asked.

'There was mutilation.'

'After death?'

'Yes, thankfully.'

'That's what I heard.' Sheen threw a pointed look at his files. 'If any thoughts spring to mind, you'll be the first to know. Pass my best wishes to Sue, tell her to drop by if she needs a chat.'

'A chat?'

Sheen shrugged, 'All right then, tell her to see me if she needs any advice on anything local. You know, the same as you do.'

'Am I missing the subtext here?'

'I wouldn't want her to think that she was only welcome up here as a substitute for you. She's far more attractive than you for a start, probably because she behaves better.'

# TWELVE

Marks arrived at the briefing room half an hour before the starting time. The usual manpower shortages had been exacerbated by a spate of political protests and the loaning of officers to neighbouring counties. Pulling together a large enough team had forced him to lean on the goodwill of other departments. He'd rung around while he'd waited at Addenbrooke's and come back to a list of three names. DCs Sandra Knight, Kev Holden and Jack Worthington. 'Well thanks very much,' he'd muttered. He asked them to come in a few minutes before the rest of the team, but it was only Worthington who bothered. He knocked and waited until he was invited to sit before picking a chair. He certainly knew what constituted good manners, but he'd also worked out how to cultivate one of the most aggressive-looking personas possible.

He'd probably been a handsome kid, he still had the symmetrical features and strong jawline, but permanently set in a hard-eyed scowl. The shaved head and the hint of a tattoo protruding from his neckline didn't help. He'd had his nose broken on a couple of occasions too; he was not going to be top of the list for any tasks involving gentle questioning.

'How's your local knowledge?' Marks asked.

'Doormen and low-level dealers.'

'Rough sleepers?'

'I've stepped over a few. Am I going to know this one?'

Marks had a photo ready. 'Known as Ratty.'

Worthington shook his head. 'Nope.'

Marks put the photo back on the desk. 'No reason you should, but he was an addict and if any of your contacts might be able to identify him then use your initiative. We really need his name.'

Worthington moved to the furthest corner of the room as soon as other officers started arriving. He slouched low in his chair and looked up at no one.

Kincaide picked the seat closest to the front. He stared across at Goodhew once, then made a show of dividing his attention between his notebook and Marks. Gully sat amongst a clutch of uniformed officers, even Sheen had joined them and chose the empty seat to Gully's left.

Holden and Knight were both present too, arriving separately with no comment from either on their lateness. They sat at opposite ends of the same row, just as they had when Marks and they had all been new recruits. Holden had been toned back then, 'a bit of all right' Knight had once commented. There had been a lot of pints and takeaways in the intervening years; they showed up in Holden's gut and Knight's frequently stony expression. Sandra Knight's chair was the closest to Goodhew, and she seemed to catch his thought.

'It's like the class of '77 reunion in here.' Her strong Derbyshire accent had never faded.

Marks managed a polite smile. 'Not quite that far back, Sandy.'

'It's when we both left school, love. We would have both been in the same school year you know.' She'd always used the word 'love', probably unaware of how often she dropped it into her sentences or the way she gave it varying degrees of warmth and sincerity, depending on the recipient. 'I mightn't have known you and Kev until a few years later but we're all the class of '77. You're feeling your age.'

Holden nodded. He was a relic from the days of shell suits and night-clubs, of standing on the terraces and smoking at the bar. Had he and Marks really been in the same school year? At that moment Marks had to agree with Knight; he truly felt his age.

He held up the photograph of Ratty and the room fell quiet. 'We know him as Ratty and he was brutally murdered at around midnight last night. He has had a small amount of contact with us in the past, but the personal information we have on him is virtually nil.' Marks paused, realizing that he'd started in the wrong place. 'Young and Charles have been seconded to Bedfordshire to assist with human trafficking operations, Clarke to London and therefore, for the duration of this investigation, we have borrowed DCs Jack Worthington, Sandra Knight and Kev Holden.' Marks nodded towards each in turn but didn't move on when he reached Holden. 'DC Holden, is this someone you recognize?'

'I don't think so. I've seen a lot of faces over the years.'

'You can't put a name to this face then?'

'I've been dealing with vehicle theft for five years, I don't s'pose he was pinching cars somehow.' He grinned at the end of the sentence, then glanced around the room as if he'd been clever or funny or both.

Marks now wished he'd pulled Holden and Knight up on their lateness in the first place. He turned to Sandra Knight. 'And you?'

'Sorry, love, the face looks familiar but so do plenty. Once we have a name I can flush him from every database possible. Right now I can go with the nickname but it probably won't throw much up.'

'You have some tattoo knowledge, don't you?'

Knight smiled broadly and sat taller, raising her voice a little as she spoke, 'TAI stands for the Tattoo and Artificial Identifier Database. It holds descriptions and images of body art, piercing and any artificial identity-related items that are not recorded elsewhere.'

'Such as?'

'Usually unregulated or extreme cosmetic surgery items, unique dental work and the growing trend for implant body modification . . .' She paused for the murmur of curiosity to ripple through the room. 'You'd be amazed at some of the things people do to themselves, then to go on and commit a crime . . . Well, it's only a matter of time before we match the description to the person. Tattoos are tame by comparison, but the volume of them is what makes TAI a challenge. If this Ratty had tattoos I'll put them in and see what we come up with.'

'Kincaide, do we have any possible witnesses from the market?'

Kincaide shook his head. 'There wasn't a single stallholder near the market at the time of his murder. Dr Addis was in the building when the call came in though. I took him with me and that meant we rapidly had an estimate on time of death. I don't think the autopsy will change that much. Seems long odds that we'll find a witness at that time of night.'

'It does, but we have to look at all possible avenues here, Michael.'

Kincaide tilted his head back and deliberately paused, 'CCTV isn't going to help us much, it's notoriously poor around the market. We could check it as a last resort, sir. Identifying where we don't need to look will save more wasted time.'

'More?'

'More than necessary,' Kincaide replied, but Marks was certain that wasn't what he meant. Kincaide resented police time being spent on this case.

Kincaide moved on, 'We believe that the deceased had been eating a bag of chips. There was litter with the body and what appeared to be, chip grease on his fingers. I suppose that's waiting on the autopsy test results too, but I've visited the Gardenia in Rose Crescent and they confirm that Ratty did purchase an open bag of chips from them late yesterday evening. I'm looking for earlier sightings to work out which route he took to Rose Crescent and searching for footage of Ratty and anyone following him before then.'

Marks nodded. 'We need to bear in mind that this attack shows signs of premeditation but nothing, as yet, that points to Ratty being the specific target. The results from the autopsy may well open up several lines of enquiry but the clear focus until then *must* be on the threat this person poses to the community at large. With this in mind we will be issuing a carefully worded statement.'

Kincaide's eyes flashed angrily. 'To create panic?'

'To shake out some quick answers. Of course panic isn't the objective, but increased vigilance is likely to bear fruit. And that's increased vigilance from all of us, Michael. Dismissing issues facing any sector of society will only threaten the outcome of this case I don't expect any of you to turn away from fully engaging with the homeless community. I will not tolerate it and this is the only warning I will give on the topic.' He ran his gaze in a slow and deliberate sweep of the room.

'I will class every corner cut and late arrival as a sign that this case is receiving a less than diligent response from this team. I am expecting this to be my last major case before retirement and I will not see it fail for the wrong reasons. Is that clear?' He didn't wait for any response, instead turned sharply towards Sheen. 'Does Goodhew have everything available from you?'

Sheen nodded. 'Enough to keep him busy for a little while.'

Marks shifted his focus to Goodhew. 'What do you have?'

'Faces that know Ratty, people he was seen with. All vague but need to be followed up.'

'Report straight back to me and Michael as soon as you find any details of his identity.'

Marks finished with clear instruction to each person present. He'd felt the lack of harmony in the room and had no doubt that he was the root of much of it. He pressed his lips into a hard line and did his best to make it clear that he didn't want chat and questions, just to see them silently exit and hurry towards the tasks in hand.

The room cleared until only Gully remained. She hadn't made any move and sat with her elbows on the armrest, her fingers interlocked. It was clear she waiting for him. Apart from the two of them, Kincaide was the last to leave. He glanced across but moved on quickly too.

'You and Goodhew were both very quiet, Sue.'

She leant back a little and stared steadily at him.

'Goodhew was. And so was I, sir.' She pressed her lips together in much the same way as he'd just done, but then added, 'For two very different reasons I'd guess.' There was an unexpected coldness about her.

'I'm sure that's the case,' he agreed. He closed the door and moved towards her. 'Is there something you need to discuss, Sue?' Now wasn't a good time for anything other than the current workload but he could sense that pushing this aside until later would be a mistake; he was used to the way she quietly pushed herself to speak out even though she hated to be in any kind of spotlight. She usually said what she needed to say despite her natural reticence and involuntary blushes. This time it was clearly different.

# THIRTEEN

There had been a dance going on in Gully's head. Logic and conscience, patience and discretion constantly pirouetting around each other, changing partners faster than second-rate celebrities. She'd thought it through – the whole situation – and made a plan that seemed sensible and pragmatic. She'd thought through the how and when . . . and now, somewhere in the middle of that thought, she'd begun to explain it out loud.

'I'd made up my mind about how and when I'd say it but after this morning,' she paused, letting the anger flow, knowing that whatever she was about to say would be unchecked. Glad that the decision to speak out no longer seemed under her control. 'After this morning,' she repeated, her mouth tightening with rage, 'I am not going to waste time considering your feelings when you support people who are so spiteful and insensitive.' She glared at Marks and, for once, his expression seemed easy to read: bewildered. 'I know about Goodhew's grandfather. I've been spending time in the archives and I found the case file.'

She saw his eyes widen a fraction, enough to betray his surprise, 'Why in the world were you digging through that lot?'

She didn't want to discuss that.

'When I first came back . . .' she said, then let the sentence drift off. She doubted Marks would stop her to rake over the uneasy return to work after the death of her closest colleague, Kelly Wilkes. 'One file led to another. And then I asked around and found out that you're not the only one who knows.'

'It isn't a sealed file.'

'No, except Gary doesn't know, does he?' She ploughed on without needing an answer. 'Sheen told me the background but he can't answer why it's always been kept from Goodhew. I don't even know how that's possible when he's the most astute and inquisitive person I've ever met.'

'Because it wasn't that clear-cut, there was more to it—'

'I decided to tell him.'

'Sue?' Marks sounded calmer than she'd expected. 'Sue?'

'What?'

'You haven't already done it, have you?'

'Do you think he'd be so calm and unfazed if I had? I decided to wait until he was back at work, we figured . . .'

'We?'

'Sheen and me. We thought he should come back because he felt it was time. He would have got here just as you left and Sheen said he'd talk to you, give you the chance to tell him first, but now Gary's back and all day I've been crossing paths with people who've been here longer than I have, and I bet they all know.'

Marks shook his head at that but it seemed more defensive than sincere. 'Not all,' he added.

'But Norris on the front desk? Sheen, Knight and Holden? I've even seen that the pathologist Sykes commented on the file. So does that mean Dr Strickland too, and Dr Addis, and anyone else over forty?'

DI Marks's expression softened suddenly and he sat on the chair alongside hers. She waited for him to speak and in the minutes that followed felt her cheeks flush and the desire to cry clogging her throat. She felt sorry for her outburst, ashamed to have lost control. But she had no desire to apologize for either.

When Marks eventually spoke his voice was quiet, his words carefully placed. 'Gary was eleven, his sister nine, and both at school when there was a disturbance at the house. There had been a previous break-in at the property and perhaps the men involved thought that the house was unoccupied . . .'

'In the middle of the day?'

'Unlikely perhaps, but it was a line of investigation. Joseph Goodhew, Gary's grandfather, was assaulted. A single punch actually. He collapsed and died a short time afterwards without regaining consciousness, and the autopsy concluded that the blow may not have killed him at all if it hadn't been for an existing brain injury which caused a fatal haemorrhage.'

'It's still murder.'

Marks nodded. 'I know, I know. But it was the second break-in at the house and nothing had been taken on either occasion. We were looking for two men responsible for a seemingly motiveless – and failed – crime. The case was struggling from the start; he was a man who'd collapsed and died – that's how the press saw it. It was barely reported and, in all honesty, quickly sidelined by other cases.'

Collapsed and died were the very words Goodhew used when she'd asked him about his grandfather.

'The family took Gary and his sister abroad for the weeks that followed. They were back in Cambridge for the funeral, and as far as I remember didn't stay around for much else.'

'It doesn't explain why he doesn't know.'

Marks hesitated for the first time. 'No,' he said quietly, 'it doesn't. As far as I was concerned it was a case we'd all left behind by over a decade. Then his grandmother made an appointment to see me, told me that he planned to apply to work here at Parkside. I told her that I wouldn't – couldn't – conceal anything that was in the public domain. She just asked me not to raise it first.'

'But why?' Gully shook her head, puzzled. 'They always talk, it's not like they're estranged or don't get along . . .'

'Perhaps he never questioned what he was told.'

'I don't buy that.'

'That's how it is. Now it's your turn. Tell me about this morning?' He studied her carefully as he waited for her to reply. 'You said spiteful and insensitive?'

Gully took a deep breath and exhaled slowly.

'It doesn't matter, I spoke out of turn.'

'But it clearly does.'

'If there was something you weren't happy with, then I think you would change it, wouldn't you?'

'Of course.'

'Then you're either happy with it or blind to it, sir.' She knew she'd pushed her luck as the words came out. They sounded less like a valid observation and more of an insult when she heard them out loud.

'I need to know what exactly you're referring to, Sue.'

'So you can understand?' She guessed he was close to losing his patience with her but she still pushed her luck further with an angry smirk. 'Because Gary's been given that option?'

'Now that's enough. I cannot stop you from disclosing this to Gary but I'd like you to hold on. I've been planning to tell him when I retire. Can you give me those three weeks?'

'I guess.'

'During the briefing you, Goodhew and Kincaide were the only ones who didn't seem uncomfortable or shocked at the photograph of Ratty's injuries. Even Worthington's face twitched. So I'm guessing you'd seen him already.'

She looked away then nodded silently.

'Because I know you were at the scene well after Addis had declared him dead, after Kincaide had, no doubt, recognized the body. When a constable being used on the periphery had no reason to be pushed to make an unnecessary identification. So you see, I'm not entirely blind. Or happy, come to that.'

Gully didn't speak until Marks finished and gave her leave to go. She paused at the door. 'Thank you, sir.'

# FOURTEEN

The Fitzwilliam Museum stood in a slightly elevated position, adding further height to the already imposing columns which dominated the frontage. It wasn't far from her home overlooking Newnham Common but she wasn't dressed for walking so it was a taxi that dropped Ellie Goodhew at the courtyard entrance of the museum.

She paid the driver then took a moment to let the stillness of the mid-afternoon settle her a little. This wasn't going to be a meeting that she would enjoy but she took comfort in museums, in the way that the trials and achievements of previous generations reduced her own worries. Maybe it was because of the Fitzwilliam's location, on a tract of land that put trees, the river and Laundress Green between it and the city, that made it feel disconnected from the rest of town. She was glad of that, and always thought that the building wouldn't have looked out of place facing out across the Grand Canal in Venice.

At that moment Venice had a huge appeal. She sighed and made her way inside and through to the café. She was early, but not surprised to find that Marks was already there.

He stood to greet her, 'Ellie, how are you?'

She smiled. 'The same as ever.' She wasn't looking forward to the conversation but her fondness for Marks was genuine.

She waited at the table while he ordered drinks. As he queued, he glanced around and when he returned with the tray asked, 'So why did you choose to meet here?'

'You chose the time, the least I could do was decide where, and I like it here.'

His eyes glinted with the first spark of a challenge. 'You would have thought it through more than that. You and your grandson have a similar opaqueness.'

She relaxed in her chair and kept steady eye contact, 'Then, I'd say because I can have melanzane parmigiana and San Pellegrino for a late lunch, and divert myself by pretending I'm enjoying Italy instead of dwelling on what you're about to suggest.'

Marks hadn't touched his coffee yet but still straightened the cup on its saucer. 'It's funny how you'd like me to believe that Goodhew's attributes have been inherited from his grandfather.'

'Gary and I both learnt from him. Goodhew's the smart one, I just see the obvious.'

'Which is?'

'You're about to retire and you want to tell Gary; to hand on your notes and leave a clear desk.'

'Leave a clear desk?' He mulled over the words. 'That's an image I haven't seen for many years. And you're right.' Marks was facing the gift shop, the rack of postcards that protruded into the corner of the café providing the only splash of colour. He stared off in their direction. 'How do we know he won't turn up here?'

She smiled at the question. 'There are two dozen museums in Cambridge; if Gary suddenly decided to visit one it would be the anthropology museum every time.'

'All those bones and sunken heads?' Marks didn't seem convinced. 'Personally, I never know where he'll turn up next. I wasn't entirely convinced he'd return to work either.'

'That's not true, Anthony, we both know what drives him.' *For now at least* she added silently.

Marks sugared his coffee, tearing the end from the sachet and sending a steady trickle of grains into the froth. He stirred it so slowly that she wondered whether he'd disturbed a single grain and they'd be lying in a syrupy puddle by the time he reached the bottom of the cup.

'I have a perfect storm brewing. Gary's back and I've cobbled together a team by grabbing any resources I can. Knight and Holden are both with me.'

She leant in closer. 'It's an old case and Gary was just a kid, there's no reason to think they'll know, is there?' She remembered both as young officers, Knight had been forthright, Holden unsubtle: she doubted whether either would stay quiet once they realized the connection. And once they worked alongside Gary, the connection might be made. 'I wouldn't want him to find out from either of them.'

'You know there's always the chance he already knows?'

That was another familiar theme. Privately she suspected that on one level he did, that buried just out of reach of his conscious mind was the accurate picture of his grandfather's death. 'He doesn't.'

'But Sue Gully does.'

'Oh,' she said flatly. 'How?'

'She found it in the archives, saw the surname and address and read the files.'

'And she will need him to know, I can see that.'

He nodded but didn't have to, she knew that time had almost run out. 'I never imagined that it would work out like this. I thought I'd be keeping it from them for weeks or months, not years. Just until we had the answers.' She'd valued all the time she'd spent with Gary; the bond between them that had grown. She had never hung on to many regrets but if she could have gone back and changed this situation she'd have done so a hundred times. 'I should be the one to tell him.'

'I'd be happy to be there, if it helps.'

'For moral support? He'll be shocked enough when he realizes we know one another, I think he'll find the secrets the hardest part to take.'

Marks drained his cup, screwing his nose up as he took the last mouthful, 'He'll feel as though he's been lied to.'

'Because he has.'

'He'll come round.'

'We'll see.' Ellie's gaze wandered past DI Marks to the condiment table. At the back of it stood a wooden posable figure, just like the one she herself had owned when she'd first tried to draw. He seemed to be looking in their direction, his paddle-hands upturned as if he was also asking the perpetual questions. How could she tell Gary and his sister about their grandfather's murder without revealing the terrible suspicion that had prompted her to keep it from them in the first place? 'I'll need to tell Debbie too.'

'Is she still in Australia?'

'She can fly home. And I'll track down their father. It'll take me a couple of weeks at most to get them here.'

'I thought persuading you would be hell.' A slow smile grew on Marks's face. 'You've always been against this in the past, why now?'

'You said about a perfect storm. I think it's about things coming into alignment – it's the same idea I suppose but it just sounds less daunting. You're retiring and so is Sheen, maybe the desk clearing applies to him too. Gary's older and wiser and so is Debbie. Then you told me that Sue knows. Of all people she doesn't deserve to be put in that position. Sometimes, when that alignment happens, it's better to go with it than to resist it.'

He nodded. 'Now I'm retiring, I can't decide whether the job feels like it's lasted a lifetime or should be just starting. But I'm ready to move along now.'

He took his jacket from the back of his chair and stood to put it on. She stood too and touched him lightly on the arm.

'I've never said this before but I really do appreciate all the support you've offered Gary over the years.'

'I've given him more latitude than I should have, I know that. And he should have chased promotion and moved on by now, but his logic isn't everyone else's. I'm glad to have had him on my team, but relieved to have survived the experience.'

# FIFTEEN

The next morning, Goodhew had started at Jimmy's on East Road. The shelter was situated within a significant part of the buildings of the Zion Baptist Church. Sheen still called it 'the night shelter' out of habit; it now stayed open twenty-four hours every day.

The church itself and its companion building, the old Sunday school, were both large and uninspiring from the outside, giant chunks of grubby cream and red brick. Perhaps it was the building's size and ugliness that made it affordable for the charity; he'd always found it apt that it was very different on the inside. Today there were few people around and none of them knew Sam. By the time Goodhew left the building, three men stood in the doorway; all were thin and shared the same complexion, weathered skin over monochrome. Goodhew stepped onto the pavement then turned to speak to them.

'I'm looking for Sam?' The man nearest to Goodhew had his gaze fixed on the traffic and didn't seem to notice anyone around him. The younger of the other two leant back against the wall; he wore skinny jeans and 1980s Nike trainers. Whenever Goodhew spoke he looked back and forth between Goodhew and the older man. It was a few minutes after ten but each held a can of cheap cider, a carrier bag holding the next six-pack at their feet.

'Have any of you seen Sam?'

The two exchanged glances, then the man furthest from Goodhew spoke. 'What are you then? Her social worker?'

'DC Goodhew, Gary Goodhew.' The man seemed bemused when Goodhew reached out to shake his hand. 'What's your name?'

'Will John do?'

'For today. Have you seen her then?'

'Not this week, mate. What's up?'

'Did you know Ratty?'

The silent man continued to ignore them, but the other two nodded.

'When did you see him last?'

John shrugged. 'I dunno what today is.'

'Monday.'

There had been a pause, but Goodhew waited until John realized he was still expected to give an answer.

'About a week before they killed him.'

'They?'

'It's always they, isn't it? The great unseen *they*.' He raised his can as if *they* were somehow worth toasting. 'And now they want Sam too?'

'*I* want to speak to her. She might know Ratty's real name – unless either of you do?'

They didn't, but John reached out and jabbed the silent man in the arm. 'Vic, where's Sam?'

Vic's gaze wandered away from the traffic and settled on Goodhew. 'Sam who?'

John raised his voice, 'Sam and Mooch.' Then louder, 'Sam and Mooch.'

The skin around Vic's lower eyelids had a permanent droop, forming a veined red hammock that glistened with moisture, his nose looked damp too and when he finally spoke spittle flew out faster than the words. 'Mooch, she likes the river.'

'Give it a go, mate, Vic's full of shit though.'

It hadn't been the most reliable lead of his career but Goodhew had worked his way towards the river in any case. In the summer months the riverbank, cemeteries and public gardens would have been amongst the first places Goodhew would have checked; in a wet and bitter

February he would have tried every other likely doorway or squat first. But, based on Vic's 'information', he'd decided to check Christ's Pieces and Jesus Green on the way to the river, then from Jesus Lock Bridge, following the river downstream towards Stourbridge Common. If that failed he'd planned go back to Jesus Lock Bridge via Midsummer Common and head upstream towards Newnham.

It began to rain as he crossed Christ's Pieces. His jacket kept out the worst of it but it wasn't many minutes before the wet made the denim of his jeans begin to cling to his thighs. Perhaps it would make him better equipped to spot the sheltered places.

The area around Jesus Lock Bridge had been deserted, the bridge itself shining darkly, water dripping from its steel elevations. He didn't check his watch but guessed it had to be close to noon. He set out along the towpath, and was estimating how long it would take to complete a fruitless walk from here to Stourbridge and back to Newnham, when Mooch ran from the shadows under Victoria Bridge and onto the path ahead of him.

She planted her feet squarely and barked half a dozen times in one quick volley of yaps. She backed away as he walked closer, then turned tail and scurried into the gloom. He found her huddled alongside Sam, sharing space on a small pile of flattened cardboard boxes. Sam sat cross-legged in a sleeping bag which she'd folded down to her waist.

'Sam?'

'You're that policeman, right?'

'That policeman?'

She angled her head back and stared up at him. 'Ratty knew you.'

'That's right.' He couldn't hold a conversation standing over her. 'OK if I sit?'

'Whatever. You're soaked, though, you'll make the path wet. Miserable fucking weather. So what do you want?'

'I need to find out more about Ratty.'

'Bit late for that.' She spoke every sentence in the same way, quickly, with a cocky tone that rose in the final couple of syllables. Teenagers often spoke like that too, especially when they were being challenged in front of their mates. It made sincerity difficult to spot and sometimes worked as a pretty good tactic for deflecting questions.

'Who he knew and where he went could help us find his killer.' She didn't reply. 'Will you answer some questions for me, Sam?'

'I don't want to go to Parkside.'

'Here's fine. I'll need to write it down though.'

'You know you won't find witnesses, don't you?'

'Why not?'

'Because Ratty was invisible. No one would have chosen to look at him, so no one would have seen what happened, right?'

'Someone's seen something.'

'And why will they care? They think that people like him are destined to die in the gutter.'

'Plenty don't think so and they're the witnesses we need.'

'We?'

'My questions and your answers?'

She tried to sound casual. 'I got nothing to hide.'

He took that as a 'yes'.

'When did you last see him?'

'Earlier that day, I'd been down by McDonald's.'

'Rose Crescent?'

'Well it wasn't Paris, was it?'

The only other McDonald's was a drive-through on the edge of town, but detail, as always, was everything.

'Do you need to know which bit of pavement I was on too?'

'Sam?' he nudged.

'I'm telling you, aren't I? I was down there and I'd got a few quid and a bloke bought me a coffee, that happens sometimes if you sit near enough to a takeaway. Ratty came down and blagged half my drink and a couple of quid for later.'

'Did he mention anything unusual, anyone he'd met perhaps?'

'No. And his mood was just the same as any other day.'

'Was he often on Market Hill?'

'Yeah. He'd been going on about that choices bloke.'

She said it as though he ought to know exactly who she meant. From memory he ran himself up and down the aisles of market stalls and still couldn't imagine who she meant. 'Someone he met?'

'No. Famous dead bloke, went on about choices.'

'Thomas Hobson? You mean Hobson's choice?'

'That's it. He was something to do with Market Hill, right?'

Goodhew nodded. 'And a few other places round town.'

'Yeah, Ratty went on about them too.'

'Was that just recently?' Choice led to change. Perhaps there was a reason that Ratty had been dwelling on thoughts of Hobson.

'Yeah, the last couple of weeks.'

'Really?'

'Yeah, then a couple of months before that. It was one of his favourite topics, he liked to make out that he had options.' Mooch nudged her arm and Sam let the little dog clamber into her lap. She scratched Mooch's ears as she spoke. 'Choice? That really makes freezing your balls off OK, doesn't it? There you go, you've had all I know about Ratty.'

'It would help if you can remember anything about his background.'

'Like what? I'm not the font of everything like he was.'

'Do you know where he lived before Cambridge?'

She shook her head, then stopped. 'We were down here last summer and he pointed that way and said he'd lived down there as a kid.'

Goodhew looked downriver, in the general direction of Chesterton. It wasn't much of a lead.

But then she smiled at his misunderstanding. 'You're looking in Cambridge? That's what I did. Ratty said I was stupid. Not just me then. He said, "Same river, different town," but he didn't tell me where he meant.'

'That's the kind of thing, what else?'

'Said he knew stuff about you.'

'Ratty said that about everyone.'

'Fair point.'

'What about his real name?'

'Everyone called him Ratty. I'm Sam because it's my name. I thought maybe his real name might be something really shit so I asked him, he said it was a nickname he'd been given thanks to a kids' TV character. Wouldn't say which one though. And that really *is* the lot.'

'Thanks Sam, you have been a big help.'

'If I believe that, I know you have to be pretty desperate.'

He clambered to his feet, the effects of the cold and wet already chilling deep into his flesh. He rubbed his thighs briskly as he tried to restore his circulation. Sam hadn't shivered, in fact she barely moved and seemed to ignore the weather with either stoic determination or a poor sense of touch.

'It's all helpful,' he assured her.

'Right. I still think you're flogging a dead one.'

'If he had family then it's important they know.'

'It's been in the paper.' She reached into her sleeping bag and pulled out a folded page of newsprint. 'If I've seen it, they'll have seen it too.'

'That only says that a body was found, no description.'

She shrugged and tucked the page away. 'I reckon I care and they don't. But if you stick his photo in the paper they'll come running out then.' One corner of her mouth curled into a smile. 'It's easier to show some love for someone when they're too dead to crash on your couch.'

# SIXTEEN

There was no brightness in the sky on any horizon now. The weather wouldn't improve for the rest of the day, and the rain filled the air with nature's version of white noise. As cold and wet as it was, Goodhew walked across Jesus Green, glad of the solitude. His thoughts started with Ratty, then drifted on to Sam and Mooch. He didn't want to believe that a girl and her dog were the sum of the people who cared about Ratty.

But when Goodhew had almost died, he'd discovered that the people that really mattered could be counted on the fingers of one hand. And even some of those he'd steered away from, finding it far easier to shrink his circle of contacts to the bare minimum. And that was without the misadventure of whatever it was that had led Ratty to abandon a conventional life. Further ahead, other pedestrians appeared as inky smudges through the mist of rain. There had been several occasions when he'd tried to track Ratty down, usually at awkward times of day or in the cold or wet; times Ratty might have sought shelter if any had been on offer. But Goodhew chose to believe that there was someone out there who needed to know that Ratty had died. Who could help them put the real name to his battered face.

The smudges of people began to solidify enough for him to be able to pick out the broadest details of each. Seeing a little more clearly made the greatest of differences; he pulled out his mobile phone and called Bryn.

'Gary?' Bryn shouted down the phone. 'Hang on.' After a brief delay the noise of Bryn's workshop became muffled and instead he could hear a kettle being filled. 'Let me guess, you've bought a car and need it serviced. No, that's not it, you've phoned to distract me from looking after customers' cars. You're unemployed so you want my dad to sack me?'

'Bryn, shut up now. I'm not buying a car and you like distractions. I need you to speak to Maya for me.'

Maya had been Bryn's on-off girlfriend for a few months now; anything over a week was probably a record. She was a free spirit, sometimes elusive, but the 'off' times were her choice and seemed to infuriate and attract Bryn in equal measure. He wouldn't mind any excuse to phone her.

'Depends what it is,' Bryn replied, but it was easy to hear the cheerfulness in his voice.

'I need some information about a tattoo – a couple of tattoos actually. How well does she know local tattooists?'

'She probably knows them all – doesn't mean she's on speaking terms with them all. They're always knocking each other's work.' Goodhew heard the kettle and Bryn rummaging around for a pen. 'Tell me what you're after.'

Goodhew described Ratty's tattoos. 'It doesn't matter who did them, I just need someone who can identify the man they belonged to.'

'I see,' grunted Bryn. 'You're no longer unemployed then.'

'I went back on Sunday.'

'Boredom get to you?'

'Maybe it did a bit,' Goodhew conceded, 'and there was a murder.' He hesitated, then added, 'Someone I knew a little.'

'OK Gary, I'll phone Maya now.'

'Keep it low-key, can you?'

'I'll tell her it's a favour for a mate. I'll phone you as soon as I can.'

# SEVENTEEN

Goodhew sent a duplicate text to Kincaide and Gully. 'Ratty possibly from a town north of Cambridge and along the River Cam, nicknamed after kids' TV character.'

Only Gully replied. 'Ely, Littleport, Downham Market, King's Lynn? What else?'

'Initial AR on tattoo on his neck.'

'That's it?'

'That's it. Going for change of clothes, back in soon.'

By the time he returned to his flat the first twinges of back pain had begun. Instead of just changing into dry clothes he stood in the shower, turning the jets on full and switching the temperature in two-minute intervals between cold and as hot as his skin could bear. Gradually the discomfort settled and he switched off the water after one final hot rinse down. He walked through to the lounge, and as he pulled on fresh jeans he noticed that his phone had received a new message. It had come from Bryn. Goodhew translated his friend's dubious text abbreviations: Maya had found two possibilities. Garry Brown at Second Skin in Newmarket and Laura Alps on Forehill, Ely.

Ely stood on the River Cam, Newmarket didn't. It took him just a couple of minutes to find the tattoo shop where Laura Alps worked. He dialled and as he waited clicked 'search images' and found a pink-haired girl with cat-woman mascara smiling out at him. It was Laura who answered.

'I've got a couple of minutes. Depends what it is.'

He introduced himself. 'We're trying to identify the owner of several tattoos, a swallow on the neck with initials "AR" . . .'

She cut in before he could finish, 'Maya gave me the description, didn't say why.' She continued, sounding cautious, 'I might recognize the mermaid.'

'Do you have the man's name?'

'Not really, no.'

'Not really? Did you know him as Ratty then?'

'Something like that, I never really knew for certain.' He waited for her to add more detail. She didn't. 'Was it one of your tattoos?'

'That mermaid? No way, it's a piece of shit.'

'Did you do any of his tattoos, Laura?'

'No. He came by sometimes, always talking about getting a new one. I never told him to stop wasting my time so once, maybe twice a year, he'd wander in, hang around for a bit then wander out again. I don't think he ever had money.'

'Do you know if he had family in Ely?'

'No. He never said, always cut off any questions by saying he liked to mind his own business."

Ratty was one of the nosiest people Goodhew had ever known and in different circumstances the comment would have amused him.

But he said nothing and Laura continued, 'He was always on something, drunk or a bit incoherent. Apart from the last time.'

'When was this?'

'A couple of months ago, I guess. He came in and said he wanted a tattoo but couldn't afford it. It was the same as the other times but without the bullshit.'

She let out a small surprised 'oh', 'I do remember something. He said he might get the money together for his fortieth.'

'I'll need to come by with the photos of the tattoos to get a formal identification, will you be there for the rest of the afternoon?'

While he'd been speaking to Laura on one phone, he'd been texting Gully from his mobile. He made himself a coffee, found a T-shirt and was about to pull it over his head when he caught sight of a police car pulling up in the street outside. He guessed what that meant and threw the T-shirt across the end of his settee; what he needed now was a shirt and something that would pass as a suit.

It took just a couple of minutes to join Gully, she already had the engine running and pulled away from the kerb as soon as he'd shut his door.

'Where are we going?'

'You were right about Ely. I'm not 100 per cent, but I think he was Aaron Rizzo.'

Goodhew repeated the name slowly, trying to mesh it with his image of Ratty. It didn't suit Ratty at all. 'I thought the *R* in *AR* would be Roland.'

'As in Roland Rat? So did I, but I went on the Internet and made a list of famous TV rats, then began with the ones with names starting with A or R. I only found Rizzo and Roland.'

'Who's Rizzo?'

'From *The Muppets.*'

Goodhew looked blank.

'You're kidding me?' Gully exclaimed.

'I know the pig, the frog and the bird.'

'What bird?'

'The big yellow one.'

'Really?' She grunted in disapproval. 'Rizzo was easier to check than Roland so I went for that first, I entered 'Rizz' as a text string to see if it threw up anything similar. Only match of the right age, Aaron Rizzo, aged thirty-eight. Only living relative was his brother Matthew, lives in Ely.'

'And now we have a name we can go for medical records.'

'Exactly. Marks wants us to speak to the brother, and get back to him as soon as we have a yes, no or a maybe.'

'And all in the time it took me to walk back here and take a shower?'

She frowned and glanced at her watch. 'Heading for two hours, Gary. Did you black out or something?'

'I was thinking.'

'And?'

'Nothing that wouldn't have occurred to you.'

Matthew Rizzo lived in a mid-terraced house, narrow with aluminium 1970s framed windows and dried-up rain marks on the glass. The front door was solid, apart from a single spy-pane in the upper-centre. A man's face appeared, rippling behind the textured glass. He opened the door and held it wide, inviting them in before either had had the chance to explain why they'd come.

There was a mat and a coat hook directly behind the door, but rather than a hallway, they'd stepped into one corner of the sitting room. Books lined the longest wall, two guitars and an amp stood by the window, and the only door stood open and led to the kitchen. Gully could see outside through its windows.

'Do you live alone?' she asked.

'With my girlfriend, she's at work.'

Goodhew nodded, 'Please sit down, Mr Rizzo.' He paused.

'Yesterday morning we were called to investigate the death of a rough sleeper. It was reported in today's paper.'

Matthew nodded too. He'd paled slightly but he kept his gaze fixed on Goodhew, probably willing the words to come more quickly, but it wasn't the time to rush.

'Although the man was known to us we need to establish his identity.'

Gully found herself studying Matthew Rizzo's face for any signs of familial likeness but couldn't see it.

'We knew him as Ratty.'

She spotted the brief flicker of his eyes, the twitch of his fingers; the name meant something.

'It could be,' he conceded. 'Maybe. What did he look like?'

Goodhew kept his initial description to height and build. 'We need someone to make a formal identification, but we also need to be as sure as we can before we ask you to do that.'

'Of course.' Matthew Rizzo didn't move though, instead he took a few breaths and stared in the direction of the front door. 'What happened to him?'

'He was the victim of an assault, which is the most I can really say until we can confirm his identity.'

Goodhew glanced across at Gully. She picked up on the cue. 'I'll make some drinks,' she offered and retreated to the kitchen. The silence between the men stretched out for at least a full minute, enough time for her to remember how she'd once hated the getting-the-drinks part of this. But with Goodhew it wasn't sexism that sent her to the kitchen; he was better at this role. He knew how long to wait before nudging Matthew Rizzo back into conversation.

'Did your brother have tattoos, Mr Rizzo?'

'A few.'

'Can you describe them, when you're ready?'

'He had fancy script on his arm at one time but he had another tattoo, a mermaid, over the top.'

'Why?'

Matthew Rizzo swallowed, fighting to control his voice and managing to keep it in check. 'We were in a band together. Back in the nineties. The Rizzos, and we were doing OK for a while, pubs mostly, but I didn't want it tattooed on me. I'm not crazy.' He shook his head. 'That was Aaron's job.' He paused, then asked, 'Do you think it's him?'

Goodhew gave nothing away. 'Do you have any recent photos of your brother?'

'Not recent but I have one from back then, before the band split. Would that help?' He hurried up the narrow staircase and Gully heard a drawer open and then shut again. He returned with a large square frame filled with a display of nine six-by-four prints. He passed it to Goodhew just as Gully brought the drinks through. She and Goodhew stood side by side, both drawn, she was sure, to the same image in the top right-hand corner.

The man was early twenties, thin but not skinny. He was holding an ice cream in his left hand, his short-sleeved shirt bearing his tattooed forearm and leaving 'The Rizzos' clearly visible.

There was no doubt that it was Ratty.

Goodhew dwelt on it for a few seconds longer. 'What did he play?'

'Bass. And he sang.'

'And you played guitar?'

'I teach it now, but yes.'

'When did you last see him?'

'Before Christmas. I don't know exactly. He'd come by un-announced, and I've seen him in Cambridge a few times.'

He took a sip of his tea. 'I've imagined this moment so many times. Thought of the circumstances you'd tell me and I would have guessed hypothermia or overdose, accident maybe. But not assault.'

He had barely touched his drink but put the mug on a side table, took a grey wool coat from the hook beside the door and stood ready to leave. 'Poor kid,' he said. 'Just couldn't get his head straight.'

Goodhew phoned ahead and arranged to meet Marks at the morgue. Matthew Rizzo was silent throughout the journey, and Goodhew's own thoughts settled on wondering how presentable they'd managed to make Ratty's body.

Marks was waiting in the doorway and led Rizzo through to a small anteroom that was equipped with chairs, a TV set and the obligatory box of tissues. They both sat, the TV in front of them.

'The body is in the next room,' Marks explained. 'When I turn on the screen you will see the face of the deceased. You just need to confirm whether or not he is your brother. Is that clear, Mr Rizzo?'

'Of course,' he replied.

Ratty's picture flickered onto the screen. Goodhew heard the brother's sharp intake of breath, registering shock both at the realization and at the contusions visible across the side of the head. Despite that, Ratty's face had been cleaned up more than he would have thought possible.

Matthew Rizzo drew another slower breath, sitting taller as he did so. 'Yes,' he confirmed, 'that's Aaron. Without a doubt. Now please tell me what happened to him.'

He nodded occasionally, listening silently as Marks explained, leaving the injuries until last.

'Mr Rizzo, it's because of the unusual and very specific nature of these injuries that I would like your assistance with an appeal to the public.'

'To give permission, or more than that?'

'Once your wider family know, then we can arrange appeals for information via the news media. And if you feel you would be able to be directly involved, it would certainly help.'

Rizzo didn't reply immediately, he shifted his attention back to the now blank TV screen. 'Whatever you need,' he said, 'but first I need to see him. Properly, not through that link-up.'

'Are you sure?'

'I'd feel like I'd let him down if I didn't.'

# EIGHTEEN

He held the words in front of him and the slightest quiver of the sheet was just visible in the bottom right-hand corner of the TV screen. The information bar almost obscured it and read 'Matthew Rizzo, brother of the victim'. Although his hand shook he remained composed, barely glancing at the sheet.

'My brother had struggled with some long-standing personal problems but we never totally lost touch with each other. He was my only sibling, my only close relative, and I had always hoped that he would, eventually, turn his life around.'

Goodhew had been trawling through CCTV footage for hours. He'd been sitting in what he'd hoped would be a quiet part of the incident room but now was gathered with everyone else around the large TV set that was mounted in the opposite corner.

Almost everyone else, he realized, as he noticed that DC Kev Holden was seated with his back to them all.

'Mind if I join you?'

Goodhew turned away from Holden. Dr Addis stood next to him. 'Of course not.' They watched Rizzo for a few seconds before Goodhew spoke again.

'Are you here to see me?'

'No, no, Kincaide asked to see me. I signed the death cert but I spoke to a couple of witnesses. I think he just wants to make sure he has a full statement.'

'He's being thorough then.' Goodhew could hear the note of doubt in his own voice and turned back to the screen.

Rizzo was finishing now. He spoke directly to the camera, 'Aaron has died after a senseless attack which has robbed me of my only brother. I would like to ask anyone who knows anything, however small – please will you help find my brother's killer. There will be a number given at the end of this appeal, please ring.'

The camera switched away from Rizzo and back to an on-the-spot reporter. Her words were immediately drowned out by Kincaide. 'Eye contact with the camera; he was good,' he chuckled. 'That's what I call a victim impact 101. It ticked all the boxes. He'll get the phones ringing.'

'We needed a photo of the victim up there.' DC Knight pursed her lips. 'We're looking though.'

Ratty's brother's photos were too old. Their only recent ones were shots taken post-mortem; an identifiable shot from the CCTV was needed urgently. Goodhew caught Knight's eye and tilted his head in the direction of the desk. She nodded, and moved towards him, then stopped and turned back towards the screen when she heard Marks's voice.

He read out a carefully prepared statement, outlining the details, 'We currently believe that this is an isolated incident but it was also a very violent assault which led to the death of Aaron Rizzo. Mr Rizzo suffered serious head trauma and some very specific injuries to the eye area.' Marks looked up from his words, and for a second Goodhew thought he had finished speaking.

'For several reasons this case is one of the most disturbing we have encountered. The person who carried out this attack is dangerous. Issuing this kind of appeal so early in a case is an unusual step.' He paused again then fell back to reading from his script, referring to the eye injury again.

'The eyes are always very emotive,' Dr Addis whispered.

'Why?' Goodhew asked. 'Because people call them the windows of the soul?'

'Cliché maybe but clichés come from somewhere, and I do know that they are the most likely exclusion on a donor card.'

'It's so they can see in the afterlife.' That was Worthington, and there was no way of telling whether or not the statement was serious.

'They'll be pissed off when they find out there isn't one,' Kincaide chipped in.

Goodhew and Knight turned away. Holden still faced away from the rest of the room, but Goodhew could now see that there was nothing on the desk in front of him.

'Is Holden OK?'

Knight glanced over, then gave a disapproving grunt. 'He's a lazy so and so. He'll catch a nap if he gets the chance. How far are you through the recordings?'

'I've almost finished with the Petty Cury approach to the market. I'll get to the end of that then I'll give you your desk back. I'm sorry, I've drawn a blank I'm afraid.'

Knight shrugged. 'It's the way it goes, love, frustrating, but I'll tell you what,' she dipped her hand into her jacket pocket and pulled out a recordable DVD in a clear jewel case, 'I just picked this up from the art dealers in Rose Crescent.'

He nodded at the pile that waited next to his keyboard. 'It's turning into a big collection.'

'Too many hours to search through, it's always the way.' She dropped the disk onto the pile and walked away without comment. Goodhew looked back across the room; the tail end of the appeal was still on the screen but no one appeared to be watching it now. Kevin Holden's chair stood empty and the other officers either chatted quietly or had turned back to their phones and computers.

Dr Addis took his coat from the rack but detoured to Goodhew's desk on his way to the door. 'I don't think you should doubt Kincaide, he will be thorough.'

Goodhew gave a non-committal grunt; he knew Addis a little, he'd been an on-call doctor since his own early days at Parkside, but he wasn't sure that Addis was qualified to comment on Kincaide.

Addis cocked one corner of his mouth into a lopsided smile. 'You're right, it is none of my business, but he is being thorough, it's just the way he's treating other people . . .' Addis raised his brows so they rose above his rectangular-rimmed frames.

'Like who?'

'He and I had agreed the identity of the victim before he sent Sue in to take a look.'

Kyle had unlocked the back door and slipped back into his mother's house. He knew her routine, Leah's school hours and his invisibility to the see-no-evil neighbours. He'd switched on his sister's laptop – she'd left it on the kitchen table and put the news on in the background as he boiled the kettle and heated soup. Kyle liked the twenty-four-hour news running; sometimes there was a comforting numbness in its monotony and, at others, he found an uncomfortable addiction in undulating between hating the bulletins on overseas conflicts and being unable to look away from them. The local news usually broke this up with safer stories, ones where it was OK to turn away. He dropped two slices of bread into the toaster and waited for them, drumming the tip of his knife on the worktop.

Kyle didn't know which words made him turn back.

Or whose voice it was, until he saw the steady gaze of the officer staring out at him. DI Marks, according to the caption.

The reporter thanked him.

Marks thanked the reporter.

An incident room phone number flashed up on the screen and Kyle stood in front of it trying to glean some clue. He wasn't sure what he'd heard. Something that had hooked him away from his thoughts, that had brought him back into the here and now from wherever his mind had just wandered.

He pushed aside yesterday's post and a mug of cold coffee that would have been there since his mum had had breakfast. He tried to recall his last train of thought. Of course he had been somewhere on the infinity loop of Hannah, Lila, IED death and Harry, but he had a feeling that he'd been at a particular point, having a particular thought. He tried to replay the item but a timer circled on the screen.

'Come on!' He gave up and backtracked to the news index so that he could reload it from a different screen. His fingers hovered above the track pad. By the time it was ready to watch his agitation had begun to bubble. He began the playback: a murder victim, a homeless man known as Ratty had been identified. There was no photo, and the name meant nothing. The body had been found amongst the market stalls. Everyone knew the market but again, to him, it meant nothing.

He skipped forward by thirty seconds. The victim's brother was talking now. Skip. Skip. Skip. He paused, then skipped back, staring at the name across the bottom of the screen.

Matthew Rizzo.

He paused it and closed his eyes. 'Mr Rizzo', wasn't that the name Mrs Fielding used? He pictured her, a compact woman with tightly permed greying hair. In his imagination her lips were pressed shut in a thin and disapproving line.

What did you say?

He screwed his eyes more tightly shut. *Tell me, tell me, tell me.* What he needed to know was in his own fucking head. It was no good. He snapped open his eyes and flicked his hands out in exasperation. The mug of cold coffee rocked, then slopped across his hand. 'Shit.' He wiped his knuckles across his jeans then ran his cuff across the keyboard. No harm done, he told himself. He closed his eyes again, concentrating on slower, calmer breaths. On the third he heard Mrs Fielding's words, 'No, Mr Rizzo always pays up front.'

Kyle opened his eyes slowly this time. Mr Rizzo. It wasn't a common name. Matthew Rizzo's face was frozen on the screen.

Was he Mrs Fielding's Mr Rizzo? Or was it his dead brother?

Or a coincidence?

Kyle returned to the start of the playback and promised himself that he'd watch every second of it this time. And physically at least, he made it to the end. About halfway through they began a description of the injuries. The words had been carefully composed, enough to give a sense of the horror. And the urgency. But stopping a couple of steps away from painting an overly graphic picture. Except Kyle already had a similar picture very clearly in his head, and he drifted back to his infinity loop: watching her eyes seep and her face turn into Hannah's, imagining the blood spill and being overtaken by the cold and creeping instinctual fear of death. Then picturing Harry and feeling the

94

crushing force of fear. Because of Lila. Because of what Hannah had done. And now because of Rizzo.

Leading to death.

Threatening Harry.

Kyle scrambled to his feet, lurched towards the doorway and vomited across the carpet.

Ann Fielding had seen the news but it wasn't until she sat with her mid-afternoon pot of tea and open copy of the *Cambridge News* that she began to think more deeply about Mr Rizzo.

'Aaron Rizzo, a familiar face amongst the city's rough-sleeper community.' And the age would have been about ten years adrift except that the article made a point of saying that he looked considerably older.

She was surprised there had been no photo, but would she be able to recognize him when she'd only seen him once? Even that would sound ridiculous. But she didn't see how the two Mr Rizzos could be one and the same. She let the tea brew until it turned the splash of milk in her cup to the colour of ginger biscuits, she sipped it as she considered the pros and cons of even mentioning the garage.

'Mum?'

She hadn't heard the front door open so the sound of Joanna's voice from the hall made her start. 'I'm through here,' she replied. 'I need your opinion.'

She waited until her daughter entered the room then slid the newspaper towards her, waiting again as she read. Finally Joanna looked up and shrugged. 'You don't know him, do you?'

Ann began to shake her head. 'Not exactly, but you know I rent out my lock-up? His last name is Rizzo, isn't it?'

'Aaron?'

'I don't know. He says "Mr" when he calls but I'm wondering whether he said Aaron that very first time.'

Joanna crinkled her nose the way she'd always done whenever she was puzzling something. 'He wasn't homeless. Quite smart, I think you said.'

'But how long ago was that?' Ann was asking herself as much as her daughter. 'Four years? Maybe five?'

'He always pays on time, doesn't he? He wouldn't do that if he was homeless.'

Joanna was right, he had always paid on time too, a year in advance at that. The money came hand delivered in mid-November: 'I'm sorry to miss you, I hope you don't mind me posting this. Happy Christmas.' Or similar. Always in time for her to splash out on the presents. 'If there's no connection then I don't want to upset him, I wouldn't find anyone else who'd pay up front like that.'

Joanna shook her head. 'They've found his brother and they're looking for sightings in the days before he was attacked. I think you can ignore it.'

Ann had reached that conclusion once already, only to find that it still niggled her. She chewed on her bottom lip as she tried to pinpoint her concern.

'Mum, if you're worried, then phone. It won't hurt.'

'I don't know what to say.'

'That you rent a garage to a Mr Rizzo and you're wondering . . .' her voice trailed away. 'What exactly?'

Ann shrugged. 'That he might be the dead man I guess. I don't know, it's a feeling.'

'Do you have his phone number?'

'It's in my phone. I could ring him I suppose?'

Surely this wasn't such a complicated decision, but she looked at Joanna, wondering exactly when her daughter had become the adult in their relationship. 'I'll do that.' She dialled the number but the line was dead. 'Perhaps it's wrong.'

'You've phoned him before haven't you?'

'Once or twice.' It didn't sound much for several years' rent. 'Maybe I used the home phone and wrote a different number in the phone book.' That didn't sound plausible either but her endlessly patient daughter left the room to return with the book.

'I'm sorry,' Ann said, 'I feel as though I've made a big fuss over nothing.'

Joanna passed her the open book. 'No you haven't,' she said and pointed to the page. 'His name is Aaron.'

'Oh.' she frowned. 'I should have looked in there already.'

Joanna glanced towards the window, an unremarkable view of tufty grass, a small fir tree and cotoneaster spreading up the rear outside wall at the back of the block of lock-ups. 'What does he keep in the garage, Mum?'

# NINETEEN

Public appeals were far trickier than in the days of just a few TV channels. Only a fraction of the possible audience now saw them the first time around, so there would be a brief pause after broadcast, then, hopefully, a trickle of calls would begin. Social media picked up the baton from there and the link to the footage would daisy chain its way from news sites to local front rooms. That was the theory at least.

Sue Gully sat across the desk from DC Sandra Knight; neither of their phones had rung. Knight looked as though she was glaring, even though she wasn't. It was her usual expression. She just had one of those faces.

While they waited, they'd both been watching the footage from the CCTV cameras in the vicinity of the market. Knight had nabbed the Rose Crescent footage, Gully watched a narrow view of a row of phone boxes and the corner outside the Cambridge University Press book-shop. The picture seemed clear until the first pedestrian. 'This one's triggered by movement sensor,' she said.

'Saves you watching a whole load of nothing.'

'Yes, but look.' Gully twisted the monitor towards Knight and rewound the footage by a few seconds. The picture seemed to jump, 'By the time it starts recording the person's almost through the shot.'

They caught a grainy glimpse of a shoulder and trouser leg. Sandra

Knight's scowl darkened. 'You'll still have to watch it, even though it won't be worth squat in court.'

Gully wrote down the time stamp and a brief description of the image. Of course Sandra was right but it still amounted to a whole lot of hours wasted.

'And you'll have thrown away plenty more years by the time you're my age.'

'That's good to know,' Gully muttered.

But Sandra hadn't finished, 'Don't waste those years on men. At least in here you get the chance to take a few of them out of circulation.'

'Men?'

Sandra laughed without a hint of amusement. 'Funny,' she clarified. 'Them, the scum, that's who I'm talking about. We get the ones we can and in my head I have a little list of the ones who will have to wait.'

Apparently Sandra was 'good fun once you got to know her'. Gully couldn't remember which unreliable witness had told her that one. She plugged on with the footage, careful not to give any sign that might hint at boredom. When her phone rang they both reached for it.

'PC Sue Gully, how can I help?'

'Hello, yes.' The voice was female. Sounded in her sixties, maybe older. 'It's about your Aaron Rizzo,' she began, and Gully could hear the worried waver in her tone.

'Can I start with your name?'

'Sorry, yes, it's Ann Fielding.' There was someone else with her and Gully heard a woman's voice encouraging her. She started to say something about rent money and Christmas, then paused. 'My daughter will explain,' she said, and Gully could hear her hand over the phone.

'I'm Joanna, my mum rents a garage to a man named Aaron Rizzo, you know, a lock-up. She is worried because the name is the same. We've tried calling him, but his phone is dead.'

'Let me take a few details,' Gully spoke steadily but she could already tell that Joanna and her mother weren't timewasters and, as far as the police were aware, there were no other Aaron Rizzos locally.

Sandra looked over from the other side of the desk, turned her monitor towards Gully and waved in its direction.

99

The figure on the screen was a familiar skinny form. 'Is that him?' Sandra mouthed.

Gully nodded, then reached out to hold the monitor still. Can your mother describe Aaron Rizzo?'

'Slim, late forties.'

'Height?'

'She's not sure. She says average, but she's indicating about five eight or five nine.'

'Taller than that.' She heard Ann Fielding's voice in the background. 'He was at least six inches taller than me.'

'Which could be five eight, couldn't it, Mum?'

Gully didn't need the image on the screen to remember Ratty clearly but she studied it carefully in any case, keen to make any possible connection between him and Mrs Fielding's man.

She asked Joanna to pass the phone back to her mother.

'What were his teeth like?'

'In what way?'

'Just good or bad. A full set or gaps?'

Ratty's mouth had black stumps low in the gum, looking like cracked mint humbugs dissolving between the few remaining good ones.

'Unremarkable, I suppose.'

Gully nodded, feeling a little disappointed. As unusual as the name seemed, it was hardly impossible that there could in fact be two Aaron Rizzos. Gully began telling Mrs Fielding that there was nothing to worry about.

'What do I do about the garage now?' Mrs Fielding asked. 'He won't be in touch until November and with no number for him . . .'

'Give me his mobile number and any details you have, we'll double-check before you open it up.'

'I already told you, it's dead,' Mrs Fielding cut in.

Gully nodded patiently, 'But there are still things we can check.'

'There's no point,' she sounded stubborn now, 'because I can't open it anyway and I'm not spending money on a locksmith.'

'You don't have a key then?'

'He replaced the lock then added two more. There's no way of getting in.'

'Three locks?' Gully asked.

Ratty's image was still frozen on Sandra's computer screen. She couldn't believe he'd rented this lock-up, but suddenly she couldn't believe that there was no connection either. She stared at Ratty. The man had been in his last few hours when this had been taken. Perhaps he really hadn't had any inkling of what was about to happen to him but, for her own part, she couldn't deny the feeling that something was happening now and the investigation was about to slip down a darker path.

# TWENTY

Gully shot a quick sideways glance in Goodhew's direction. 'You haven't even asked where we're heading.'

'You've found some new information about Ratty and it involves a visit?'

'No points for that, Gary. A man named Aaron Rizzo has been renting a domestic lock-up in Cherry Hinton for almost five years. I thought you'd want to take a look as soon as.'

Hills Road stretched out ahead of them in its usual waking hours' state of congestion and chaos. The vehicles that moved made a stop-start weave between parked cars and others butting out from side turnings. Every traffic light ahead seemed to flash a different colour. Pedestrians and cyclists criss-crossed. Cherry Hinton stood at the other end of this.

'Does Marks know?'

'Of course.'

'What did he say?'

'Just to let him know the outcome; the description of this other Aaron Rizzo is nothing like Ratty but the locks were changed and none of us like coincidence do we?'

Five years. That was the kind of stability that didn't exist in Ratty's world. It gave Goodhew an uneasy feeling.

'Gary?'

'Do you have the key, Sue?'

'A locksmith will meet us there with a master.'

'Shit. Lights, Sue. Get us there before he attempts to open it.'

Gully responded instantly, ramming it into a lower gear and hitting the accelerator on the first wail of the siren. They screamed through the traffic, jumping the lights at the junction of Station Road and again as they took the left-hand turn into Cherry Hinton Road. Although Gully never needed much encouragement to use the emergency lights, her driving remained quick but economical. It never felt like speed for the sake of it. He gripped the arm rest as they turned and he knew she'd appreciated the urgency in his tone.

Two turns from Cherry Hinton High Street and they arrived at a short cul-de-sac of about twenty garages. A white van was parked at the entrance and, thankfully, the driver waited inside. The garages had all been identical once; prefabricated block walls, corrugated roofs and tinny black metal doors. Hadn't the 1960s been glamorous? Now each had its unique scars; dents and rust flecks and replacement locks. The man clambered from his van as Goodhew opened his door.

'His name's Vernon,' Gully called and hurried to remove her seat belt.

'Which garage?' Goodhew asked.

'Number twelve,' she said, slamming the door behind her. None of the garages were numbered, but Vernon gave them a quick nod before unfolding a sheet of paper.

'I parked alongside. Look.'

He handed the sheet to Goodhew. It was a photocopy of a street plan. Goodhew looked up from the rectangle representing the whole block and moved closer to the garage door closest to the back of Vernon's van.

'Sue,' he said quietly, 'get SOCO down here.'

'Why?'

'This is the detail we were missing.' He took his phone from his pocket and began photographing the door; the eight-inch-high tufts of grass at the bottom, the extra padlock at each corner and the dark green

103

paint flaking from a dent made by a boot mark in the metal. There was nothing else to make it stand out from the others.

'You want me to open it then?' Vernon crossed his arms and made no move to take any tools from the van. 'What's in there?'

'We don't know,' Sue replied at almost the same moment as Goodhew spoke.

'Evidence,' he muttered. *The reason Ratty died*, was his guess.

Gully turned away to speak into her radio, then turned back and shook her head. 'They want Marks to phone you before they send anyone out.'

'We'll wait.' Goodhew stared at the screen of his phone until the moment it began to vibrate. 'Sir . . .'

It wasn't Marks but Kincaide, who cut him short, 'You've requested SOCO for a potentially empty lock-up garage, is that correct?'

'It's been rented under Ratty's real name.'

'Which proves what?' Kincaide snapped. 'That someone had something to hide? Or that Ratty still possessed enough organizational ability to hang on to the smallest of boltholes?'

'Ratty wouldn't . . .'

'Why didn't I know about this until control tries to get hold of Marks? You're supposed to keep me informed.'

Goodhew fixed Gully with his most resigned expression, she rolled her eyes in reply.

'It's a private garage and we have the owner's permission to use a locksmith, therefore there is no issue with access. If you find a pile of nicked bikes – or whatever – then call me back and I'll see about a SOCO. OK?' Kincaide exhaled with a frustrated growl. 'Just get the fucking door open, Gary.' He cut off the call, beating Goodhew to doing the same.

Goodhew turned to Vernon, whose expression had become increasingly apprehensive. 'We've been instructed to go ahead.'

'Yes, I heard that from here.' Vernon took a step backwards towards his van, 'How do you want me to do this?'

Goodhew inspected the door, there was one locking handle in the centre of the door and a hinge and latch clasp about eight inches up from each bottom corner. Both clasps were fitted with padlocks. 'Do you have the keys for these two?'

'No, just the master key for the main lock.'

Goodhew had enough in his pocket for that one; no wonder people added additional locks of their own. 'OK, you have screwdrivers though? Good, unscrew the bottom plates and we'll open it that way.'

A couple of minutes later and he sensed Gully at his shoulder. 'Do you already know what's in there, Gary?'

He kept his gaze fixed on Vernon. 'Why would I?'

She studied his expression. 'You seem too certain.'

He shook his head. 'I'm just guessing, Sue. And I hope I'm wrong.'

'Personally, I wouldn't stick my neck out and try to arrange SOCO if I hadn't already seen proof of a crime.' She arched an eyebrow, clearly expecting more detail than he could offer.

'Fair enough, but tell me what you think is in there?'

'I don't know.'

'Come on, in about ninety seconds he'll say *all yours* and we'll roll that up, what do you think we'll find? Give me your best guess.'

He stole a glance at her. She too was watching the garage door. She chewed on her lip. 'It has to be a secret,' she said.

'Such as?'

'Something illegal. But we don't *know* that's true.'

'Forget that. This is just hypothesis. The Ratty we knew couldn't organize his life from one day to the next. What's the alarm ringing in your head, Sue? What do you think we're about to see?'

Vernon finished unscrewing the second of the hinge and latch clasps and reached in his pocket for his keys.

'Sue?'

'It's what got Ratty killed,' she breathed, 'that's what I think.'

It took Vernon far longer than ninety seconds and his efforts were sound-tracked with occasional tuts and mutterings. Goodhew offered his help but Vernon waved him away with, 'Sometimes they're stubborn.' Finally he twisted the handle to check that he'd been successful in unlocking it, but made no effort to open it.

'All yours,' he called and stepped away.

'All ours,' echoed Gully. 'So far, so accurate on that front.'

They waited until Vernon left. Goodhew passed Sue his phone and removed his jacket, throwing it onto the roof of the patrol car.

'Film from where you're standing when I open it, then move into the doorway but stay out of the garage, one of us in there will be enough. Film everything you can.' He took a pair of thin gloves and a small roll of evidence bags from the glove box and pushed the bags into his pocket. He turned to check that Gully was filming then put one gloved hand on the garage door handle and turned it. 'Nothing lost if it's empty, eh?' With that he pulled, stepping back as the bottom of the door swept upwards.

Gully watched through the phone screen; it flickered as it adjusted to the darkness, then the flashlight kicked in, illuminating the space in front of her with a harsh but steady beam.

She and Goodhew had had a similar logic about this garage but she had no idea what specifically either of them thought they'd find. Maybe piles of stolen goods, black market cigarettes and alcohol, a hidden vehicle used in a crime. Something that said *crime* as soon as the door opened.

Not this.

The space was empty apart from a small chest freezer standing on a square of unpatterned maroon carpet. She felt the first small wave of unease.

Goodhew cleared his throat. 'The garage is mostly clean and clear. The only item present is a small chest freezer. It is standing in the centre of a piece of carpet measuring approximately one point five metres square.'

'Is it plugged in?' she asked, then immediately realized that there would be no electricity supply.

The garage was of standard size, she reckoned that had to be about 2.5 by 5 metres, and the carpet had been positioned centrally so that there was a gap of 50 centimetres between it and the walls on either side and at the back.

He glanced upwards, above him was nothing but bare wood rafters; the freezer remained the only item of interest.

He turned to Gully and the camera. 'Sorry Sue, you will need to come a bit nearer. I think we should have a close-up of the lid and seal in case opening it causes any damage. The camera light will be useful.'

She focused the camera on one side then moved across the front of the freezer until she'd filmed the edges that were about to be opened. 'Ready,' she told him and trained it on the front seal. Goodhew positioned his hands so that his thumbs could push up against the corners of the lid and leave any possible prints on the handle intact.

Gully kept watching via the phone's screen.

What got people killed?

Drugs, greed, debt, jealousy, secrets and lies. Hundreds of things, most of which came back to love or money. Where did Ratty fit in?

The lid popped quietly, opened smoothly. She heard Goodhew draw a sudden breath and she whipped the camera out of her line of sight so she could see clearly.

'Oh god,' she gasped, and sucked in a lungful of putrefied air. 'Close it, Gary, quick.' She pressed her face into the back of her sleeve and he did the same.

'Film it first,' he told her and she managed to raise the camera again and point it back into the freezer. Her hand shook but the wobbling beam of light showed more than enough.

Goodhew closed the lid slowly. 'That'll do, Sue.'

And as one they hurried back into the light, closing the door behind them. She shoved the phone back into his hand, then radioed in while he phoned Kincaide. By the time she had finished speaking his call was also done. She heard her own voice coming from his phone and watched his face as he replayed the moment they had discovered the body. His earlier obvious revulsion had passed and now he stared at the screen. He played it back several times and the sirens were just a few streets away by the time he spoke.

'What did you see?' he asked.

Contorted limbs and grave wax. The shape of a huddled person. Her skin leathering, the strap of a bra and a mess of brown hair, all still oddly feminine. 'A woman's body.'

'Did you see her eyes?'

'Like Ratty's?' she guessed.

'I think so, it was hard to tell.'

# PART TWO

# TWENTY-ONE

*I made the permanent move to Cambridge in the late eighties when I inherited my father's house. That sounds impressive but, after the mortgage and bank loans had been settled, it wasn't as much as I'd hoped. Just as my mother had struggled bringing me up, I continued to struggle to complete my education. That money was a start though.*

*My first flat was a single room above a block of shops in Perne Road. Downstairs was a chip shop and the furniture in the two rooms was permanently impregnated with the fumes of cooking fat. The building was a dark and ugly flat-roofed affair overlooking the roundabout at the junction of Radegund Road. It was noisy, hot and polluted but they were also some of my best times. I lived there when I met her.*

*I'd had girlfriends – enough but not too many I suppose. Certainly enough to know what I liked and thought I needed. Besides, I was in the process of laying down my future; the flat was temporary, my education all but done.*

*Chicago's was the mainstay of Cambridge nightlife back then. People often said 'I don't like nightclubs' then immediately gave some reason why they were there. I was one of those and found myself there on more Saturday nights than not. There was something addictive about feeling that I might miss out if I didn't go. It often pushed me into a last-minute dash for the bus.*

*Most times I'd see some of the other students and mingle with them until two or three of us were ready to attach ourselves to any nearby group of girls.*

*The night I met her panned out differently. I'd made it inside ahead of the others and grabbed a prime spot with a good view of the dance floor and en route to the bar. Arriving early felt lame, I bought myself a bottle of Becks and tried not to glance too frequently at my watch. I briefly felt self-conscious.*

*But of course that's exactly what nightclubs are designed to protect you from – mirrors and pillars and irregular angles positioned so you can find a safe corner before the senses are pounded with bass-heavy music, alcohol and the cigarette smoke masking the sweat in the air.*

*It was through one of those angled and mirrored panels that I first caught sight of her. I saw her checking her lipstick in a compact. She completed the move swiftly and discreetly before slipping both items back into her bag with a smooth movement. She rested her hand back onto the table, her fingers forming a gentle curve and the corkscrew curls of her dark brown hair falling over one shoulder.*

*She glanced at her watch twice in the minutes I studied her but, apart from that, didn't move. Her expression remained quietly confident, calm with the hint of a smile. Whoever she was expecting never came but she didn't seem surprised at that either. I found myself wondering who he was and whether she'd give him another chance.*

*She checked her watch one final time, I checked mine too and it was exactly quarter to nine. His time seemed to be up; she hooked her bag over her shoulder as she stood and turned towards the door. The move was understated but precise with no hint of pique or embarrassment.*

*Somewhere in those fifteen minutes I'd become hooked and watching her leave would have been like letting her walk away with the last page of a chapter that may still have proved vital. So I followed her.*

*From a distance, of course.*

*A man caught up with her in the cut-through in front of Woolworths. He looked a little older than me, groomed in a way I wouldn't have known where to start. She moved quickly and listened to whatever it was that he tried to tell her. In my head I added words to his gesticulations; don't be silly, I'm here now, I am sorry, don't spoil the evening.*

She was polite but firm until I saw the man's expression become more frustrated and I knew he'd get nowhere.

Finally she walked away from him, along Market Street towards the market square itself. I watched her until she was almost out of sight before I realized that I still didn't feel as though I'd read that final page.

And as I hurried after her up Rose Crescent, I wondered whether I could be part of her life. It made sense that I'd seen all of that for a reason – not serendipity or any of that shit – but because my subconscious was letting me know that it was the moment to move forward. And the more I watched her over the next few days the more convinced I became that it would be just a matter of time.

Just as life had turned unexpectedly that first time I saw her, it turned again twenty-one years later. I came home early – my hours were more predictable back then – and I found her sitting at the breakfast bar, cradling a mug of coffee and lost in thoughts that were clearly taking her somewhere else entirely. I stood in the doorway and watched her for several seconds before I spoke.

'Nothing to do?'

She was startled enough for the coffee to lap the lip of the cup but not to overflow.

'Too much to do,' she replied.

Afterwards, when I replayed the moment, I wondered whether her voice had been too monotone, if she'd spoken a little too unguardedly and revealed more than she'd intended.

'Too much?' I queried.

She shook her head and seemed apologetic.

'Have you been crying?' I asked.

'No. Why?'

'Your eyes look red.'

I studied them carefully but after a few seconds she moved her chin away from my hand.

'I fell asleep.'

'When?'

'About an hour ago.'

'You went to bed?'

'No.' She glanced through the open doorway to the lounge. 'I'd just loaded the washing machine and sat down for a few minutes. Next thing I knew I'd been asleep.'

She made a 'cheers' movement with her mug.

'Hence the coffee,' she added.

When I looked at the settee and armchairs later I couldn't see a depression in any of the cushions, no sign that she'd been sitting down even briefly, but right then I heard the raised pitch of the machine completing the spin cycle and looked at the almost empty coffee mug and decided to take her word for it.

'So everything's fine?' I asked.

She nodded. 'Of course.'

I pulled the second bar stool across so that I could sit next to her. 'I'll make you a coffee,' she said and moved away from me. I watched her refreshing the water and reloading the dispenser with my favourite arabica.

I made several attempts at small talk but she kept her back to me, fiddling with cleaning the milk jug and wiping down the flurry of coffee dust that sprinkled the worktop. If I had made her turn to look at me, what would I have seen?

I only wondered that later, when it was too late. Somewhere at the back of my mind an alarm bell was ringing. I just didn't bother listening to it. Learning to listen carefully came later, once I understood the importance of words to my work.

She dried her hands on a tea towel then wiped them again on the front of her jeans before turning to face me. 'I'll pick up the kids in a minute.'

'I don't mind going.'

She shrugged. 'Don't worry, Jenna's out at the usual time but Charlie's staying for art club.'

I opened my mouth to say that I was still happy to go, perhaps my wife caught the thought more quickly than I could voice it.

'I thought I'd take the car, grab some shopping in between, cook something special for dinner.'

Something special.

\*    \*    \*

*'We don't run an art club,' the school secretary told me, 'only chess club on Tuesdays.'*

*By the time 4.30 had slipped past and I'd phoned the school they had already had an hour's head start.*

*I tried to guess where she might have taken them; nowhere sprang to mind. I thought of friends of hers that she might have confided in but their numbers were in her phone and the address book in the hallway drawer. She'd taken both.*

*It was this realization that allowed the truth to slowly dawn. Her wardrobe and drawers told me nothing, but the girls' beds were bereft of the two items they would never be without; Charlie's threadbare yellow rabbit and Jenna's bear, Rolo.*

*People talk about doors opening as a positive thing but a door opened then and I stared out at the first view of what life without them might be like.*

*All my adult years felt as though they had been for them. In those minutes, as the obvious finally hit me, I knew she'd gone but I also knew she'd made a terrible mistake. The girls were mine and no one would ever love her the way I did.*

*I promised myself right there and then that I'd find her and bring them home.*

*'I need a break' the note read.*

*I didn't find it until a few hours after she'd gone. She'd left it tucked under one of the bottles in the drinks cabinet like a silent dig at my alcohol intake. I could hear her voice as clearly as I would if she'd been in the room.*

*'You never get though an evening without a few glasses, do you?'*

*The note itself was brief, she promised to contact me in a 'week or so' when, in her words, I was likely to be 'less volatile'.*

*I kicked a hole in the plasterboard when I read that. First the alcohol, now the outbursts; I could almost feel her smiling as I proved her right again.*

# TWENTY-TWO

*But days turned to weeks, and anger to desperation. I was coming through the front door when the phone began to ring. In my hurry to answer I forgot to wonder if it might be her. Her voice sounded distant yet achingly familiar.*

*'It's me,' she paused, then added her name as if I might have forgotten.*

*I bit back the urge to say anything that might have made her hang up again.*

*'How are you?'*

*She started to speak but cut herself off quickly, too soon for me to even know what the first word might have been. 'We won't be coming back.'*

*'You have to.'*

*She didn't respond to this either, instead she gave me the details of her solicitor. It was a Bedford address.*

*'So is that where you're living? Bedford?'*

*'I'm not prepared to give you our address. Just contact through them. I want this to be the last time we speak.'*

*I felt a strange shift in my world, as though that moment had split my life in two. Her voice was without any hint of emotion.*

*'I'll need to see the girls.'*

*'I've thought about that.' She stopped there as if that half-sentence was a full explanation.*

*I should have kept control of the conversation then, told her that I had too and made my own demands. Instead I just asked, 'And?'*

*'I will be seeking sole custody. No access.'*

*'You can't do that.'*

*The unreasonableness silenced me for a few seconds. It felt longer – a gap where my brain and mouth wouldn't sync. Even if they had I would not have had words for the feelings of outrage passing through me then.*

*'What would you do if I was there right now? It really is a good thing that I'm only on the phone, isn't it?' Her voice sounded too calm.*

*'This isn't a game. They are our daughters.'*

*'Why would I force them to see you when I'm not prepared to put myself through it? Answer me that?'*

*'You said you needed a break. I want you to come home.'*

*I took a breath then managed to keep the anger from my voice.*

*'How much clearer do you want me to make it? I'm not coming back. I want a divorce. We want a life without you.'*

*'Why?'*

*'You know why.'*

*'No, I don't. We've been together for over twenty years.' I gripped the handset tighter. 'I can't stop thinking about you. You can tell me if there's someone else.'*

*'It's not that.'*

*'Then come back. I want you and Jenna and Charlie back home.' I sounded pathetic but once I began to plead I couldn't contain any of it any more. 'I'm sorry, please.'*

*I promised her I'd be different. That I'd be less this, more that, all the things I thought would make me the person she wanted. And at that moment, I thought I could change. But I remember thinking it could be just as appropriate for her to change to be what I needed. That flashed into my head but I pushed it away again, that would be for later, once she was back.*

*I don't know how long I tried to convince her but, by the end, I'd broken down into sobs. She waited silently until I had to ask her whether she was still there.*

*'I wanted to phone you but I needed time to clear my mind first. But*

*I waited much longer than that before I left. I spent these last months watching you, making notes of the way you treated us. Taking note of the petty humiliations and subtle spite that, in isolation, look like nothing. If we had had children sooner then I would have left you sooner. They are not growing up with you.'*

And suddenly I hated her, every ounce of wanting her was crushed. *'Fine to father kids but not to live with?'*

*'That isn't what I said – listen to yourself, you're losing it now.'*

*'I'm like any other decent man. I just want to see my children.'*

*'Stop.'*

She began to say something else but I shouted her down. I didn't actually give a shit what she had to say. *'Stop? Don't tell me what to do. Don't tell me anything – the one who leaves is always in the wrong, remember? Remember?'* She had always said that, now at least I could throw it back in her face.

*'I remember. I do. And I am in the wrong because I shouldn't have had children with you.'*

*'But you did.'* My jaw was clenched and I glared across at the kitchen calendar, noticing for the first time that its pages were out of date by almost two full months.

*'I'm sorry for what is my fault, but I've made up my mind. The divorce will go ahead.'*

I heard a tremor in her voice but it didn't make her sound any less determined.

*'The house will be sold and I want half its value. Not half the equity.'*

Our mortgage was close to paid off but the difference between half the value and half the equity probably meant that she'd get an extra £30K.

*'And,'* she continued, *'that extra will be full and final settlement. I don't want any ongoing maintenance payments. It's a clean break.'*

*'No chance.'*

*'Imagine what I've put together over the last few months. The details would ensure I get full custody, so don't fight it or you'll lose even more.'*

And I lay awake that night but instead of thinking of her, I started making lists of the things she might have seen, personal notes that I

*thought I'd kept secure with un-guessable passwords. I hadn't done*
*anything then but the documented evidence of the things I would like*
*to do would be enough.*

*I let her and my girls go that night.*

*They were as good as dead to me.*

# TWENTY-THREE

His ever resourceful post lady had left him a note: 'I signed for your package, it's by the basement steps – Geo x'.

The cardboard tube was dry and unscathed. Goodhew carried it up to the top floor and leant it on the doorway leading through to his flat. It contained a street map of Cambridge. He'd been considering ordering it for some time but had only made the final decision after his first day back. There had been no urgency but now it seemed like a fitting way to mark his return to work.

He made coffee and stood at his window as he drank it. He looked across at Parkside Station, as he had so many times in the previous months; he'd been back for a matter of days but he already felt the draw of it. The unlit corners in particular. From up here he could feel detached enough to view the darkened windows and revisit the day.

He turned his attention away from Parkside, looking south-easterly in the approximate direction of Cherry Hinton and the woman's body they'd found this afternoon. Finding a body was a trigger, and there was nothing he or Marks or anyone could do for the victim or their family except try to catch the person responsible.

Or, in this case, prevent it happening again.

The thought made him pause, the mug close to his lips and his hand cupped around it even though it was now barely warm. He finished his coffee over the next ten minutes, trying to catch the thoughts that danced around the edges of his mind. They were too young as yet. Finally he turned away from the glass and called his grandmother. She would not care about the time.

'I've bought a map,' he told her. 'How do you feel if I put it up in the study?'

'It's your house, Gary.'

It *was* his house, but it had belonged to his grandparents for years before and some of the rooms remained unused and unaltered. Goodhew had the strongest memories of his grandfather in the library and, apart from Goodhew's flat in the roof space, it had been the first room he had begun to use. And, consequently, the only room he'd altered. There were still some books and papers and a few items of furniture, but mostly his grandfather's presence remained because he existed in Goodhew's thoughts. Bringing the settee and jukebox down from his flat hadn't disturbed that and, when Goodhew had emulsioned one wall and used it as a huge notepad he'd felt that his grandfather would have been pleased.

*It's your house, Gary.* She invariably said exactly that. The house was his without any strings. But still. He didn't want his grandmother to think he was just wiping out the past.

'It's a big map,' he added.

'To cover up your graffiti?'

'No, it's going on the other wall, from the door to the corner by the window.'

'The whole wall?'

'Pretty much, it's come in a dozen rolled-up sheets that need positioning. I could actually do with a hand pasting it up . . .'

'Pasting? I don't think so, I could supervise though. You'll need to make sure it doesn't slant at all,' she laughed. 'I could just imagine how irritated you'd be with that. And when is this *makeover* taking place?'

'I didn't have a particular plan, although I did wonder . . .'

'You thought you'd do it right now, didn't you, Gary? Do you know what time it is?'

'I'm not tired.'

'And I'm not your mother,' she replied and hung up.

He knew what that meant and had fresh coffee ready for them by the time her taxi drew up. She stepped into the flat and continued to speak as though twenty minutes and two miles hadn't just punctuated the sentence, 'so I won't tell you what to do, but just because I'm helping you it doesn't mean that I wouldn't like you to sort out your *sleeping arrangements*.' She made the phrase heavy with innuendo, and shot him a knowing look. 'People with well-balanced lives do not hang maps at midnight.'

He closed the front door and followed her to the second floor. She draped her jacket across the back of the settee. She wore blue cigarette trousers and a loose shirt; both looked brand new. She must have spotted his doubtful expression. 'They're the closest I could find to decorating clothes,' she told him. 'Where is this map then?'

He pointed to the roll of papers next to the now empty packaging in which they'd been delivered. 'I took them out and rolled them the other way to try to unbend them.' Even from a few feet away the cerise veins of main roads stood out in the distinctive Ordnance Survey map colour scheme.

'A street map?' she sighed. 'Oh, it's Cambridge, isn't it? Couldn't you have gone a little wider?'

She'd probably expected Europe, or the Pacific or, more likely, the whole world. 'I did,' he told her cheerfully. 'It stretches north to Waterbeach, south to Great Chesterford and from Cambourne across to Bottisham.'

'Yes Gary, everywhere that's right on our doorstep.'

'Come on, you'll see.'


It took three hours to position it and paste all the sections to the wall. They sat across from it now with fresh coffee and a plate of slightly burnt toast. His grandmother pointed at it with a triangle of toast. 'You're right,' she admitted, 'it's striking.'

Layers of history were visible with the pattern of old streets, older footpaths and water courses crossing between the more recent developments. The current life of the city showed up even more clearly. From here he would be able to see the most direct routes, the nearest pubs, shops and schools, the routes of buses and corners of Cambridge that he may have overlooked. He moved closer to the wall, the location

122

of his house appearing just above his eyeline. He looked up a little further to the location of Market Hill then traced the route with his gaze, down the wall and across towards his right hand; a different view of familiar streets. He found the position of the lock-up garage in Cherry Hinton and touched the spot with the tip of his index finger.

The body might have been dead there for much of his time as a DC. It was not the city's fault, but a shadow had passed across it in any case.

'You do realize that it will be out of date in no time?'

She was right of course, but despite the swathes of new development in and around the city he hadn't given that any thought at all.

'I can replace it when I need to.'

'Will you need to if it's only art?'

He'd already found himself picking out the shape of familiar roads, spotting sites of older crimes. 'I'm not sure why I wanted it, maybe to help me think.'

'Not art then?'

He shook his head, 'No, it's not.' And he knew then that it was as much about where he was going as where he'd already been.

# TWENTY-FOUR

Goodhew swam first, but still arrived early. He tried sitting at the desk that had once been his, but now it seemed totally alien and he returned to the one he'd used the day before. He typed up his report on the discovery of the body, stopping at various points to repeatedly watch the footage recorded on his camera.

He'd found it hard to concentrate, there should have been more news overnight, maybe an update from Marks or even Kincaide. Something to engage him more than this. Just before seven, PC Ted Moorey came in holding a selection of stationery items and a box file. He was skinny with tufty hair and acne scars; he didn't look old enough to drive. Goodhew introduced himself. 'We didn't meet properly yesterday.'

'Cool. I'm Ted.'

*Cool.*

'There's a briefing in here first thing,' Moorey told him. 'The DI wants everyone in.'

Goodhew watched as Moorey added to the board, pinning it with stills from CCTV and photos of Market Hill and the garage. They didn't take up much space and the board still looked too sparse, considering the crime. There were no photos from inside the lock-up yet, but they would be added soon, along with shots of the female victim. Goodhew's gaze locked on to the gap between the prints; everything anyone needed to know lay in the gaps.

Moorey pointed at Ratty. 'You knew him?'

'Not well.' An image of Ratty slipped into view, then back out again. 'We crossed paths sometimes. Of course I'd wondered about his past . . .'

'Because he was homeless?'

'Partly, and partly because he was interesting. He liked to think that he knew everybody and everything round town and, at times, it felt as though he did. He could lie low for weeks then turn up with the most insightful comments. I didn't know anything about him personally though.'

'So he wasn't exactly a friend?'

'No.' Goodhew shook his head. 'He helped me with information now and then. He usually protested, then pointed me in the right direction in any case.' A new and unexpected image of Ratty flashed into his head. 'One time I was trying to find a possible witness in an assault case. Ratty knew him. I stood out of sight and he said he'd give a cough when he saw the guy. He started coughing and couldn't stop, hacking and wheezing until I thought he'd collapse.' He smiled at the memory.

'What happened?'

'He swore at me. A lot.' Goodhew removed his jacket and sat back in the chair. 'He would disappear for weeks at a time, at least there would be weeks when I wouldn't catch sight of him. Last summer he was one of a group of homeless people who became ill after taking PMA, two died and when the call came in . . . well, I wouldn't have been surprised if he hadn't made it.'

Ratty had rented that lock-up for almost five years.

The carpet carefully placed. The freezer too.

Goodhew hadn't seen much of the woman; tangled brown hair, no grey at the scalp.

The freezer was small so she had to be too.

He slid his face into his hands and closed his eyes. He thought back through from his time as a PC, when he'd probably looked too young to drive and had been on the periphery of every important case. *Verity Coe – missing.* Longer than five years, but possible. He moved his thoughts forward by a couple of years. *Megan Albert – missing.* Possible. *Anne-Marie Hills – possible runaway.* But certainly too tall, she'd been a hockey player, about five foot ten with short dark hair. Her name threw up the memory of her snapshot in the papers, the other names were harder to picture. *Lila Rasnikov* – missing and also possible. *Belinda Duff – contact lost with family.*

He opened his eyes to find Moorey standing beside his desk, mug of coffee in hand. 'I got this for you, people are arriving.'

'I wasn't asleep.' Goodhew picked up a pen and wrote the names then crossed them through until just a couple remained.

'Who are they?'

'Some names I had in my head, that's all.'

He looked up at Moorey, who pressed his lips together and forced a smile. 'People are arriving,' he repeated.

Moorey had repositioned the display board slightly to ensure that it really was in the clearest part of the room, a rectangle of space in front of Goodhew's desk, and DI Marks therefore stood only a couple of feet in front of him as he addressed the large group that had assembled in the room.

'The body discovered yesterday is an IC1 female. As yet we have no formal identification and no cause of death. Due to the state of the body we also do not know an approximate date of death. More to follow on all those points.'

Goodhew glanced over his shoulder; every officer's attention stayed with Marks. No sideways glances or scribbling of notes.

'What has been recovered, however, are her fingerprints, and I'm expecting data back on those at any moment. I can also confirm that Aaron Rizzo, the man known to us as Ratty, has been positively identified by his brother and this has now been verified via medical records. His identity is therefore not in question. His background and the investigation into his death will form one major strand of this investigation, as will determining the true identity of the man posing as Aaron Rizzo. We need full details of how the payment for the garage was made, who hired the lock-up, whether he signed a contract and whether any of the neighbours came into contact with him or anyone else visiting that lock-up.'

Goodhew had assumed his own involvement with Ratty would

126

continue but Marks looked beyond him, his focus falling on Kincaide. 'Michael, stay on this one, Worthington and Knight, you too. Find people who knew Rizzo, go wider with the CCTV footage in the hours before; see if he was picked up on cameras elsewhere in the city centre.'

Knight shook her head, 'I can try but the coverage is patchy at best.'

Marks moved on without comment.

'Regarding the identity of the female victim . . .' With no warning Marks stepped closer to Goodhew's desk and put his hand on Goodhew's list. 'I should not have to remind you of this but there is to be no speculation and absolutely no mention of injuries suffered by her, or Rizzo, rumoured or otherwise, to anyone outside this room.'

The phone in his jacket's breast pocket buzzed softly and a single glance at the screen seemed to tell him everything he needed to know.

'We have a provisional identification.'

The room stilled, suddenly expectant.

'Lila Rasnikov. Too soon for DNA but jewellery, fabric, hair and height all match. I will be seeing Miss Rasnikov's parents next, we need to keep them informed of progress.'

He took a moment to survey the room then wrapped up the briefing with a final run-through of priorities and tasks.

Once people began to disperse his attention switched sharply to Goodhew, 'Belinda Duff, Megan Albert, Lila Rasnikov and Verity Coe. Where did you get that list?'

'They're names I remembered; missing women with a connection to Cambridge.'

'Grab your jacket, I want you to drive.'

# TWENTY-FIVE

Goodhew's first year with the police had been a year for firsts; the first time he'd found a dead body, the first time he'd held a man's hand as he took his final breath and the first time he'd broken news to a bereaved relative.

They were driving towards Milton to meet Lila Rasnikov's family now, but Marks was silent and Goodhew's thoughts were drawn back to that first time. Perhaps it was the same for Marks too. He guessed that the first time left the deepest impression on each of them. For Goodhew it had been 29 December, exactly halfway through the hangover days between Christmas and New Year. Three young men, all within a year of Goodhew's own age, had driven from the car park at the Fleur De Lys pub, doubling back at the first roundabout then accelerating across the Elizabeth Way Bridge as they headed towards the city centre. They hit the second roundabout at sixty, jumping the lights before a lamp-post came close to slicing their car in half. When Goodhew arrived the engine's fan still ran and he'd had to reach inside to silence the stereo.

He checked each man for a pulse; two were clearly dead and the faint signs of life disappeared from the driver before Goodhew had had any chance to administer first aid. There was nothing he could do beyond squeezing the man's hand and hoping that he knew he wasn't alone. The driver's father was one of the first on the scene. Thankfully he arrived after the paramedics and fire engines and was kept back from the car. Breaking the news of the deaths to him right then went against protocol, procedures and training, but a single look from the car to the father convinced him otherwise.

And now, despite hating the news they'd be giving, he was glad that they were visiting the family at the earliest moment possible.

'It's different when you have your own children,' Marks spoke and Goodhew realized that his boss had clearly been following a similar train of thought. 'I can't help putting myself in their shoes, then I have to tell myself not to. Bringing our own experiences won't help at all.'

'I know,' Goodhew replied, but the comment was enough to push Ratty to the front of his thoughts. And Kelly Wilkes, and his grandfather. He pushed the images aside. 'What do we know about the Rasnikovs?'

'They seem to be a tight-knit family, both Lila's parents' relatives live locally. The dad's a driver, the mum works part-time in the office of a local builders. Lila was the middle child, one older brother and a younger sister, and they all want to be present when we visit.'

The family house was located in Milton and looked about forty years old. The road outside was clogged with parked vehicles. The closest parking space was fifty yards away and, by the time they'd locked the car, the front door of Lila's parents' house was open and a solidly built man filled the entrance.

He neither smiled, nor shook hands, his only greeting was to step back and let them through. His wife stood in the hallway and they all followed her into a dining room. The table accommodated six chairs and a young man and woman already waited there.

Goodhew's guess that they were Lila's siblings was immediately confirmed by Nikolas Rasnikov, who introduced his wife as Nina and the two children as Peter and Gia. Gia was slim and no more than five foot four, just like the body in the freezer. Her hair colour and its slight wave appeared identical too. He looked away. Marks waited until they were all seated.

'We received information yesterday, which led to the discovery of the body of a young woman.'

No one moved, everyone seemed frozen as they waited to hear the inevitable. They would all know it was inevitable too; there was no other reason for Marks to begin this conversation unless the body was Lila's, but they still hung to every word as if there might be some other outcome possible.

'Based on initial examination, I'm here to tell you that we are expecting the body to be confirmed as Lila's.'

'But you don't know for sure?' Nina had seen a glimmer of possibility.

Marks shook his head. 'We have some formalities but clothing, appearance and blood type all match.'

Nina shook her head too, she pressed one hand over her mouth and reached to her husband with the other.

'Will we be able to see her?' Mr Rasnikov's voice was hoarse already. 'To identify her?' He looked at his wife then back at Marks. 'We'll both need to see her.'

'All of us,' Peter added.

His sister – Lila's sister – stayed silent the longest. 'How did she die?'

'We're awaiting the autopsy report.' Marks replied without any hesitation. 'When we have that and the formal identification we will be able to give you all more details . . .' He carried on speaking but Goodhew realized that Gia was staring at him and he'd been staring back, seeing Lila's face brought to life in her own, but this time he didn't turn away.

'Gia how old were you when your sister went missing?'

'Fifteen.'

'What do you remember?'

'I was busy at school and busy out of school, mostly with my mates. I remember I kept thinking that Lila had it easy.'

'Gia!' Her father muttered her name in disappointment.

'I thought everyone did except me, but Lila especially. I know that's not the case now, don't I? But I'm just saying how I remember it then; you'd hurt your back, mum was stressed, depressed – whatever – and Pete just cared about his student loan. I was in the middle of it with Lila telling me that the things upsetting me were things that didn't matter at all.' She shrugged at Goodhew. 'You asked.'

He gave the smallest smile of thanks.

'Why ask Gia these questions now?' her mother asked.

'Every angle is important,' Marks assured her, 'and casual details confided to a close friend or sibling may be exactly the information we need.'

Nina nodded and leant closer to her husband. Peter tried to comfort his sister too but her grief was showing itself to be different to that of the others. She pulled away from him, scooping up her bag and standing unsteadily. 'Lila didn't have a boyfriend, not that I knew, but if she had she'd have only told me, Mum, because you were always so obsessed that something awful was going to happen.' She brushed her hair away from her face with a shaking hand. 'I look back now and I don't understand why we were so bloody depressed when we had such a better life than this one.' She left the room and Goodhew expected to hear the door slam in her wake but there was just silence, eventually broken by a howl of anguish from somewhere upstairs. It was then that Nina began to sob.

# TWENTY-SIX

Leah's geography homework lay across the table: 'Should Tourism in Antarctica be Encouraged?' She left her books spread out, as if she had some kind of intentions towards it when she had absolutely none; handing in the answer 'NO!' would get her in more trouble than not handing it in at all.

Instead she sat on the floor with Harry. She'd screwed a sheet of paper into a ball and kept rolling it towards him, making a pantomime of retrieving it then backing up to roll it again. He laughed every time she pounced on it and made surprised faces. She loved the way the tiniest upset became a major drama, and the way that the tears could disperse in seconds and all be forgotten. She took a second sheet of paper and folded it into the shape of an emu's head, she drew on eyes and pretended to snap at her own nose with its beak. Harry looked less certain, so she made the emu pick up the ball and pass it to him, then she took it back with her other hand only for the emu to steal it again and hand it back to him.

Harry squealed, 'Ball.'

When he started to lose interest she clapped her hands together, 'Cuddle?'

Harry flung himself into her lap and she hauled herself onto her feet, pulling him up with her and balancing him on her hip as she walked through to the kitchen.

Her mum was scooping microwaved mash onto plates of spaghetti hoops and scrambled egg. 'He's got legs, Leah.'

'He likes me picking him up.'

'I've told you before, you'll make a rod for your own back.'

Leah mouthed the words as her mother spoke them, then shrugged. 'My back, my rod.'

'You'll change your view when you get a dose of the real world.'

Leah cocked her head and arched one eyebrow. 'So, I should be more like Hannah then?'

'Don't even push my buttons on that one, my girl.' And, as if to underline her irritation, she grabbed the ketchup from the fridge and kicked the door closed behind her. 'She needs to make up her mind. If she's going to be a mother then she needs to act like one. She needs to spend more time with Harry and stop using us like free childcare.'

'Kyle wanted him here.'

'Yeah, easy for Kyle to drop him here then bugger off and expect us to do it all. That's why you shouldn't carry that little lad around all the time, the sooner they learn to stand up on their own two feet . . .'

Leah scooped up a teaspoon of mash, blew it, then aimed it at Harry's mouth. She was well practised at knowing when to let her mum's words pass her by. 'I told you, Kyle said that he didn't want me or Harry over at their house.'

'I know Leah, but his idea of danger . . .' she sighed and shook her head, 'Kyle isn't in the real world half the time. We can't see someone in the shadows every time he does, bless him.'

'He really was scared, Mum.'

Her mum placed her hand on Leah's shoulder. 'Leah love, that's the point, he clears off at the drop of a hat and he doesn't know when he's imagining things. He'll come back when he wants to get help,' she removed her hand again after giving Leah a gentle shake, 'and, until then, we just help ourselves. You'll be fine at Hannah's.'

'Can't I babysit here?'

'Leah.' The fleeting softness had gone from her mother's voice once more. 'There's no difference. I'm working tonight so it's you alone with Harry either way. And he'll be in his own cot there – better for him than shunting him between two bedrooms.'

Leah recognized her mum's decisive tone and knew she wouldn't be able to sway her. 'Will you come to get me?'

'Of course, as soon as I've cashed up.' With the late licence, drinking up time and an hour of banter from the band Leah doubted that would be this side of 2 a.m.

'I wouldn't leave you to walk, you know.'

'You might as well, you don't care about what I have to say, do you?' Leah snapped, then pushed Harry into her mum's arms. 'I need to get changed then,' she added. Really what she wanted was to scream at the frustration of being a couple of days shy of fourteen and still having no say in anything.

She reached the top of the stairs but, instead of going to her room, pushed open the door of the one that had once been Kyle's. There was a dip in the bed covers as though he'd been lying there recently. She flung herself onto it, with her face on his pillow. It felt as though her whole life had been punctuated by Kyle leaving then coming back. Basic training and home. Afghanistan and home. Afghanistan, hospital and home. Missing days. Missing weekends. And each time a little less of him had returned.

'Come home soon,' she whispered. And if he'd walked in at that moment she would have pleaded for him to stay, to leave Hannah and bring Harry and forget the things that haunted him. But, for all her wishful thinking, she knew that Kyle's mind had filled with the kind of problems that dwarfed a normal life; threats that were real, if only to him. Nothing she could say would be enough to steer Kyle home. He had to find his own way and in his own time. And when he gets back he'll find Harry safe and waiting for him. Leah pushed herself into a sitting position. That *was* what mattered, not whether Kyle's current state of mind claimed that there could be a threat of monsters or evil, or Hannah's poor parenting, but whether Kyle would come home to find his little son both happy and healthy.

She still wasn't pleased to be babysitting at Hannah's house but now she felt less worried. It was, she decided, all about perspective; Kyle's worries might not be real, but Harry certainly was. Harry was the priority here.

She went to her room to change her clothes and that was when she saw the envelope lying on her bed. She recognized Kyle's handwriting at once. She opened it to find a birthday card, but no long written message. The real message was the card itself; he might be struggling, to have temporarily cleared off, but he wanted her to know he hadn't forgotten her or gone very far.

# TWENTY-SEVEN

Goodhew had opened his front door to find Gully on the doorstep. 'Come to check on me?' he'd asked as he stepped aside to let her through.

'No,' she replied, 'I'm sure being in the thick of the investigation is suiting you. Better than being on the outside anyway.'

That was true.

'I actually came to see if you wanted to grab some food? I've just finished and I haven't eaten.'

'Of course.' It was almost eight o'clock, but he didn't ask what she'd been doing in the time since her shift ended.

That had been almost two hours ago. They'd walked towards the city centre, stopping at Savino's for coffee and panini. Now they sat back in Goodhew's grandfather's old study, each with a mug of coffee. Gully nodded towards the map. 'Is it supposed to be decorative or functional?'

'It'd be hard to look at it and not think of work, wouldn't it?'

'It's weird for anyone to sit at home thinking of their job – you know that, right?' she commented. But immediately added, 'How were the Rasnikovs?'

It was the first time either of them had mentioned the case, and he knew what she was really asking; had there been anything untoward about Lila's family. 'Nothing stood out,' he replied. 'Lila's younger sister was the most openly distressed, but sometimes the kids are the ones who seem to bounce back quickly too.'

'Did you?'

The question caught him by surprise. He guessed she was referring to his grandfather's death but it was unusual for her to raise the subject so he queried what she meant.

'You were about twelve, weren't you?'

He could have ended the conversation right there, just as he guessed he mostly would have done in the past, but it didn't seem so hard to go on either. 'He died in July '92, so I was still eleven.' It was always surprisingly easy to cast his mind back to then. Often quicker than recalling the events in between. 'It was my last term in primary.'

Gully watched him. Expectant.

He thought he could remember everything about that moment, each face in the classroom, the smell of the sticky floors and the sound of running and the netball bouncing on the tarmac out in the playground. 'It was after lunch. In maths. We broke into separate groups for numeracy and I was with nine or ten other kids. We were doing fractions with Miss Moore, and I remember struggling to concentrate, staring at the page, dropping my pencil.' He heard the uneven rolling sound made by its hexagonal sides. 'Our classroom had one of those doors with the reinforced window in it. I crawled under the next desk to find my pencil and was still down there when our headmistress, Mrs Stone, appeared behind the glass. She took me out into the corridor and told me that my dad had come to pick me up, she said that my grandfather had been taken ill.' He tilted the mug until the coffee lapped close to the rim. 'Actually, he was dead already and I don't even think I felt surprised.'

'But you must have been shocked?'

'I felt numb, suffocated. As though something had fallen on me.'

Goodhew shrugged and stared across at the map; it filled the wall that had once been hidden by floor-to-ceiling bookcases. His grandfather's death had sliced Goodhew's childhood in two. Before then it had been constantly full; the house – his house now – had brimmed with books and photos and furniture with drawers. This study held the best memories, drawers packed with trivial souvenirs or travel tickets or letters or, best of all for small boys, models and gadgets. Every single item seemed to have a story attached and his grandfather kept them all in his head, ready to share with Gary.

Goodhew had suspected that they were made up from scratch each time so, sometimes, he'd pick an item again, just to check. But his grandfather never tripped up and the new version of the story would always match the first. And sometimes his grandfather told him extra details, and sometimes he would say, 'More when you're older.'

The house and its stories had seemed endless. Their conversations too, and Goodhew could still remember many. His grandparents had been the epicentre of his childhood; the starting point for exploring Cambridge, the place to read books, do homework and to avoid his parents' almost constant fights.

Then it had all gone. The summer had been there but he hadn't been part of it. The rest of the world seemed to go on oblivious and became invisible to him for a while. He didn't remember much of the funeral service, the house being emptied or being enrolled in a new school. His twelfth birthday had come and gone, then, at the end of August, his father drove his grandmother to Heathrow. She held tight as she hugged him and his sister. 'I need to go,' she whispered, 'I love you two so much, and I'll see you at half-term.'

He realized that he'd been silent for several minutes. 'I don't have contact with my mother's parents. They live abroad and I haven't seen them since I was a kid.' Goodhew tilted his mug and watched the surface of the coffee transform from circle to ellipse. 'You know, I was always closer to my dad's parents than to my own mum and dad.' He looked up fully. 'Are you close to yours?'

'I am actually. I'm the oldest of three. Did you know that?'

He felt as though he should've done but couldn't remember Gully talking about her family any more than he spoke about his own. 'No, I didn't.'

'That's funny, Gary, I always assume you know everything about everyone around you. You're so quick to dig up information whenever it suits you.'

'Honestly?' He found himself studying her expression as he spoke, alert for the first sign of disapproval. 'I used to gather details on most people, minor titbits like dates of birth or noticing where they shopped and the car they drove.' She frowned and he hesitated, then added, 'I stopped doing it with people I knew, it felt wrong.'

'Then why do it in the first place?'

'When I was a kid I wanted to be a detective and I thought I should train myself to look for details and remember as much as I could. I wasn't in Cambridge for secondary school, my sister and I boarded. It was a game I played to pass the time there.'

A small smile crept to her lips. 'You're funny. I just played netball at secondary school.' Then without warning her smile faded again. 'Kelly was the first person I've lost, you know. How does it feel when you start to get over it?'

'You don't go back to where you were, but it becomes more manageable.'

'Like the edges of it blend in with the rest of life?'

Goodhew nodded. 'Something like that,' he replied, but he really didn't have the answer. His grandfather's death had left an unfillable gap that he should have come to terms with many years ago. A crushing sadness suddenly blindsided him. He wondered whether he'd been carrying it all along or whether Kelly's death had brought it back. Or if, somehow, Sue had triggered it.

'I'm going to walk you back to your place now.'

She looked surprised at his abruptness and muttered an apology as she gathered her jacket and gloves.

'Don't,' he told her. 'Don't apologize.'

She told him that she didn't need the company walking home but they walked together anyway. Mostly in silence. She probably thought he was too closed, too uptight. But in reality it had been the most open conversation he'd had with anyone except his grandmother. Finally, as they turned the last corner before her home, he reached out and touched her arm. 'I'm sorry, Sue, I don't know why I find it so difficult.'

'I think I understand,' she told him. 'I'll see you tomorrow.'

# TWENTY-EIGHT

At half past midnight Leah sent Hannah a text asking her when she'd be back.

Leah knew that it wasn't *so* late compared to some clubs, but Hannah wasn't supposed to act like she was free to party when her son was so small and with a schoolkid as a babysitter. Leah also guessed that her point of view wasn't entirely fair; but just because Hannah was her nephew's mum it didn't mean Leah had to love her. And just because she was her brother's ex-girlfriend it didn't necessarily mean hating her.

But she did.

Leah had thought she'd be pleased when Kyle left Hannah, but the way he'd done it had been a mistake. Leah had imagined that he would kick her out then come with Harry to live at theirs. In her mind's eye Hannah would have just dropped off the face of the planet.

Instead Hannah had just sent her a text, 'Back in ten minutes, thanks for babysitting.' She knew, from experience, that an 'I'm on my way' text from Hannah meant Leah should 'be ready to go'. There'd be no hanging around to tell her how her son had been without her. She never asked anyway.

Leah got it, and she'd be ready by the time Hannah walked through the door, but she wouldn't be leaving that second, her mum would be coming to get her.

She'd just switched off the television when Hannah turned up. Her mood had lifted since she'd been out, she buzzed, bright-eyed and

140

insistent the way alcohol affected people a couple of hours before they pissed themselves. 'Everything OK?' she didn't wait for an answer. 'Sorry to kick you straight out but it's bed for me. I'm knackered.'

Leah stayed on the sofa. 'My mum's finishing at one, said she'll be here by half past.'

Hannah didn't look at her. No eye contact whatsoever – Leah had noticed that about her; it happened whenever Hannah didn't want an argument. 'It's just round the corner. I'll text her and tell her you've gone straight home.'

'She won't like it.'

'Why not? You've walked back plenty of times in the past.'

*But not at this time of night.* 'Kyle told me not to.'

'If it bothered him that much he wouldn't have fucked off, would he? Huh?' Hannah turned and made eye contact then, raising both caterpillar brows and giving Leah a scornful glare. 'Exactly, you don't have an answer for that one, do you?'

Leah knew she would have to walk out now anyway or face a slanging match. So she didn't comment, just zipped up her anorak and moved towards the open door. She wanted to question Hannah, to ask her why she was in such a rush to make her leave. And why Hannah never asked about Harry. Or cared that Kyle had gone. But Leah knew that there was little point; if those questions had triggered any answers they would be lies, or at least partial ones.

She pulled up her hood and walked away with her head down. She didn't turn to look along the road, but could see enough in the very corner of her vision. Perhaps Hannah would think she'd missed the taxi parked a few doors further along. It was a proper one, London style with the well-lit and roomy interior. There was a passenger, a man, talking to the driver, hand on the door and about to alight. Leah wasn't surprised. Of course not. She doubted he was the first; in Leah's opinion Hannah just took things when she wanted them.

Leah turned her attention back to the path and found a pace just short of a jog; running would sound like panic. A swift walk would allow her to pass quickly in and out of range of anyone listening. Maybe there was no one around, but it didn't feel that way. She glanced ahead then back down at the uneven footpath just in front of her.

141

'Just stop here,' Hannah had told the driver. The cab pulled up at the side of the road and she spoke more softly to the man on the seat beside her, 'I'll wave at you, I don't need the babysitter gossiping, OK?'

He shrugged, a big-shouldered lazy movement. He moved his hand from her lap as she stepped out. She hurried across to the house with her key ready when Leah opened the door. *Good girl.* She even had her coat on. Leah looked eager to say something, but then, she always did. Hannah had little time for any kid, but Leah had become invaluable so she forced a smile. Told herself to be patient.

Leah hesitated, 'My mum's finishing at one, said she'll be here by half past.'

For fuck's sake, the last thing Hannah needed right now was Kyle's mother getting in the way. Hannah's expression hardened, she stared at the centre of Leah's chest and felt the girl's discomfort. A couple more nudges and she was out the door. Scooting back home and so much in love with little Harry that she knew Leah would forgive her for almost anything.

She waved at Rick, then moved away from the door, leaving it ajar as she brought a couple of bottles of beer back through from the kitchen.

She thought she'd kept it casual; the door on the latch, drinks on the sofa. What did all that really matter, though, when she guessed that neither of them cared too much about the detail?

He closed the door quietly behind him. 'Nice place,' he said.

'Liar,' she replied.

'What's the deal then? Has your bloke gone? I don't want anyone walking in on us.'

She sat on the settee, the rough weave rubbing against the back of her bare thighs. He stood in the centre of the rug in front of her; she began to feel as though she was being interviewed. Perhaps he was nervous. He didn't seem it though.

'It won't happen. I kicked him out.'

He picked up the bottle of beer and held it by the neck. He didn't drink any, just swung it like a pendulum. 'What about the kid?'

'He won't wake up. Why all the questions?'

'Just asking. Come here then.'

She'd kept her shoes on, there would have been about a foot difference in their heights otherwise but the solid black platforms reduced that to about five inches. They made her teeter slightly, at the start of the evening when they were still unfamiliar and now because she knew she was drunk.

She joined him on the rug and he wrapped his hand around her waist, then he started to kiss her; he was good at it, his mouth was firm and hungry but it wasn't what she wanted. She edged back towards the settee, pulling him with her. She wondered whether she'd need to lead it but he suddenly swung into the seat and dragged her down, rolling onto her and pinning her between the sofa's arm and his own body. She reached for his shirt buttons but he pushed her hand away and slipped the shirt over his head in one easy move. She pressed the palms of her hands flat on his pecs, then slid them up to his shoulders. There was a vanity about him, a self-obsessed arrogance.

He was all about self-indulgence and she knew she'd been picked for that. And vice versa. She tugged at the lace side of her knickers, rushing to free herself and hoisting her short skirt a few more inches.

He ran his hand along her inner thigh, then stopping with his knuckles pressed against her clitoris. He twisted his hand over and slipped his thumb inside her. He sank his fingers through her pubic hair and pressed them into her skin.

He kept very still for almost a minute, the only sound was of her breaths, each swift and deep like almost silent gasps. Her gaze was fixed on him and she didn't know whether she wanted him to stop or needed him to go further. The sensation came close to pain, but not quite. Deliciously not quite.

She pushed her thighs wider and pulled at the belt on his trousers.

'Don't,' she breathed.

He massaged his thumb some more, pressing down harder with his fingers.

'Don't do it or don't stop?' he loomed over her and she saw no warmth in his expression.

She still didn't know what she wanted but, 'Don't stop,' found its way to her lips. 'Don't stop,' she repeated.

'Not here, upstairs,' he muttered, pulling his hand away sharply and grabbing her wrist.

She hurried up the stairs ahead of him, still wobbling on her heels. She made it through the bedroom door but had no time to even turn towards him when she felt his hand on the back of her skirt, dragging it downwards. She rushed to release the waistband before it ripped. As the skirt fell to the floor he turned her and she dropped back onto the bed. His jeans were gone and he stood naked in front of her. Gloriously naked. He leant towards her and she smiled, drawing her legs up either side of his. She felt him now, hard and determined between her thighs. She drew her legs wider as he thrust himself inside her. The first moments of deep pleasure pulsed through her.

She closed her eyes, and stretched her head back, exposing the flesh of her neck and breasts for him to enjoy. She thought she'd feel his mouth on her skin but only his hands touched her. Those strong hands gripped her roughly and forced her legs wider still. She felt release. Relief. Freedom. Nothing that passed between them now would be anything more than self-gratification on either part. No guilt or burden, just more miles than were bridgeable between her and Kyle.

She'd needed this for longer than she knew.

# TWENTY-NINE

A chain of events, that was the expression. And from Michael Kincaide's experience that usually involved steps that became progressively more unfortunate. The bad day at work that led to drinking, drinking that led to an argument and so on until they were called out to scrape some poor sod off the pavement. That chain seemed to hold together, tagging on poor choice after poor choice until the catastrophic moment of collapse and unravel. In his experience a chain of events was designed to go only in one direction.

It was now only Thursday but he'd already had a gutful of pretending that Ratty's murder stood on equal footing to other deaths. At first the press had managed just a couple of inches in a sidebar and it had taken a bereaved relative and the public's thirst for details of anything twisted before the details of mutilation had given the case any kind of kudos. But the bottom line was that Ratty had beaten the odds by staying alive as long as he had, and there were many, many scenarios where he could have been discovered in the same spot, just as dead, and no one would have blinked.

Kincaide's burgeoning irritation had only been increased with Goodhew's piss-taking cryptic clues regarding Ratty's real name. Goodhew had clearly known more than he'd let on and had used that information to find the other body. By the time Marks had held that briefing Goodhew had been restored as the bright-eyed nerd at the

145

front of the class. Sitting still and quiet had taken Kincaide's full quota of will power. That had been the first link in the chain, swiftly followed by the sight of Goodhew driving DI Marks to see Lila Rasnikov's family.

Kincaide had stopped for two pints and a chaser in the Free Press before the convivial mix of locals and intellectuals also became too deeply irritating. Home wasn't any better with Jan bleating on about the body found about half a mile from their own house. He'd made the mistake of mentioning Goodhew.

'He's back is he?' Her voice had a Punch and Judy shrillness and kept repeating in his head, even through a couple more cans and an oversized glass of whisky. And so, link by link, the chain of events had driven him towards the inevitability of no sex followed by a hangover. He began vomiting sometime in the small hours when the green light from the LED display of their alarm clock would have still been too painful to look at. When he finally emerged from the bathroom it read '5:22AM'.

'You brought that on yourself,' Jan muttered.

*Bitch.* He glared at the back of her head. 'I'm going in early.'

'You're still pissed. I hope you get pulled over and banned.'

And that would have been the case had Kincaide's law on chains of events really been true. Instead it all fell in his favour; at 6.55 the phone rang.

'Mike?'

Kincaide recognized the nasal tones of Andrew Gould, fingerprint technician and another general nerd. 'How's it going, Andy?'

'We've got something on these prints.'

'From the lock-up?'

'Yes, it's taken longer than we hoped, not at all straightforward actually,' he took an excited breath and began to talk about *whorls* and *humidity.*

'Andy, wait.' Kincaide's head was already banging. 'Just give me the bottom line. Are there any names?'

There was only one. Kyle Phipps.

It took Marks less than twenty minutes to arrive at Parkside. Kincaide waited within sight of the foyer, and relayed the details as they headed upstairs. 'Kyle Phipps is twenty-two years old. He signed up to the army just over four years ago, he hadn't been in trouble prior to that but was cautioned for being drunk and disorderly while home on leave in 2011. No charges though.'

'Is he still serving?'

'I don't know, that's all we have on our system.'

'Home address?'

'Absolutely. Two in fact, he's registered in a rental on Barnwell Road, with his girlfriend Hannah Davey, and their kid, Harry. And before that with his mother and sister just over the back, in Peverel Road.'

Marks nodded slowly. 'We'll visit both properties. You and I can start at Barnwell Road, that looks the most likely. I'll send people out there now, meet me downstairs in five minutes.'

Kincaide arrived at the front doors before Marks, and stood and watched as the first couple of cars pulled out of Parkside Station with their blue lights flashing. The pulse of the sirens made his brain throb, but he really didn't care.

Apart from a few hours in the middle of the night, the traffic ran constantly on Barnwell Road. They were the best places to approach with full lights and sirens; the occupants would often be too immune to the sounds outside to notice yet another police car or ambulance.

Marks and Kincaide arrived ten minutes after the first officers who had, by then, positioned themselves front and back of the property and could confirm that Kyle Phipps wasn't on site. Kincaide followed Marks into the front room; the occupants, a man and a woman, sat at opposite ends of the settee. Despite the distance between them, their body language was very similar and both sat on the edge of their seats and stared with disinterest at the floor in front of them. The man had the build that Kincaide associated with rugby players; strong arms and solid upper body, a heavy jaw and what looked like an extra-thick skull. He sat with his elbows on his knees and his hands locked in between.

Her hands were clasped and resting in her lap. A toddler sat at her feet, gripping a toy car in each hand.

147

Marks glanced round. 'I'll get over to the mother's house in Peverel Road.'

Kincaide nodded and waited until his DI had left before positioning himself across the room from Rick and Hannah.

'What's your full name then, Rick?' Kincaide asked after receiving just a first-name introduction.

'Rick Gowan. D'you mind telling me what's occurring?' He spoke with the remnants of a Manchester accent.

'Rick Gowan.' Kincaide repeated the name as he jotted it down and ignored the question. 'What's your relationship to Kyle Phipps?'

'I'd never heard of the bloke until the last hour.'

'So your relationship is with his girlfriend?'

'It's not a relationship . . .'

'Ex-girlfriend,' she cut in. 'Kyle is my ex. I met Rick last night.'

'I see,' Kincaide did see. He saw at once that Rick would be irrelevant to this investigation. The whole scene had one-night stand stamped on it and they both had that unwashed look of people who'd chosen morning sex over having a shower. 'So, Miss Davey brought you back here very shortly after you met? I see. And were you aware that this is the home of Kyle Phipps?'

'Like I said, I'd never heard of him. She said she lived alone with her kid.'

'And, as far as you've seen, that appears to be the case?'

'D'you think I would have hung around with another bloke in the house?' He sniffed loudly and shot a disparaging glance at Hannah. 'She didn't act like there was anything going on.'

Kincaide nodded. 'And you don't expect us to turn up on the doorstep after a night out either.' He spent only a few more minutes with Gowan before sending him on his way. The poor sod hadn't had a clue what he'd let himself in for. Kincaide looked across at Hannah, and tempered his sympathy for the guy with the observation that Gowan hadn't done too badly either.

Hannah wore a short dress – if she'd been standing it would have curved around her bum and stopped near the top of her thighs. She shuffled back on the settee, unabashed, crossing her legs at the ankles and leaving him with a view of thighs, hemline, cleavage, face. She had sunbed perma-tan and blue-black mascara. Her appeal probably wouldn't last beyond her mid-twenties; but it held an attraction. He realized that he hadn't spoken for a minute or two. His presence seemed to amuse her and the first hint of a smile curled her mouth.

'One moment,' he told her and slipped into the hallway. DC Holden stood at the back door, cigarette in hand. Kincaide nodded in the direction of the living room, 'Sit in on this one with me.'

He nodded and pinched out the cigarette. 'Sure.'

Holden took the space Gowan had occupied.

Hannah's demeanour had changed in those few minutes and her expression had changed to irritability. 'Go on then, ask away.'

'Where's Kyle?'

'You already asked that and I still don't know.'

'I didn't ask you, I asked Mr Gowan. Rick, from last night,' he added, just in case she couldn't remember.

'I don't know where Kyle is, and I don't care. He hasn't left me with a penny, the bills aren't paid and he hasn't seen his kid. You think I should be waiting till he comes back, right?' She folded her arms across her chest. 'In the past he's been away for months at a time and last night was pretty much the first time I've gone out and enjoyed myself.'

'Pretty much?'

'I do go out with the girls sometimes. Look, if it's over between me and Kyle, what's the problem? Nobody held a gun to his head and made him move out. He wanted out, well he got it. And I'd had enough by then anyhow.'

Harry pulled himself onto his feet and attempted to climb up beside her. She pulled him onto the seat. 'Come on, little man.' Her voice softened when she spoke to the toddler and some of her defensiveness disappeared when she spoke to them again. 'Why d'you want Kyle then?'

'He's a possible witness in a serious incident.'

'What incident?'

'We're investigating a murder.'

'What murder?' She looked uncertain then, her attention shifting from Kincaide to Holden and back again. 'What do you think he's done?' she asked quietly. 'Oh shit.'

'What's on your mind, Miss Davey?'

She frowned at the baby as though he might have the answer, then continued to frown as she looked back at Kincaide. 'Do you think he's killed someone?'

'Is that a possibility?'

'He won't talk to you.' She looked thoughtful, then tapped her temple. 'You know he's not right, don't you? He has issues.'

Kincaide and Holden exchanged glances; Kincaide knew nothing of this and Holden gave a subtle shake of his head.

'Such as?'

'He was in Afghanistan and it fucked with him.'

'We are aware that he served in the armed forces.'

'He's been screwed up ever since.' She looked down at her son again. 'You can't take risks when you've got kids and I'm a good mum, you can ask anyone.' It was always those words 'you can ask anyone' that cast doubt. 'This time when he started to have another meltdown, I'd just had it. He thought someone was coming after him and I thought, let them come. I can do better than that.'

Kincaide hadn't expected the whole truth from her; he was well aware that some people were persistent liars. He imagined she'd be the type who'd be happy to lie if it made her life run more smoothly. And she had lied, he just didn't know which parts were fabricated yet.

Peverel Road followed a ragged 'D' shape, built in the years when all estates were designed with wide verges between the houses and the road. In fact there was enough space for every house to have a clear view of the arriving police cars, and within ten minutes several of the doorways had spectators standing outside, exchanging commentaries with their neighbours. Marks parked directly in front of the Phipps's house, the front door was opened almost immediately and he was pleased to be able to slip inside before any of the spectators started with their inevitable questions.

Julie Phipps was slim, the kind of build that had more to do with work and worry than good diet and exercise and, although she initially sat down to speak with him, she seemed to find it hard to stay still. She offered him tea, and frequently glanced at either the window or the door, and it felt as though he never managed to grab her full attention. Her daughter, Leah, sat across the room. She wore headphones and he could pick out the compressed slivers of what sounded like a Ramones track escaping. There was no possibility of her hearing anything above that and yet, within a couple of minutes, he found himself wondering whether she could lip-read; her facial expressions were far too synchronized with their conversation.

'We're looking for your son, Mrs Phipps, can you give us any ideas as to where we might find him?'

'No, and I mean that. He's always had the ability to clear off when he was a kid, lie low when he thought I'd be angry. I could never find him back then and that was before the army trained him how to do it properly. Well, that's what they say anyway, I'm not sure they trained him for much except getting killed.'

Leah dropped her headphones onto her neck, pausing the music mid-bar. 'You don't actually think that, Mum. Before he joined up you were like, I hope they take him, knock some sense into him. Sort him out. Then when he's away, you were like, he's so kind, I hope the army doesn't knock all that out of him.' She raised an eyebrow at Marks but, apart from that, her expression stayed detached. 'Underneath she's worried.'

Julie scowled. 'Just butt out, Leah.'

Leah turned to Marks again. 'Do *you* want me to go as well?' she asked lightly.

Marks turned his biro over in his hand and pointed the lid at the window. Goodhew had just parked outside and was walking towards the front door. 'See him? I want you to tell him about your brother, and if there's anything at all that might help us find him, please don't hold back. It's important.'

'I know.' She sobered then and nodded. 'I really do.'

# THIRTY

They sat in her mum's kitchen, at two stools pulled up to opposite sides of the breakfast bar. He'd introduced himself but hadn't suggested she called him by his first name, or implied that he was there for her, or used any of those other trite phrases they repeated on the TV. Her experience of the police came down to that, watch them on telly, avoid them in real life.

At first Leah leant back with her arms folded while the detective, Goodhew, leant closer, one elbow on the work surface with his cheek cupped in that hand. Kyle had often sat much like that and the two of them had a similar build, tall and lean. Although the detective was a few years older than Kyle, and with green eyes where Kyle's were hazel, she liked the idea that there was the smallest similarity and changed her own position to mirror his.

The only other person there was a policewoman who stood near the door to the hallway. It was a joke; she should either have sat with them or cleared off, there couldn't be a discreet distance in a room the size of a shed. 'Why's she here?'

'This is PC Dawn Marsden, she's here to give you any extra support you might need.'

PC Marsden gave the tiniest nod, acknowledgement that she was in the room, but remaining dutifully detached. 'So if you give me a hard time she'll stick up for me?' Leah thought he looked too serious to work out that she was trying to wind him up, but he just looked quietly amused as he produced a retractable biro from his pocket.

'How old are you, Leah?'

'Killer first question,' she replied. He probably already knew the answer but she also knew that, if he didn't, any age from about eleven would have seemed plausible. It wasn't that she was particularly short for her age but she was, as other kids in her year seemed happy to point out, skinny, flat-chested and baby faced. 'Fourteen.' She paused. 'I'm in year nine,' she added. She had no idea why she thought he needed to know that, and suddenly she really felt childish.

He squiggled on his notepad and didn't seem to notice. 'There's quite an age gap between you and your brother then.'

'About eight years.' She studied him carefully, still weighing him up. 'We have the same dad though, if that's what you're wondering.'

'I wasn't actually.' His gaze flicked up from his pen. 'Go on,' he said.

'He's dead. People always assume he buggered off, but it was a brain tumour when I was four. I don't really remember him.' Her instinct had been to challenge him because she knew it as the best way to feel in control. Except that he seemed to understand exactly what she was doing.

'And Kyle was twelve?' He was looking at her but his focus shifted a little, giving her the slightly disconcerting feeling that he was seeing right inside her head.

'I guess.'

He pressed the tip of the pen into the pad, leaving a deep full stop at the end of whatever it was that he'd just written.

'What do you want to know about Kyle then?' she asked.

'Anything that will help us to locate him. We need to find him, Leah.'

'Because you're trying to catch him or protect him?'

Goodhew frowned. 'Do you know where he is either way?'

She shook her head. 'He wouldn't like me talking to you. Neither would Mum, except she's worried.'

'About?'

She ignored him. 'Tell me something. He was a soldier and you're in the police, why doesn't that make you both on the same side?'

He could have dismissed the question for any number of reasons, instead it seemed to interest him. 'We are I suppose, it's never occurred to me to look at it that way. I doubt many people do. And if your mum's never been much of a fan of the police, your brother's not likely to be either.'

'I don't know anyone around here who is.' She watched his expression, making sure she hadn't imagined it. 'You remind me of him.'

He looked surprised. 'What, Kyle?'

'Just a bit. There's always more going on in your head. His mind doesn't stop. He watches people and he thinks he knows what they're going to do. That's how it was before he left this time.'

'When was this?'

'A few days ago.' She shrugged.

'What did he say to you?'

'He told me that he wanted Harry here with me and Mum, didn't want me to walk around with Harry in the streets. He said it wasn't safe.'

'In what way?'

She shook her head. 'It's almost impossible to know what's real and what's only in his head. I thought he was losing it again, but it's all gone to shit with him and Hannah so maybe he was just trying to get Harry away from her.'

'Then why leave? Why not live here and fight for custody?'

'She *is* a crap mum.'

He shrugged. 'And how's he doing as a dad? I guess not as well as he'd like?'

She couldn't think of an answer that was truthful but still loyal to Kyle. She looked down at her hands and saw that her fingers had woven themselves together. 'He loves Harry, and second to Harry, he loves me,' she said finally. 'I don't think he'd let either of us down – not in a really bad way anyhow. So, if you find him, you could bring him back, right?'

'Maybe. It would depend.'

She silently rechecked her logic; what was the worst he would have done? Her first instinct said a fight, and it was most likely, or something else when he'd been drinking. Even then, the thought of little Harry would have held him in check. Right? And this way the police could find him and they'd all sleep easier knowing he was OK. She took a deep breath. 'Ask me whatever you think will help.'

'Names first, anyone he spent time with, people he likes, anyone he's fallen out with . . . whoever comes into your head.'

'He hasn't mixed with anyone much since he got injured.'

'Why do you think that is?'

She had her own theory, mostly based on the snide comments from the kids that hung around outside the chip shop, that everyone who knew him assumed he'd come back dead or seriously screwed. That his old mates had written him off already. The kids at the chip shop hadn't been far wrong on either count. She pressed her lips together for a moment, then spoke: 'Things aren't like that any more I guess,' she began. 'Kyle said that people move on. What's the point of having mates at school when you're going to hit sixteen and ditch each other anyway? He says they've all just grown up and it's fine he's lost touch with them.'

'But you don't think so?'

'No, I don't.'

He nodded slowly. 'What about before that, before he signed up? Or anyone he stayed in touch with after that, for example when he first came home on leave three years ago.'

Two names sprang to the front of her mind; there were others of course, work colleagues, old school mates and then lads from the pub who existed only as disembodied first names. 'Tina, his ex-girlfriend, and JP.'

'JP?'

'Jean-Paul Hewlett, they met at college, used to hang out sometimes. It went on for about a year I guess, a little longer maybe, then they had a row. JP smacked Kyle in the face, gave him an actual black eye.'

'Why?'

'Kyle wouldn't tell me, but why would he?'

'You must have some idea?'

'Look, I was only eleven or twelve and they'd probably been doing something they shouldn't have.' She paused, and tried to think. 'I'm not saying Kyle was up to anything illegal, just something that he wouldn't tell me about . . .'

'It's fine, Leah, I just need to get hold of him.'

'OK. I don't know where JP is now but his family run a hotel in Tenison Road, the end nearest the railway station. It's called the Beaumont.'

His notebook was rectangular and small but he seemed to have noted everything she'd said without needing to turn the page. 'And Tina?'

'Tina Cooney,' Leah exhaled loudly as she said the name, 'I really liked her. Kyle was dumb to leave her for Hannah. My mum told him that too, but she says you can't tell Kyle anything.'

'And how can I find her?'

'She worked at Sarianna's, d'you know it?'

He shook his head.

'It's a hairdresser's, in Cherry Hinton.'

His pen stopped moving and a flash of interest sparked in his eyes. She drew a breath and, several seconds later, realized that she still held it. She had no idea what she'd said that might have been significant.

'Do you know Mill End Road in Cherry Hinton?' he asked.

She exhaled slowly, doing her best to be silent and controlled. Yes, she knew it very well. 'I've heard the name,' she admitted. She didn't add that she'd been there because of Kyle. Or that she'd heard that the police had found a body. She hadn't connected the two until that very moment; why would she when Kyle's last mention of the place had been so long ago?

'Have you ever been there with Kyle? Do you know if he's been there?'

She repositioned herself, wriggling backwards on the bar stool. 'I don't remember. Maybe I've just seen the signpost.'

'OK,' he closed the notebook and placed the pen on top so that it cut a diagonal across it. 'I understand.'

She bit on her lip and managed the smallest of nods, even though she couldn't see what he now understood, and didn't want to ask either. His expression suddenly seemed impenetrable and she wondered if she'd made a mistake by saying anything at all.

# THIRTY-ONE

Goodhew pushed open the door of Sarianna's, all six women in the room glanced then, as if it was a prearranged routine, and five of them looked away again. One of the two hairdressers turned towards him, tail comb in hand. 'Can I help?'

'You used to have a hairdresser named Tina Cooney?'

'Still do.' She pointed the comb towards the back of the shop. 'Tina?'

A bead curtain separated the salon from what he guessed was some kind of storage room. A woman in her early twenties pulled the strands to one side. She had pixie-cut dark hair and wore flat pumps and a white and pink beauty therapist's uniform. 'Not a hairdresser though. Nails mainly.'

By the time he'd introduced himself he could feel all the other eyes back on him again.

'Come through,' she held the curtain to one side. 'Their ears will be burning,' she added loudly, then took him through to a cream-walled treatment room. 'It's this or out there with the ladies.' Her tone stayed light but he could see the curiosity written on her face. The furniture consisted of a couch, a single chair and a narrow side table stacked with a display of nail polishes and beauty products. He picked up the nearest – 'Self-heating organic salt body scrub' – then placed it back amongst a variety of other tubes. 'Everyone's job is complicated to someone else, isn't it?'

She leant against the wall. 'Yes, you're right there.' Her expression seemed unguarded and gentle.

'I believe you know a Kyle Phipps?'

'Kyle?' She blinked. 'Yes, we went out for a few months. I haven't seen him in a long time though.' She paused. 'Is he OK?'

'We need to find him.'

'So that's a no.' She wrapped her arms around herself.

'You worked here while you were going out with him. Did you live round here too?'

'No, I lived with my mum, not far from Kyle actually. I thought I'd bump into him but I never have. Although I heard he's got a little boy now.'

Asking an ex an opinion on their former partner had limited reliability, but he asked in any case. She allowed herself the smallest of smiles.

'If I said that, underneath it all, he has a good heart, I'd just sound like every other girl that's ever claimed that her bad-boy boyfriend is just misunderstood.'

Goodhew nodded and the silence from Tina ran on a little too long. She reached to the side table and picked up the nearest bottle of nail varnish, checked the lid was tightly sealed, replaced it then moved on to the next. 'So, what's he done?'

'He may be a witness. Does the name JP mean anything to you, Tina?'

And for the second time in less than an hour he saw a simple question cause a visible jolt. But Tina didn't avoid answering as Leah had done. She straightened the row of bottles for a moment then turned to face Goodhew.

'Are you here because of the murder? The woman in the lock-up?'

'What makes you ask?'

'My dad lives down Mill End Road. Those lock-ups are in two blocks of eight, the body was in one block and my dad's garage is in the other. My dad never used it, but JP and Kyle did.'

'They rented it?'

'Not at first. He just let them use it because Kyle was my boyfriend, but when we split up Dad said it had to be on a more formal basis and that's when he started charging them. Just a few quid each week, but it was the principle that they ought to pay that mattered to Dad.'

'Then Jean-Paul and Kyle fell out?'

'No one calls him that, but, yes. That's what I heard from Dad. I don't know what it was about though.' She began to say something else, hesitated, then spoke anyway, 'Kyle isn't an angel, but I wouldn't think . . .' She shook her head and stopped.

'You wouldn't think what?'

'I wanted to tell you that he's a decent bloke, that he wouldn't have anything to do with that woman's death. But I don't know the first thing about any of it, do I?' She reached towards the door handle. 'I hope he didn't, that's all.'

# THIRTY-TWO

The streets around Cambridge train station had been born out of waves of development and redevelopment; the builder's merchants relocated, leaving the land available for modern townhouses, while some of the large sixties' offices had recently given way to new flagship sites, equally uncharismatic but shrieking of investment. The towering shell of Foster's Mill had been hidden, swathed in printed tarpaulins to hide its transformation into modern living space, while the railway station's porte cochère had been filled by commercial ventures and, at the other end of Station Road, the remaining genteel houses had long since been converted to language schools and legal practices.

There had been losses, but Tenison Road remained mostly intact and, at the station end, several of the large gable-fronted properties had been converted into either bed and breakfasts or small, independent hotels. The Beaumont sat amongst them. It had once been two adjacent houses and the hotel's logo was displayed across matching canopies above each front door.

Goodhew wasn't sure which way to enter until he spotted the small gold and black sign that read 'Reception'. He walked through the downstairs and was near the back of the house by the time he found anyone. A grey-haired man of about sixty sat at the dining table closest to the window. He had a copy of *The Times* open in front of him at the puzzle page. 'Killer Sudoku,' he said. 'Supposed to be good for the brain.'

'Do you work here?'

'Brian Hewlett, co-owner.'

'You're Jean-Paul's father?'

'That's right.'

'DC Gary Goodhew. Is JP around?'

Hewlett closed his paper and Goodhew thought for a minute that he was about to stand, but instead he leant back and bellowed in the direction of the other side of the building, 'Jeeps!'

Goodhew heard no reply and, after the briefest of pauses, Hewlett yelled out again. 'Get down here. You have a visitor.' He turned back to his puzzle for a few more seconds, then, without warning, he closed it, folded the paper into three and dropped the newspaper and pen into the waste bin beside the table. 'Take a seat,' he muttered. 'I have things to do.'

He passed his son, who stepped aside to let him through the doorway, neither spoke. JP was a couple of inches taller than Goodhew, broad-shouldered, wearing jeans and a black rugby shirt. Goodhew recognized the green and gold cross logo immediately.

'Cambridge '99 Rowing Club?'

'Yeah, success is labour's reward,' he quoted the club motto. 'I row for the county and dad still thinks I'm a freeloader. All because I'm spending free time on a "hobby" instead of wallpapering the family empire.' He pointed in the general direction of the upstairs rooms. 'And now you're here he probably thinks I'm a criminal too. Thanks for that.'

'I'd like to ask you a few questions about Kyle Phipps. I understand that you and he were friends?'

JP's expression darkened. 'Briefly. Very briefly actually.'

'I heard it was longer than that.'

JP shrugged, 'OK, so it was a couple of years. What do you want to know?'

'We need to find him.'

'Well, I can't help you there. I haven't seen him since before last Christmas, when I'd seen him drunk in town a few times.'

'And did you speak to him?'

'No, I saw him from a distance and walked the other way. The last time I had a proper *conversation* with him was in the summer of 2011. I don't know the exact date.'

'When you had a fight?'

'When I punched him.'

Goodhew could tell from JP's tone that the story would follow without much prompting. 'I need to know about the lock-up you and he had in Mill End Road.'

'What about it?'

'Why you had it. What you did with it and why you fell out.'

They'd both been standing until then, but JP kicked the leg of the nearest chair so that the chair swung out from under the table. He sat heavily and Goodhew took the opportunity to sit, too.

'We met at college, we were both at CRC. I was studying hospitality,' again he gestured at his general surroundings, this time with an open palm, 'because this is the Hilton. Kyle was doing catering. He had no interest in being a chef, just kept on about wanting to join up, but his mum had told him to hang on until he was eighteen and he needed to study something to kill the time. We ended up in the same bar on the same night a few times and Bob's your uncle.'

'And the lock-up?'

'We had an entrepreneurial moment, bought a job lot of bikes at an auction with a plan to rent them out. This place is close to the train station, so I'd thought we might get something going from here. I was right too because bike hire at the station itself has opened since then and they're making a killing. Anyway Kyle's girlfriend's dad let us put them in his garage. We thought we'd paint them all up in pale blue and yellow.'

'The colours of your rowing club?'

'Yeah, the colour scheme was my idea. When Kyle was able to join up he lost interest in our plans, almost overnight. Left me with all my spare cash tied up in a bunch of bikes over in Cherry Hinton.'

Goodhew frowned, he couldn't quite see the logic but asked the question in any case, 'And that's why you fell out?'

'No. I was irritated and I probably wouldn't have bothered with him much after that, but we agreed that we'd still fix them up and sell them off one at a time so that we could at least end up with some profit.'

'And?'

'And things kept turning up in the garage when he was home on leave. A few tools at first, a socket set he said he'd borrowed, a jet washer and a lawn mower. It didn't take me long to suspect they were stolen. I told him to keep it away from me, I didn't want anything to do with it, then I turned up one day and he was dismantling a whole frigging motorbike. I told him to get rid of it and I started moving faster to get shot of our push bikes until the last time I went when there were just a couple of them. I opened the door and the first thing I saw was a Snap-on tool box, on wheels. I mean . . .' He raised his hand and dropped it again. 'He was there already, and he just shrugged, didn't give a shit. So I just smacked him one and I didn't give a shit either. I took one of the last two bikes and rode away.'

'And you're sure all these items were stolen?'

'Absolutely.'

'And he didn't retaliate?'

'No.' JP flashed a quick grin. 'Hitting him was out of character for me but isn't it ironic to assault someone because they're breaking the law?'

'I can see that.'

'I just did it, then afterwards I thought about how stupid I'd been. I think I was lucky that I caught him by surprise; I had always felt like he was one of those people you didn't want to cross.'

'And to your knowledge, was he ever violent?'

'I don't know, I just saw that he had the potential.'

# THIRTY-THREE

Goodhew stood in the corridor, leaning back against the wall and listening to the conversation in the adjacent office. Kincaide's voice had been raised several times in the past few minutes. Marks was far harder to hear but Goodhew was able to pick out most of his boss's words.

'It's not negotiable, Michael.'

'I don't want to work with him. He is already taking the piss out of me.'

'So you said, but nothing you have said proves that.'

'When he identified Ratty he clearly held back information. He told me Ratty lived up the river and was named after a kid's TV character. No one would find a name and address from that. No one.'

'Sue Gully did.'

'So Goodhew says, and that's my point, people actually believe his bullshit.'

'That's enough,' Marks snapped and it was the first time that any of his words had been louder than any of Kincaide's.

Kincaide fell silent for several seconds then spoke firmly. 'He's done it again.'

'How?'

'When he wanted that garage opened he already knew it would be a crime scene. He had more information than he shared with us. He's come back and straight away he's trying to play games.' Goodhew

164

heard movement and imagined Kincaide pacing towards the door then back to Marks again. 'You can't say he's never done it before, can you?'

'I'll speak to him but, until I retire, you two will be working together and I want you to consider this: you and Goodhew have different sets of skills – play to your strengths and let him play to his.'

'And can I ask what you think they are, sir?'

'His or yours?'

'Both.'

'You work them out, Michael, and I would add that I see virtually no overlap between his strengths and yours, so why wouldn't I want you both in the same team? Go home, find a fresh perspective on Goodhew, because I care about our effectiveness, not your petty issues with one another.'

A few seconds later the door was pulled open and Kincaide left Marks's office, turning in the opposite direction to where Goodhew stood. Kincaide took several strides before he stopped abruptly and turned. 'Where have you been?'

'I met Kyle's ex-girlfriend and, after that, another friend of his. I came to update Marks.' Goodhew stayed where he was and Kincaide returned to just outside the office door.

'I need to know, Gary.'

Goodhew let the trace of a smile form. 'I thought you didn't want my opinion on anything? And by the way, it really was Sue, not me, who worked out Ratty's identity. And I didn't hold back information on either occasion.'

'So update me.'

The door opened beside Kincaide and Marks held it wide for them both to enter. 'Update us both, Gary.'

DI Marks hadn't known that Goodhew would be in the corridor, but sometimes the peculiarities of timing bore fruit. He would have seen them separately, he'd already planned that much, and it was considering Kincaide's and Goodhew's very different perspectives that had left the thoughts of their respective strengths at the forefront of his mind.

Kincaide went for the straightforward answer. The obvious one, to put it another way. And in most investigations that was precisely the job that was required. Go in, grab the facts, document the evidence.

Crime, investigation, arrest, conviction.

Bang, bang, bang and bang.

It frequently felt as though more opportunities to convict were lost through lack of evidence gathered, or lack of manpower, than the inability to identify the guilty party. Kincaide had his eye on the closure rate, he paced himself for unremarkable cases and an effective, if equally unremarkable, career.

If every member of his team had been a clone of Kincaide it would have still functioned. He couldn't begin to imagine every member as a clone of Goodhew; just processing the idea was stressful. He'd listened as the start of their exchange reached him from outside his office and in less than a minute had them both sitting at his desk.

Goodhew updated them on the visits that came as a result of his talk with Kyle's sister Leah Phipps. Goodhew had done well. Marks had persevered with Leah's mother, Julie, who had declared herself as both concerned and cooperative, but the information she had provided had been virtually nil. And, just because he was in the mood to consider it, Marks allowed himself a moment to consider how Kincaide would have fared with Leah or her mother. 'Michael, any questions?'

Kincaide shook his head. 'Not at this moment, but I'm sure I will.'

Goodhew cut in, 'I do. Is Kyle Phipps the main line of investigation?'

'Not the only one, but yes, he is the focus.'

'I understand why we need to talk to him,' Goodhew frowned. 'I don't believe he killed Ratty. Not without the picture being radically different.'

Kincaide shifted his weight and shook his head slowly.

Marks raised a hand, gesturing Kincaide to wait. 'We have a proven connection between Kyle, Lila Rasnikov and Aaron Rizzo.' *Aaron Rizzo*; that name wasn't working for any of them, they would need to accustom themselves with it before any trial, but right now he corrected himself, 'Ratty, that is.'

Goodhew shook his head, 'No we don't.'

'Of course we do,' Kincaide snapped. 'Kyle's fingerprints are in the garage Ratty rented, how is that not a connection, Gary?'

'And what's the logic? Why did Ratty rent the garage?' Goodhew asked the questions as much to himself as to Marks or Kincaide.

'There was a dead body in there. It's obvious.'

Goodhew paused, then, 'It's no proof that Kyle and Ratty were connected. What proof do we have that Ratty ever went there? None.'

Kincaide glanced at Marks and back at Goodhew, who seemed to have lost some of his concentration.

'Gary?' Marks spoke sharply.

'Sorry.'

'Listen to Michael.'

'There are two likely scenarios,' Kincaide began. 'First, that Ratty rented a garage, Kyle used it to hide Lila's body, Ratty found out and Kyle killed him as well; or Ratty killed Lila and Kyle found out, killed Ratty and tried to make it look like the same killer. The two deaths weren't so similar, it is just the eye mutilation that's the same.'

'Just? Not many people would look at Lila's body and understand what they'd need to do to copy it, or even have the stomach for it. Michael, your logic is jumping all over the place. Do you think Ratty killed Lila? Or do you think Kyle did it?'

'Like I said, they are the two most likely scenarios.'

'No.' Goodhew tapped Marks's desk top with the tips of his fingers, then slapped his palm down, but his tone was decisive rather than angry. 'No, I really don't believe that Ratty killed her. That's not some blind belief either, the Ratty I knew was withdrawn, he didn't want to confront people, in fact he'd go out of his way to stay clear. He would not have hunted someone down in order to kill them.'

'And your point is?' Marks asked. 'Someone who keeps a low profile won't be a killer? That's a hard-to-follow theory. It sounds more likely that your familiarity with Ratty via your police work could be distorting your judgement.'

'OK, I wasn't explaining it clearly. I was about to say that Ratty's ability to kill would have been driven by fear or threat or panic. A crime where he would have to plan and organize, in order to kill for self-gratification? No. There wasn't self-indulgence or self-gratification in Ratty's life. Never mind the practicalities of how a homeless man organizes rent and arranges a chest freezer in the first place . . . not impossible, but not likely either. And then Kyle—'

Kincaide interrupted, 'You don't know Kyle, none of us do, you can't pretend he wouldn't kill, you just don't have a shred of evidence.'

'Kyle has a connection to the garage and has personal problems, of course he's a possibility. We don't have enough information to know. Do you really believe that Lila Rasnikov's murder was the killer's first time?'

'I don't see why not.'

Goodhew shook his head. 'It won't be, and I haven't seen any signs that Kyle escalated to this, never mind the fact that he was only nineteen when Lila died.'

Kincaide scowled. 'Plenty of teenagers kill.'

Goodhew scowled back. 'A few do, but not like this.'

Marks pressed his fingers to his temples and considered Goodhew and the destabilizing effect he could have on an investigation. The balance had to be kept between that and the unteachable thought processes and talents for reading people that Goodhew possessed. He was like a trained dog that sniffed out what wasn't audible to the rest of them – because they didn't hear something it didn't mean it didn't exist. It didn't mean it was relevant either.

'Gary, I'm listening. If neither Ratty nor Kyle is a killer, what's your theory?'

'I don't have one yet.'

'So just give us your thoughts.'

'Just this, the killer's done it before and that murder – or murders – is what we need to discover.'

'We are cross-referencing old cases nationally. We're not going to overlook possibilities like that, Gary, but that can't be the main thrust of the investigation. We have to work with what we have, and that's to treat Kyle as our main suspect.'

'It might not be a known case, sir, it could be an as yet undiscovered body like Lila Rasnikov's.'

'And what can we do about that? Right now, nothing.' He continued to direct his words towards Goodhew, 'I believe our investigation is following the most relevant route and I don't want you undermining it or Kincaide's authority. Have I made myself clear?'

168

Goodhew nodded and Kincaide glanced at him, then nodded too.

Kincaide looked satisfied. From where Marks sat, Goodhew just looked like Goodhew, and Marks doubted he'd done anything at all that would keep him on the leash.

# THIRTY-FOUR

That afternoon Goodhew had returned to Parkside out of obligation, rather than because it would be the most productive thing to do. He'd known how he'd feel as soon as he stepped through the door, the old feelings of airlessness and frustration would be back. They weren't about Parkside itself, he didn't think he was so fickle that his earlier energy has just dissipated, it was more about his attention being called away from the part of his brain that wanted silence and open space and the opportunity to listen for the answers. He could feel the tension rising because the case looked fragmented and he needed to turn it over in his mind to find a new angle, another way in.

Marks had Ratty and Kyle Phipps right at the heart of it. Goodhew had juggled with the thought; Marks was correct – up to a point. There might be one killer, there might be two, but he doubted it was either of these two men.

He'd left Marks and Kincaide, headed towards the stairs and reminded himself of the simple truth; the case might look fragmented but it wasn't. There weren't enough facts yet, that was all. He needed more and when he had them he would turn them over until he could see these broken pieces forming a single answer.

The stairwell windows had been tipped to vent. The daylight was fading and the evening air from outside had scraped through the gaps and met him as he took the final flight. Sue Gully had been waiting for him at the bottom.

'Gary? Do you have a few minutes?' She'd held an envelope in her hand but she hadn't offered it to him.

He'd glanced at his watch. 'You've finished for the day, right?'

'I wanted to catch you.'

'Can we walk into town? I want some air.'

She'd nodded, gone to change and taken the envelope with her.

Now they sat at a window seat in The Cow with a bottle of beer each and the envelope between them with its contents lying on top. Goodhew twisted them around to face him. 'I was expecting something a little more exciting, you know.'

Gully smiled and spun it back. 'A sealed envelope was always going to grab your attention more than the actual contents.' There were three notes written under one another, 'The Cow, July 2011, Overnight'. 'These are reminders for me, and I don't think there's a confidentiality issue with it written like this either.'

'What is it then?'

'Kyle Phipps, he came here on 29 July 2011. Just before closing time a couple of the punters reported a scrap outside.'

'Whereabouts?'

'In front, up by the cornflake statue.'

He knew where she meant. The statue stood a few yards in front of the pub and depicted the Greek giant Talos. In this representation he'd become a diminutive figure with something resembling a cereal box strapped to his back. Goodhew nodded.

'Phipps was bloodied but conscious. An ambulance was called but by the time it arrived he was on his feet, shouting abuse and ready for a scrap. He spent the night in the cells.'

'Not charged?'

'That's right. He was drunk and mouthy, but hadn't caused any damage; in fact he was the only one with any actual injuries. The police surgeon checked him over, said it was superficial and sent him on his way in the morning.'

'Who had hit him?'

'It doesn't say.'

Goodhew swilled the beer around in the bottle, 'You know what, it's a matter of a hundred yards or so from here to where Ratty was found.'

171

'And it's just a few minutes from here to most of the city; we're not anywhere that's exactly obscure, Gary.'

'No CCTV in this case?'

'It's patchy, a few systems trained on the shop fronts, nothing on the pavement though,' she replied.

'And there hasn't been much for Ratty either,' he said, mostly to himself.

'So many are trained on the shop fronts; the centre of Market Hill is notorious for its lack of surveillance.'

'I do know that, Sue. I was thinking aloud as much as anything. Who examined Phipps?'

'The paramedic first, then Dr Addis was on call and saw him in the custody suite.'

'No comment from Addis?'

She shook her head. 'Or anyone else come to that. Phipps was a bit lively when he came in, had a half-hearted swing at the first person who came through the door.'

'And who was that?'

'Funnily enough, DC Holden.'

His path and Holden's had rarely crossed but Holden's short temper was well known. 'It's always the same names in the thick of things. What did Holden say? That it didn't warrant pressing charges?'

'Pretty much.'

Goodhew smiled sourly. 'He enjoys throwing his weight around. Did you speak to Holden or get that from the notes?'

'Just the notes.'

'OK. Then what?'

'Once Phipps was back at Parkside he became quiet, I imagine it was an uneventful night for everyone except Phipps. And I only found this information thanks to Sheen. The name Kyle Phipps rang a bell apparently, he went through the custody records and he passed it to me to pass to you.'

'It should have come up when we ran a background check on him.'

'It did, Kincaide's aware and has had a look at it, but as far as he's concerned it's old news, along with Kyle Phipps receiving a speeding ticket and bunking out of school. I didn't know all that, though, when Sheen raised it, but it's there in the case notes.'

Goodhew tugged the sheet back towards him. 'Can I keep this?' Goodhew could see why it had been dismissed. Phipps wasn't the aggressor for one, and anyone could get felled once they'd had a few; it proved nothing about either Kyle's aggression or lack of. But it had occurred just a month before Lila Rasnikov's disappearance and not far from the scene of Ratty's murder.

'What are you thinking?'

'About Venn diagrams actually.'

Her eyes narrowed. 'Explain.'

'Marks is moving forward with the theory that Ratty and Kyle are connected, that Kyle is the main suspect in Ratty's murder and that one or other or both were involved in Lila's death. As yet, though, there is no proof that they knew each other. No sightings of Ratty at the lock-up either.'

'But the lock-up is in Ratty's name.'

'Exactly, so someone with a connection to Ratty and therefore Lila rented it.'

'And Kyle's prints were in there. So this Venn diagram comes in how?'

'People who knew Ratty in one group, those connected with Kyle in another and to Lila in the third. I was trying to picture the overlapping circles and which people might belong in the middle of the diagram.'

Her eyes remained narrowed. 'Venn diagrams? OK, I'm changing the subject now.'

'Why?'

'Do you have any idea how sad that is, Gary?'

He didn't answer for a minute, and then finally asked, 'I'm going to walk round to where Ratty was found. Do you want to come?'

She had no idea why she would, but said 'yes' in any case and within a few minutes they were standing amongst the deserted market stalls.

'About here?' he asked.

'Pretty much.' She pointed behind her, in the direction of the Guildhall. 'I was back there, remember. But this looks about right.'

Goodhew stood with his back to the railings that fenced off the steps to the public toilets. The tarpaulins on the empty market stalls interrupted his view in every direction. Bunting and extra signage fluttered from some despite the lack of wind; add in darkness and he could see how Ratty may have been caught unawares. 'Why here, Sue?'

She studied the cobbles. 'I've been thinking about that. When we thought it might be a spontaneous killing it made more sense; a fight can break out anywhere.'

'But this was planned. It's an odd location.'

'Yes, but no one could email Ratty, or phone him, so they may not have been able to prearrange a meeting that way, or know anything about his plans . . . Ratty wouldn't have known his own plans.' She kicked an old cigarette butt into a crack in the ground. 'How did you find Sam and Mooch?'

'Legwork.'

'Same thing.'

That made sense. 'Someone wanted to kill Ratty, they planned what they could and the rest, like the location, had to be spontaneous.'

'Exactly.'

'So the killer knew who Ratty was, but not in a way where he could arrange to meet him on any kind of pretext,' he added.

'I guess.'

'And he knew Ratty by sight and, for at least the last four years, by his real name.'

'You're making too much of a leap, Gary. You are assuming that Ratty's killer is the same person that rented the lock-up.'

'No, I'm not. The person who killed Ratty knew about Lila's eyes and therefore he knew about the garage.'

'Kyle Phipps knew,' she said quietly. 'It could be him.'

'I don't like it, Sue.'

'Because Kincaide does? Or for a reason that's more substantial? Because *it feels wrong* obviously doesn't count.'

'Does anyone commit a crime like that the first time? It's too sophisticated. It's not the work of someone bunking out of college or scrapping with his mates.'

'You can't keep using that one argument, Gary.' She too leant against

174

the railing and they stood shoulder to shoulder, facing the market's centrepiece fountain. It had been filled in and turned into a flowerbed; there would always be examples of things that weren't as they were expected to be. And, wrong as it was, he knew he was prepared to listen to her in a way that he would never listen to Kincaide. 'Go on then, convince me.'

'Kyle had a scrape with the police outside The Cow and around the same time he is punched by Hewlett. We don't know about the first incident but we do know that he didn't retaliate at Hewlett. Then Kyle heads back off to Afghanistan, so he wasn't avoiding conflict. I think it was self-control alone that kept him from hitting back at Hewlett.'

'And you're going to say that doesn't make him look less guilty, but more so, that it would have taken self-control to kill Lila and that he had the capability.'

'Yes,' she jabbed him lightly in the side with her elbow, 'and there may be something in his background that you might miss if you are adamant about only looking for someone else.'

She was wrong about Kyle, he felt certain of it. But at the same time she had a point. He elbowed her gently in return. 'What if I dig deeper for a connection between Kyle and Lila?'

She turned to look at him, tilting her head away as if a little distance would help her weigh him up. 'In an official capacity I hope.'

'Of course.'

'You worry me when you switch from "we" to "I" you know. Those months at home won't have changed you that much.'

Goodhew headed back towards home, but in the end he walked on past and back to Parkside. Marks had gone, Kincaide too. Goodhew made coffee, switched on his PC and surrounded himself with a pile of paperwork on Lila Rasnikov. His knowledge of her had been formed from three moments alone; finding her body, seeing her photographs and meeting her parents. Each had made an impression, nothing more. Wondering whether he could find a connection between Kyle and Lila had made him realize that he just didn't know enough.

He started with the initial call from her parents. They'd rung in at 4.05 a.m. on 6 August 2011, then three more times before 8 a.m. to report her missing. She'd been three weeks shy of her eighteenth birthday and a couple of weeks away from hearing her exam results.

She'd studied at Hills Road College: English Literature, Biology and Psychology. She'd passed them all with two As and a B, but had never seen the results.

*She hadn't decided what she wanted to do with her life.* Her father had said those words when Goodhew and Marks had visited. There had been tautness in his deep voice and he spoke unnaturally slowly, as though every word needed to be kept under control.

Goodhew found the transcripts of each of her father's calls. Goodhew heard Nikolas Rasnikov's voice in his head as he read through them.

NR: I'm concerned about my daughter, she hasn't come home.
CO: How old is she?
NR: Seventeen.
CO: And how long has she been missing?
NR: She said she'd be back late. That usually means eleven, or just after.
CO: So she was due home at between eleven and half past yesterday evening, 5 August?

Goodhew imagined a note of scepticism slipping into the emergency call operator's voice then. He thought of the twelve- and thirteen-year-olds that frequently went AWOL without their parents ever picking up the phone.

CO: Does she have a mobile phone with her?
NR: It's switched off, or out of range. We just get her voicemail. We want to make sure she hasn't had an accident or something.
CO: I understand, sir, let me take your details and someone will call you if your daughter has been in contact with the emergency services. Can you tell me who she is with?
NR: I don't know.

Each call followed a similar pattern, Lila's father's sentences became increasingly clipped, tension in the third call giving way to a brief moment of anger in the fourth. And each ended the same.

CO: Can you tell me who she is with?
NR: I don't know.

# THIRTY-FIVE

*The Isle of Ely. The water had long since been drained but the island status remained, at least in a metaphorical way. I wondered how I'd lived so many years in Cambridge without Ely having a greater impact on me. It was a mere sixteen miles away, and Ely had only ever felt like a satellite to Cambridge, a tiny town with the honorary badge of 'city' awarded because of its cathedral. And, therefore, the tourism because of its cathedral. Any commercial success more due to that and the influx of housing market refugees from Cambridge than merits of its own.*

*The day I visited had been warm and bright, with only smudges of cloud and vapour trails marking the sky. Even those floated higher than usual and reminded me of the tiny marks left from over-polishing glass. I hadn't come to view any specific properties at that point. I'd been too depressed to organize myself as much as that. So I just wandered around the centre. High Street and Market Street ran parallel to one another with cuts and passages linking them. There were other roads and shops that spurred away, but it was this simple circuit that kept the heart of the city close to the bosom of the cathedral. Family businesses seemed to hold their own here. A shoe repair shop. A haberdashers. A family butcher with rabbits hanging in the window. There were some chain stores but not enough to shake the feeling of the place being slightly disconnected from the wider world.*

*I don't remember making any decision at that point but I know I* began walking through the city with my eyes newly opened. I walked through the cathedral grounds, staring up at the intricacy of its stonework. I wondered how many years it had taken to build. Hundreds I guessed. Multiple generations of men working blindly towards a greater goal. No doubt Ely sacrificed much back then but now it reaped the rewards.

The shape of the windows – an arch with a pointed top – was repeated in the railings, and once I'd spotted it I found it echoed in other shop fronts and doorways.

I drifted like this for several hours, immersing myself, staring up at rooftops, more like an overseas tourist than an almost-local who shouldn't have been so taken by the layers of history. It should have been no different to any other market town; but, for me, it was.

From the café on the corner of the market I watched the people of Ely pass the window. It didn't seem like any kind of Cambridge overspill but a completely unconnected place. My gaze rested on the profile view of a young woman looking into the window of an estate agent.

Two things struck me at that moment: that I hadn't even thought of my wife since I'd left Cambridge and that I didn't want to leave Ely without taking something with me.

The woman had a neat figure shown off by her calf-length red raincoat. She moved slowly along in front of the property display. Her mac was belted at the waist, buckled not tied, and I liked the way her dark hair draped neatly on her back. I left the rest of my coffee and joined her at the window. She glanced at me then smiled politely.

'Anything new?' I asked.

'I only just started looking,' she told me. She was facing a board featuring new houses.

I ran my eyes over the advertisements; the place names meant little. I didn't know which were areas of town and which might be nearby villages.

'I still don't know what I'm looking for,' she nodded and I moved along again.

'Neither do I.' But something had caught my eye. 'Probably an older property,' I added.

The prices jumped out at me. Here I could afford more than just the smallest flat. Here held more for me than I'd thought it might.

*'Well, good luck with house hunting,'* I said, *as I pulled open the estate agents' door and let her go.*

*I moved to the edge of Ely, to Queen Adelaide, named, or so I've read, after the pub named after the Queen, rather than after the Queen herself. The village is cut through by railway tracks and the river, and at first glance it seems little more than a string of mismatched houses lining a road. They always give me the impression of pebbles, perhaps scattered by a passing goods train or dumped by the wake of one of the larger boats.*

*My house was partially habitable now, sufficiently sealed against the winter for me to use it as storage. I'd started on the kitchen and bathroom, and had redecorated the larger of the two bedrooms. Everything else would have to do until spring, it had been a struggle to manage as much as I had.*

*Every Saturday I would walk to the centre of Ely. I'd discovered a kind of escapism in the place – it held no memories of my wife or my girls. It also had timelessness, the feeling that it had detached itself from the rest of the county like some kind of Brigadoon, so steeped in history that it passed, barely touched by the present.*

*I'd meander through the market and crisscross via the alleyways. Even after it became home I'd still see something new in the architecture or in the local life that would stir a little curiosity.*

*I'd answer it at the bookshop. Its small-paned front hid a deep building with three floors of ceiling-height shelves. I'd always loved books, and here were thousands of lifetimes of knowledge and inspiration. I began by buying one at each visit,* Cambridge Architecture *was my first, then,* Ely: The Hidden History.

*The bookshelf next to my bed filled slowly.*

*Sometimes I'd know exactly what I wanted to buy, other days I'd let the titles lead me and I found myself wondering what I could contribute to all these life works.*

*Everyone has a book in them – that's the saying. It's not true of course, I've heard too many people recounting dreary details too many times so I know that most people have nothing to contribute. But, once I'd had the thought that I might, I tucked it away.*

It was the end of November, when the market was filled with Christmas gift ideas along with the usual produce, that I stopped at one of the stalls where a small crowd of mostly mothers and daughters had gathered. The man behind the stand was demonstrating how to marble fabric and paper. He held a pipette of dark blue ink poised above a tray of clear liquid, possibly just water. I thought of my wife. My daughters. I almost stepped away without listening to his spiel.

Then I saw the first drop of ink fall and hit the surface, spreading to a translucent film. The next pipette contained crimson and a single drip, pushing the blue away into a wider circle.

That was the way I'd felt – was feeling. I hadn't had the clarity until the moment I saw the ink hit. The emotions I'd felt I'd described with an array of words – anger, pain, betrayal, devastation. This was the moment I saw it for what it was; grief.

And as each drop fell and the concentric rings pushed away from the centre I understood what I needed. More grief would numb the grief of losing them, would put distance between me and my emotions in a way that starting a new relationship never would. I had no desire to love again; to invest in anyone just to risk having it stolen from me would be foolish, a fruitless journey with small rewards against the risk of damnation at someone else's hands.

Sometimes you need to act alone, find solutions that your instincts lead you towards.

Drop by drop the inks spread and the original became nothing more than the edge of the colour pool, a starting point that remained in order to frame and contrast the other hues that followed. My grief was just the starting point, the first stain that would make way for the others to follow. The 'more grief' wouldn't be mine, though, I needed to watch someone apart from myself in the throes of it.

I turned away from the market and headed towards the bookshop. I wanted to calculate what would be required, the number of pages, the number of words and the quality required to see them in print. Whatever was required, I knew I would achieve it. Suddenly my future plans were clear to me; the pain she had given me would be rendered into insignificance.

# THIRTY-SIX

Kyle lay flat on his back with his knees bent – he had discovered that this or the recovery position meant he could stay still for the longest time possible. Stillness meant silence, and he wanted to hear everything without risk of discovery. He'd learnt to distinguish individual sounds more clearly and give meaning to sequences of knocks or shuffles or scrapes. There were easy ones, when she went to the bathroom or washed her hair. And she made a different sound on the stairs when she was heading to bed than she did when she rushed up for something she had forgotten. He'd moved away the insulation from his end of the loft, and a feeble amount of heat had since radiated from a narrow pipe that ran parallel to where he lay.

He'd begun at his mother's house, in her loft, keeping close to Leah and Harry. He'd thought of other options but when it had come down to it he didn't trust anyone but himself to watch over them.

He chose not to think of this as running and hiding.

The lack of insulation made every noise clear. Below him now, he heard a pattern of sounds he recognized; the thin click of an eye pencil being laid down on a glass-topped table, the quiet rustle made by small movements and short bursts of steam.

Make-up and hair; Hannah was going out again.

Noises from her bedroom were the clearest but he could pick out words and movement elsewhere too. Harry was downstairs now, unsupervised as far as he could tell. Occasionally he shouted 'Mum-um' and less frequently still Hannah would call back 'Wait a minute, I'm just coming'.

'Mum-um, mum-um.' Harry's voice picked up more volume. Hannah must have closed the stair gate with Harry at the bottom.

Kyle closed his eyes and practised breathing steadily. Harry called out again and Kyle gritted his teeth and mouthed angrily as he willed her to see to their son, 'Go to Harry, you fucking bitch.' He wove his fingers together and clasped his hands tightly. 'Fucking bitch,' he echoed.

The front doorbell gave its tinny ring and, finally, he heard her moving down the stairs. The person she let in was Leah, unmistakably Leah. He heard the tone of her voice, but none of the words. He heard Harry, who had few words but had become suddenly excited.

Kyle stared upwards. He had a wind-up torch but had only used it briefly twice, the rest of the time he stayed in darkness unless the house was empty. Now he stared into the pitch black and let his thoughts colour his vision. If he was going to be discovered it would be soon. And if it happened too soon then it would have been for nothing.

But he wanted to be with his son again. He missed Leah and all kinds of immaterial everyday things he'd never even considered before. The world down there may as well be a radio show, broadcasting endlessly and never noticing its audience. He let his head fill and cloud for several minutes.

But it wasn't so complicated, all it came down to was choices.

There were only really three; and one of those was to hand himself over to the police. It was the middle road. He would take the blame and leave his family wide open to danger with no way of watching out for any of them.

No way indeed.

And so the other two were the extremes, the hunter or the hunted, kill or be killed. But he wasn't ready for either.

Lie low and wait, then, this was all he had.

The bigger answer would have to come soon, but when he was ready. Even if that meant waiting and staring into the dark, listening to Hannah having sex with a stranger while his son slept on in the room next door to hers.

Five minutes later and a horn sounded outside in the street.

Leah shouted out, 'Your taxi's here, Hannah.'

The front door clicked shut behind her and he listened to his little sister playing with Harry. He wanted to be with them so much. He imagined dropping quietly through the hatch and joining them, but it was just a diversion. There would be the right opportunity, he wasn't sure yet how it would happen. But he knew it would.

And, until then, he knew how to wait.

# THIRTY-SEVEN

Goodhew could have gone home for the rest of the evening but he knew that the silence of his flat would lead to him spending it dwelling on the case. Instead he sent Bryn a text, then caught up with him in the Cambridge Blue.

'Where's your car?'

'Back at the garage, I'm fitting a treble carb set-up, I bought a better one.'

When Bryn talked about his Zodiac he could lose Goodhew's concentration and comprehension within a single sentence. Goodhew tried to pull an appropriately interested expression, waited for a couple of seconds, then asked, 'Have you eaten?'

'A while back,' Bryn conceded.

Goodhew studied the specials board. 'There's plenty to choose from.'

Bryn shook his head. 'They serve food until ten.'

Goodhew stared at his watch face for several seconds; the last two hours had slipped away without him noticing.

'Gary, why are you back at work?' Bryn didn't wait for an answer. 'What happened to getting your head straight first?'

'Those are actually your words, not mine.'

'You meant the same thing. And, also, what happened to "if I go back it will be different"? I saw you last week and you were fine, now you've been back for a few days and you've already lost track of time.'

'OK then, what happened to, "Congratulations on returning to work"?'

Bryn made a show of rolling his eyes upwards and scrutinizing the ceiling. 'I could kill a kebab,' he said finally.

So they walked back up Gwydir Street and visited a kebab shop on Mill Road, heading towards the city centre without either of them suggesting that that was the plan.

Bryn screwed up the kebab wrapper and landed it in the bin without slowing. 'Actually, I saw your grandmother and she said that your return to work was on the cards.'

'Right,' Goodhew muttered. His grandmother and Bryn had become good friends. She was Goodhew's closest confidante but with Bryn she played pool and talked about cars. Bryn had had a half-century-old photograph of a hula girl tattooed onto his arm, without realizing the photo was of Goodhew's grandmother. His grandmother had been flattered, Bryn had found it amusing and it was only Goodhew who'd been left feeling vaguely awkward. This only added to Bryn's delight.

'We played pool, nothing else,' teased Bryn, 'and you don't have to worry, she says I'm too old for her.'

Goodhew passed him the rest of his kebab. 'Do you want to finish it?'

'Absolutely.' Bryn still demolished food like a six-foot teenager. 'That murder you mentioned, was it Ratty, your homeless mate?'

'Not a mate, but yes.'

'And it's connected with that body in the garage?'

'When do you ever follow these things, Bryn?'

'You know I don't, not really. But I saw it in the local paper and bought a copy just because I thought I recognized the photo.'

Goodhew frowned. 'Of Ratty?'

Bryn took another large bite and shook his head wordlessly.

Bryn often seemed aware of a disproportionate number of young women in Cambridge, but Goodhew was still startled. 'Of Lila, the victim?'

Bryn swallowed. 'No, the photo of the garage. I rent two, one's in Glenmere Close and it looked like the same block.'

'What's in them?'

'That one's empty, the other has a few spares in it.'

'And you pay rent? What's the point if it's empty?'

Bryn waved the question away. 'I'll use it again sometime. I don't want to give it up then have trouble getting another one later. Sometimes Dad buys a hobby car and keeps it in there while he's tinkering with it.'

The junction of Mill Road and East Road came into sight. From this distance the traffic up there flowed silently and even the siren of a fire engine turning the corner ahead sounded muted. The light of the city tinged the sky sulphurous, and a cool breeze overtook him then. Goodhew watched the glow of the lights surrounding Parker's Piece, and, as they walked closer, they sharpened. And of course that meant that the darkness between here and there had sharpened too. And through it Goodhew saw the first flicker of a possibility.

'Gary?' Bryn jabbed him in the arm. 'Where do you go when you do that?'

Goodhew frowned. 'Do what?'

'Go vacant. It's like the wheels are turning but the engine's dead.'

Goodhew looked at him blankly. 'Don't you worry about theft?' he asked.

'It happens I guess, but most lock-ups are empty, or full of crap that won't fit in people's lofts.' He mulled it over for a moment. 'I don't advertise what's in there. If I left the door wide open with everything on show then maybe . . .'

'They are easy locks to pick.' Goodhew was thinking out loud now, he didn't particularly expect Bryn to comment. 'There has to be a risk.'

'You lot ought to know whether there's been an epidemic of garage thefts. But I bet you don't even know where all the garages are. I've seen hundreds of them, with rusted locks and weeds growing up the front, those ones have never been broken into either.'

'I could make a list,' Goodhew muttered.

Bryn stopped at the pedestrian crossing and threw away the second kebab wrapper. 'If I can't twist your arm to go to a club, we could grab a late one at Revolution.'

Goodhew shook his head. 'Sorry, you'll have to go without me, I need to go home.'

'What just happened Gary? I thought we were going into town?'

187

Bryn didn't sound put out, he rarely did. Just curious. 'I'll come back with you, if you like?'

'Thanks, but no.' Goodhew shook his head. 'I have a new map of Cambridge at home . . .'

'Not the answer I was expecting.'

'Actually, it's about the garages.' Goodhew considered the logistics of what he was thinking and the speed with which he would need to work on it. 'How many could you locate on the map, right now I mean?'

'Quite a few I guess, Romsey Town, Chesterton, Abbey, Cherry Hinton, those kind of areas.' Everywhere Bryn listed lay on the east side of the city, running from Mill Road near the centre to the outskirts. 'What's this about?'

'I need another pair of hands.'

They had followed the diagonal footpath across Parker's Piece and had just past the centre at Reality Checkpoint. Goodhew looked across to his flat. He saw a person on his front steps.

'Is that . . .' Bryn began.

'It's Sue,' Goodhew confirmed.

'Did you know she'd be here?' Bryn gave him a lopsided grin. 'Are you trying to set us up?'

'Not a chance,' Goodhew answered a fraction too quickly.

Bryn's smile widened. 'It was just a joke. But if there's something I should know . . .'

'Yeah, that you're a nightmare.'

'Sue!' Bryn shouted, then waved.

She crossed the road to meet them. 'I'm checking up on you, I know you've only just come back and you're full of good intentions, and all that . . . but I'm checking anyway.'

Goodhew half turned, facing the city centre instead of his front door. 'We're going into town for a bit. Just a last drink or two. Coming?'

'We could check out Kuda?' added Bryn.

Goodhew shook his head. 'I've told you, Bryn, you won't get me in a nightclub.'

They all started towards town. Sue suggested Lola Lo, then she and Bryn bickered all the way up St Andrew's Street. Goodhew fell a pace behind them and knew it wouldn't take long before he would be able to slip back home.

It was five to twelve when Goodhew closed his front door to the rest of Cambridge. He gathered a handful of assorted pens from his flat, took them down to his grandfather's study and shut that door too. He could still detect the smell of wallpaper paste from the newly mounted map. He pressed his hand flat against it to make sure it was dry enough to take the pressure of a pen.

He drew the curtains, removing the risk of distraction more than the chance that he would be overlooked, then turned to face the room, undecided for a moment whether to begin with the map or the blank wall opposite. When he looked down at the pens in his hand it was a fat black marker that called loudest to be used. He made three overlapping circles in the plain white wall, each a half a metre in diameter, one at the top and two at the bottom. Gully could say what she liked, but right now a Venn diagram was as good as art.

He wrote Lila's name across the top circle and the names Ratty and Kyle against the other two. Only the garage connected the three of them. He marked it in the middle section, then immediately crossed it through and rewrote it in the overlap of Kyle and Ratty's circles; if Lila's only connection with the lock-up was that it had been the place to dump her body, then, for the purpose of this, it didn't count.

So far he could see only one thin connection between Kyle and Lila: summer 2011. He stared at the wall until the ink slipped out of focus. 29 July, the night of Kyle's fight, was the only date where they knew his whereabouts; Goodhew needed to start there. He wrote under Lila's name: 'Purchase history, Facebook updates, ask her family about 29 July, Could she have been there?' And the guy that had scrapped with Kyle was someone that Goodhew now wanted to talk to, someone who may have been injured too; under Kyle's name he wrote 'Paramedic and duty doctor'.

His mobile phone buzzed and he took it from his pocket – the message was from Bryn. 'Still at pub. Try East Road, Carlton Way, Hawkins Road and Northfields Avenue.'

After a couple of minutes a second text arrived. 'Lichfield Road,

Dunsfield Close, St Kilda Avenue and Teversham Drift.' Goodhew turned to the map and worked his way down Bryn's list, finding each street then colouring the road with green highlighter. Goodhew found a list of garages available to rent from the county council via their website and scribbled down his own list. Sometimes another location would spring to mind and he added it to the bottom of his sheet as he went. Bryn sent a few more texts too. Goodhew thought they'd petered out by 2 a.m., when a new one arrived.

He left it for a few minutes while he continued marking the map. It was starting to feel as though Cambridge was home to more lock-ups than houses. It buzzed again and he reached for his phone, still staring at the growing veins of green ink until the second he glanced at the screen, the new messages had come from Sue, not Bryn. 'Are you awake?' Then 'No worries, see you tomorrow.'

He crossed to the window and pulled the curtain enough to give him a clear view of Parker's Piece. Sue had reached the far side and was about to cross to Mill Road. She stopped when her phone rang and turned towards him as she answered.

'Do you want to be my voice of reason, Sue?'

'You finally admit you need one then?' She started walking back across Parker's Piece. 'Bryn bought me margaritas so there'd better be coffee by the time I get there.'

Gully stood in front of the map but faced the Venn diagram. Goodhew sat on his settee, perched on the edge of the seat as though he couldn't afford to relax. He had explained the logic and information written on both. She finished her coffee, hoping it would quickly chase away her mild tipsiness. She stood the mug on the floor. 'Why would you do this to your walls, Gary?'

He'd barely been back at work but she could already see the signs of the distraction that so often caught and overtook him. He didn't reply, but then again, it hadn't been much of a question.

'OK, what are you trying to achieve?'

'I don't want anything to be missed.'

She studied him for a moment. 'Why do you think it would? We're not far in and it seems as though you've already moved on,' she tipped her head at the map, 'to all these ideas. What if you are jumping at something else because working in cooperation with the team is just too alien for you?'

'Ouch, that's a bit direct.' He shook his head. 'But really not the case.'

She pointed at the Venn diagram. 'And you want to go back three years to find out whether Lila was anywhere near Kyle when he was beaten up? That's tenuous.'

'Yes, but I'm not going to dismiss it either. That evening is the only time before Lila's disappearance when we know where Kyle was.'

'And where do the garages fit into all this?'

'The organization of the garage where we found Lila's body was too precise. Everything seemed as though it had been planned well before she was killed. It had to be ready before her body arrived.'

'And don't you think Marks knows that?'

'Of course.'

'And even if it was, what does it prove apart from showing that the killer planned well?' She heard a slight edge to her voice and, in return, a sudden flash of stubbornness in his expression. Goodhew masked it by passing her a can of Pepsi and opening one for himself. She sat beside him on the sofa then.

'I'm your voice of reason, remember. I wouldn't work the way you do. You take risks and I couldn't stand the stress of it; I'd be wondering when my behaviour would make things blow up in my face.' She paused in the hope that the words might sink in. 'But if I believed in all that New Age hokum I'd probably know the name for the way you read situations. Do you know what I'm saying?'

'I have no idea.'

She took a couple of sips before she spoke. 'You and I could be in the same room with the same people. I'd see their clothes, their demeanour, their manners, and you would see agendas and tensions and the emotions they're trying to hide. What's obvious to you isn't always visible to me.'

'So what's your point exactly?'

'A few years ago there was a series of anonymous tip-offs passed to DI Marks. Each of them led the police towards an eventual arrest.'

She paused and waiting until he'd acknowledged that he knew what she was talking about. 'Whoever provided Marks with that information had more than public knowledge of each case. Sheen thinks it was you and I bet Marks does as well.' She was far from drunk, but aware that the margaritas were encouraging her to be say more than she'd intended. 'I *know* it was you, Gary.'

'You weren't even here then.'

'I wasn't, but by the time I arrived Marks had taken you under his wing and you switched your covert activities to the cases you were officially working on. I've seen those plenty of times. So it seems to me that it's your way of working, Gary, you've done it all along. You're good at it, but don't you think it works better when you at least cooperate with the main thrust of the case?'

She didn't actually listen to his reply. From the first time they'd worked together she'd experienced his long silences and erratic behaviour. He was a solitary and private person, and it had taken far longer for her to glimpse anything beyond that. Even his friendships with her and his grandmother and Bryn were generally kept separate from one another. Like islands. And it was the ocean between them that remained opaque. That was where his motivations lay and who was she to interfere? She studied the room, it said more about him than he said himself.

'You know what?' she said finally. 'I've just changed my mind. I think you should follow your own logic and see where it takes you; if you're going to stay up all night, you may as well do something useful with it.'

'My thoughts exactly, Sue.'

She reached over and jabbed him gently with her forefinger. 'I'm the junior here, don't listen to me, you shouldn't listen to me, I'll probably get you sacked.'

He grinned, 'A couple of drinks and your real motives come out.'

'It really was just a couple, so I *am* sober enough.'

His smile faded as fast as it arrived. 'Bryn should have made sure you got home safely.'

'You know that's sexist, it's not his job, it's mine.'

'Fair point.'

'Anyway, I followed your example and slipped away while he went to the bar. I decided to walk as far as here and would have grabbed a taxi in Mill Road if you hadn't rung me first; remember I'm not the risk taker here, am I?'

For a moment she flashed back to the moments before Kelly had fallen. She remembered the handrail of the rusting fire escape as it grazed her palm. She thought she'd hesitated for a moment then, or perhaps just imagined that she had. If it had been her caution that had held back those few feet, perhaps it had already saved her life. And cost Kelly's. Her dreams had played out many different ways since then, but whether she reached out, or shouted a warning, went ahead or trailed behind or even refused to let her friend climb, the result was always the same. Kelly fell and Kelly died.

'Do you think about her?' she asked abruptly.

'Kelly?' He nodded slowly. 'Yes, I do.'

She shuffled back until she sat deeper into the sofa and pressed her fingers into the upholstery, watching the fine cracks wrinkle in the beaten leather. 'I've had guilt because it was her and not me. That's normal, I think.'

She couldn't tell from Gary's expression whether it was normal for him too.

'It's been getting a little easier over the last few months,' she added, 'but it's the first time I've experienced sudden loss like that and I think I understand more about victims and their families than I ever did before. Nothing prepared me for it.'

He stared across at the map and her gaze followed. The green ink marking the site of roads housing garage blocks had proliferated through the suburbs.

'And yet there are people who choose to make it happen, who choose to inflict sudden loss on others.' Despite the late hour, and the last traces of alcohol that should have clouded her thoughts, the change she'd felt since Kelly's death began to make sense. 'I've started to see my job in a different light.'

His gaze was steady, his green eyes clear and sharp. 'I've always thought you would, one day.'

Unspoken thoughts of Kelly crowded Gully's head. Was there

193

anyone better for her to talk to? The skin of the sofa was soft and warm under her palm and she knew it would be easy to stay here. Just talking. Probably.

She roused herself, and he picked up his mobile from the arm of the settee. 'I'll call a taxi, it's late; you should go home now, Sue.'

It was 3.20 a.m. when the taxi Goodhew had ordered for himself dropped him in Cherry Hinton High Street, he walked from outside the restaurant that had once been the Unicorn pub. Living in one place had allowed him to build up layers of its recent history, the coming and going of people and businesses did that. Crimes did too and, as he walked through the unmoving silence of Mill End Road, he knew this street would always remind him of the moment he'd first seen Lila's body.

He turned down the short driveway to the garages, thankful that none of the houses overlooked them. They stood in two blocks of eight, facing each other across an apron of uneven beige concrete. They followed a standard design; pebble dash on prefabricated block walls, wooden door frames, metal up-and-over doors and corrugated sloping roofs manufactured from grey mottled asbestos. There were similar blocks on most estates in Cambridge, similar throughout the country. For around thirty years it seemed that Britain had been gripped by a garage-building obsession, with little change in design throughout.

The clear sky and three-quarter moon gave enough light to show Goodhew the outline of the buildings and the black rectangles of drains set in the ground. He had brought two torches, one a hand-held flashlight and the other a freestanding camping lantern. Only 'Ratty's' lock-up stood out from the rest; a foot-long streamer of police tape hung limply at one side and the word 'BASTARD' had been spray painted across the newly dented door.

The locks at each corner hadn't been replaced so it was only the locking mechanism on the handle that remained. Goodhew knew the correct tools; he'd watched Vernon the locksmith struggle to open it last time, persevering with several types of master key until he'd found the correct one. This time it took seconds for the handle to release, it was the squeal of the runners that seemed to drag on indefinitely and Goodhew expected the sounds of doors opening and footsteps approaching to come in its wake. But nothing followed.

He moved the lamp into the entrance. At first glance there was little to see; some dark patches on the floor that had once been oily pools and scuff marks where, over the years, a car door or two had been opened too wide and too quickly. He stared at the space where the freezer had stood, trying to sense whether any atmosphere lingered. There really was nothing. No cobwebs, no dust, no ghosts.

He took pictures in any case, turning slowly with his camera until he'd photographed the full 360 degrees. He took shots of the floor and ceiling, then pulled the door down from inside and photographed that too. It was only when he reopened the garage and saw the lantern light spill across the forecourt that he wondered about the other garages.

Fifteen more.

Each as anonymous as the other.

Suppose this one been chosen for a reason apart from its availability. How could you tell what was diseased without knowing what was healthy?

Goodhew moved to the centre of the open space and turned his torch on each of the doors in a slow sweep. None of the others had the hinge locks on the bottom, but he knew that already. He moved a few feet to his left and tried to turn the handle on the adjacent garage. He was unsurprised to find it locked, but jiggled it gently; it was enough to tell him that it had more play in it than the first door. He wondered whether that was simply the result of greater use until he tried his tools and realized that the mechanism was completely different. This door swung open easily, gliding on well-oiled runners. Inside smelt damp and had been piled high with sagging cardboard boxes; he flipped open the lids of the nearest two and pages of newspaper wrapped around the shape of plates and serving dishes. He lifted the corner of one page, the date read 21 August 2002. Of course that didn't mean that the boxes had been in the same place for all that time, but people hoarded and plenty did hang onto items indefinitely.

Opening the third door was swift. The lock was the same as the second and the contents were similar too; ramshackle boxes thick with dust that gave a pale grey coating to his black-gloved fingers.

Three garages proved nothing but sixteen might just tell him something useful.

It was 3.35. There was time.

He moved to each in turn, unlocked it, opened it, then walked in, around and out again. In his head he kept a tally of the details and, finally as he stood on the forecourt with sixteen open doors around him, he nodded slowly and smiled. He'd been right to compare; he now understood why Vernon had been so slow with the lock, it hadn't been any old replacement barrel but several grades higher in terms of sophistication. And out of the sixteen, it was the only one that had been changed, and, of course, the only with extra locks at the bottom of the door. But it was also the only one . . .

'Oi!' At the end of the cul-de-sac of garages stood a fence, and torchlight swung over it, waving wildly in Goodhew's direction. Instinctively he turned away.

'What the fuck are you doing?' the man shouted after him and Goodhew heard the sound of the man's boots as he scrambled the fence panel. Whatever Goodhew had been doing was 100 per cent extra-curricular, there could be no excuse, so he snatched up his lamp and ran. And kept running until he was clear of Cherry Hinton and then walked the rest of the way back into town.

He rewound his thoughts until he could continue from where he'd left off. . . . *But it was also the only one without the veneer of old dust, without the cobwebs hanging from the rafters; the only one that was cared for with discipline.*

It wasn't how much he now knew that mattered but how little he could prove, and even less that he could admit to Marks.

There was another way to look at his overlapping circles now; he re-drew them in his mind's eye as a box within a box within a box. Lila in a freezer, the freezer in the garage. The garage setup was precisely right. In his mind the conclusion remained indisputably simple; establishing the truth of it would be less so.

He needed to be in Parkside in around three hours. As he walked he drew deep breaths of the cold morning air, enough to keep his brain fed until he made it home, and when he returned it was to the settee in his grandfather's study rather than his own bed. He lay on it, with the Venn diagram and map of Cambridge within sight. He thought back to his conversation with Gully; his suspicions were really only based on what she and Marks could also see. He closed his eyes, but even then he saw the need to act. And that would be the choice between working within the boundaries of his job and accepting the need to work outside them.

Several times during the next hour he dipped into sleep, and each time jolted awake with a start. The final time brought clarity. He showered and crossed to Parkside, determined to at least start his working day as he should.

# THIRTY-EIGHT

Kincaide was already at his desk, leaning on one elbow, his face close to his monitor and frowning slightly. 'I need a PA.'

Goodhew gave an indistinct grunt in reply. He had no idea whether the comment was Kincaide's attempt at humour or if he seriously believed it. Goodhew switched on his own PC and ran through the log-in routine before speaking. 'That garage was rented out in Aaron Rizzo's name a year or so before Lila Rasnikov went missing. Suppose there was something stored there before?'

Kincaide paused with his fingers poised over the keyboard. 'Like what?'

'Just the freezer. It's more than old enough.'

'You think it was standing there all along?' Kincaide frowned and seemed to be giving the question serious consideration, but then he shook his head and asked, 'Why?'

'So it was ready for her,' Goodhew replied quietly. 'It hasn't moved since Kyle touched it and that's why the fingerprints are so perfectly intact.'

'Unless Phipps was the one who moved it.' Kincaide shrugged and turned his attention back to the monitor. Kincaide's interest had evaporated in a moment.

'Michael, I'm serious.' Goodhew glared at the back of his colleague's shiny dark hair. 'I think it's likely.'

Kincaide turned his whole chair slowly towards him. 'So, what's your point?'

Goodhew picked his words carefully. 'This isn't someone *rushing* to cover up a murder. It was planned beforehand and each part of it, even the eye mutilation, is deliberate and controlled.'

'And your point?' he repeated.

'It's not going to be the only space like that, there will be other garages set up the same. We'd need a decent-sized team to find them quickly and . . .'

'I see, this idea's too big for you to tackle alone, so now you want to cooperate?'

'Yes, there's some truth in that,' Goodhew nodded slowly. 'You wanted information brought to you first, I'm doing my best to do so.'

'Or just going through the motions?'

Goodhew shrugged, there would be little point in commenting.

Kincaide seemed to consider Goodhew's request for a few moments then his mouth formed a thin smile. 'One body in one garage and you see a pattern? Bollocks. And what list? The council couldn't begin to tell us all the lock-ups out there; certainly not the ones in private ownership nor any council owned ones re-let by their tenants.'

'This one wasn't a council let, but I would start there.'

Kincaide's expression hardened. 'You're not starting anywhere except background on Kyle. Speak to Dr Addis and the paramedics . . .' he paused to check his screen, '. . . Barnard and Asker. Find out about the night they treated Kyle and look for a connection to Lila. That's where the result will be, Gary; one bloke, one body.' He turned back to his computer, tapped for several seconds. 'Let me know how it goes, won't you?' he muttered.

Almost instantly a new email popped into Goodhew's inbox, he glanced at the screen and saw the title, 'Addis, Barnard, Asker'. Kincaide raised his eyebrows, then smiled and Goodhew could have sworn that he heard Kincaide's tongue give a quiet double-click, one breath short of telling him to trot along.

'Doctor and the paramedics it is then.' Goodhew grabbed the contact details and headed for the door. He didn't make it before Kincaide spoke.

'Don't go behind my back on this one, Gary.'

Goodhew paused long enough to study Kincaide's expression for a few seconds. 'I haven't decided what I'll do yet.'

'I've told you, you're dropping the idea of other garages. I have never understood why Marks gives you as much slack as he does, but I'm not Marks and even he will back me up if you ignore my instructions.'

'I'll visit Addis, Barnard and Asker. And while I'm doing that I'll decide how to make sure other garages are searched, that gives you a few hours to change your mind.'

'Give me more to go on, then, something that's not wild fantasy and I might take it to Marks.'

Goodhew nodded. 'OK, that's fair enough.' And it was totally reasonable although he doubted much would sway Kincaide. 'And I won't do anything behind your back,' he promised.

Kincaide brought out the emotions of a kid in a playground. *I promise.*

So ridiculous that he'd crossed his fingers as he'd said it.

Kit Barnard was at Addenbrooke's Hospital but on a break when Goodhew caught up with him. He was sitting alone at a table, resting his elbows on the surface and looking down into his bowl of soup as he dipped his bread into it.

Although seated, Barnard was clearly a good couple of inches taller than Goodhew. Close to forty, pale-skinned, with close-cropped ginger hair and heavy-lidded green eyes.

Goodhew introduced himself. Barnard didn't shake hands, just nodded. 'You'll have been here then,' he pushed the bowl away. 'Half a shift left, dog-tired and you know you need to eat.'

'But can't face it after the morning you've just had?' Goodhew sat down in the chair opposite.

'Pedestrian under a builder's van. She'll live but the leg's not saveable,' he reached back towards his bowl and turned over the contents with the spoon. He let lumps of potato and chopped tomato fall back into the liquid.

'I shouldn't have picked the soup.'

'So, how's your memory?'

'Depends. What do you need?'

'29 July 2011, you and Neville Asker attended an incident on Guildhall Street, on the corner by the back entrance to Petty Cury.'

Barnard shrugged. 'Go on.'

'The injured man was Kyle Phipps, aged nineteen at the time, superficial injuries but taken into custody for being D and D.'

'Yeah, it's ringing a bell.' Barnard had given a couple of brief nods as Goodhew explained. 'Wiry lad? Wouldn't stop talking. Yes, I remember. Just hang on, I'll grab Nev.'

Barnard slipped out through the emergency exit and reappeared with his colleague. Neville Asker was a compact man in his late thirties, tanned and muscular. He would have looked like a fitness fanatic if he hadn't been tucking a packet of twenty Benson & Hedges back into his trouser pocket.

'L'right?' he nodded. His lips didn't move much when he spoke. 'I remember him, he thought he still wanted to fight, kept shouting and lashing out at anyone in a six-foot radius.'

'So who did he hit?'

'No one after we arrived.' Asker folded his arms across his chest. 'The two of us herded him back onto the pavement. We did the whole calm and firm routine until his adrenaline finished peaking.'

'It would have been a shame if he really had done any damage,' Barnard added, 'considering he reckoned he'd come off best in the scrap he'd already had.'

'Yeah, no one else around there needed us.'

'Did he say who he'd hit?'

'No. Not that I remember.' Barnard glanced at Asker who shrugged. 'We've both done a lot of shifts since then. He might have said something like "he had it coming". . .'

'I think he said it was overdue.' Nev tapped his cigarette packet pockct. 'Didn't he say something about nicking money from his mum for fags and booze?'

'You mean Phipps had?' Goodhew queried.

Neither man replied directly.

Barnard spoke slowly as he tried to recall the details. 'I remember someone saying that, are you sure it was him?'

'Yes, you said, "Has someone robbed your mum?" and he said, "Only because she let it happen."'

Barnard grinned at Goodhew. 'He's right. I'd forgotten, but that's the guy.'

Goodhew fished Lila's photo from his pocket but didn't face it towards either of them. 'I'm particularly interested in any connection Phipps might have had to a woman.'

'Apart from his mother?'

'Exactly. Was anyone with him at all?' They both shook their heads. 'Can you recall anyone hanging around while you were tending to him?'

'Unless someone stuck their nose into what we were doing, we wouldn't have done,' Barnard said.

'You just focus on the situation,' Nev added.

Goodhew understood. He turned the photo towards them. 'Do you recognize her?'

'From that night?' Nev asked.

Barnard was already shaking his head. 'Lila something? I mean, we recognize her from the papers.'

The two of them began batting the sentences back and forth between them, passing the dialogue seamlessly. Nev started and their memories didn't seem to need jogging on this one.

'We were on duty the night she disappeared; the call came out to be aware in case anyone caught sight of a young woman fitting her description. We are called out to nightclub stragglers all the time.'

'And if one person's drunk there's a good chance they're not the only one.'

'But we didn't see anyone. My daughter was about the same age, I was happy to keep my eyes open.'

'Especially when you could've caught your Amy doing the walk of shame at the same time!'

'You're so funny, Nev.'

Nev had now taken the cigarettes back out of his pocket and was clearly hoping for another before their break ended.

He shot a knowing glance at Goodhew. 'He had a great sense of humour before his little princess turned fourteen. Sorry we can't be more help.'

# THIRTY-NINE

'Got 5 minutes?' Even if Goodhew hadn't recognized Gully's handwriting, the Post-it Note slap bang in the middle of his monitor would have told him who'd left it.

She wasn't at her desk when he first arrived, he knew she probably hadn't gone far and reached for her pad of Post-it Notes to reciprocate the message. He wrote 'Yes', stuck it to her monitor in return and, as he did so, glanced down and saw the printed sheet folded under an unopened box of Jaffa Cakes.

He slid it out and sat in her chair as he scanned it. Veronica Lake's photograph was at the top of the page, a brief biog and a full list of her films below it.

He knew the details well enough. There was a second page, though, and when he turned to it he found the identical format for Kirsten Dunst. Weird. When Gully spoke it was the first time he realized she had entered the room.

'Your two favourite actresses, right?'

'Yes, but why?' He scanned her expression and saw only a glint of amusement. Or perhaps mischief.

'You know what I was saying, that I couldn't be like you, taking risks and all that? After I left yours the other night I started mulling it over . . . And while you've been away I think I have changed the way I look at things. Sometimes I've answered the question of how to deal with a problem with, *What would Gary do?*'

He smiled. 'Don't let Marks hear that.'

'I don't always do it.' Gully picked up the Jaffa Cakes. 'Mostly I think what you'd do, then realize it's not a good idea and immediately do something completely different.'

'OK,' he replied slowly. He glanced down at Veronica Lake; she smouldered up at him, peeking out from behind a tumble of hair. He still had no idea where Gully was heading.

'But I came to the conclusion that we could each probably learn something useful from the way the other's mind works.' She pushed the box of Jaffa Cakes into his hand. 'Try dunking them in tea. And I'll take an interest in your favourite actresses and, in the process, we'll both learn more about how the other thinks.'

'I know how you think, Sue.'

'You think you do,' her eyes shone darkly, bright with a determination that he knew she possessed, but rarely showed so openly. 'I came across another case, Gary.'

'You didn't say anything last night.'

'I only saw the paperwork this morning. I thought it looked promising so I took it to Kincaide. He knocked it back of course, and that's fine,' she scowled though. She dealt with Kincaide's slights with quiet resolve.

'Except it's not. And I know he pushed you to identify Ratty when he already knew it was him.'

She shrugged it away. 'He doesn't matter. I could take this other case straight to Marks but that'll be going behind Kincaide's back. It would go down badly with everyone.'

'So? That's not a reason to let it drop.'

'No, it's not.'

He already guessed where she was going with this but she needed to say it for him to be certain.

'I want you to look into it, not for me, but with me.' Her frown deepened and she stumbled through her next few words. 'I need, want you to . . . Gary, you have to let me do the same for you. I'm fed up being on the fringes. All the hours you spend going over ideas might be more productive if you had someone to bounce them off.'

He gave a non-committal grunt and she leant back, perching on the edge of her desk with her arms stubbornly folded, as though she had absolutely no intention of moving again.

'That wasn't a *no*. I was surprised. I'm not trying to run a parallel investigation, Sue.'

'But in effect, that's what you do. And you hate the idea that something important could get missed . . .'

'And I take it to Marks if I find it, and I don't waste his time if I don't.'

She raised an eyebrow. 'Of course.'

'You know you're clever, don't you? And you really don't need any more insight into my logic, Sue. Tell me about this other case.'

'Monica Davenport.'

Goodhew looked up sharply. 'Drowning from about five years ago? What's the connection?'

'If you think it's worth following up on you'll keep me involved, right?' She flinched as the words came out. 'Damn, I didn't mean that to sound quite so needy.'

'It's fine, you have no idea how frustrating I found it when I was new here and my ideas were being sidelined.'

He rattled the Jaffa Cakes in their box. 'I'll try dunking, now tell me about Monica Davenport.'

Gully had a folder of information on Monica Davenport. She took it from her drawer then held it on her lap, just in case she needed to check any details. In the end she discovered that the facts were all easy to recall; she was tempted to flick through it just so that Goodhew didn't realize how many times she'd read through it in the last few hours.

'Monica was nineteen when she went missing. She'd been out celebrating a friend's birthday at the Graduate pub.'

'Now the Tivoli, the one that burnt out in Chesterton Road?'

'That's the one. Monica left at just after 10 p.m., headed towards the centre to catch the night bus.'

'Where did she live?'

'North-west London. She was working as a nanny for a couple with two small children, but her mum was in Histon and she'd come back to visit for a few days.'

She had Goodhew's full attention but she could also see that his brain was already trying to work out where this was headed. This one he wouldn't be able to guess.

'Somewhere between leaving the Graduate and her home she disappeared. Her friends had different opinions about how much she'd drunk varying from "she seemed pretty sober" to "I could tell she was pissed".'

'But they'd been happy to let her go alone?'

'She'd said that it was still early and not like living in London.'

'That's a bit naive.'

'Very, but there you go. The driver of the bus she might have taken did pick up a young woman passenger who alighted at the correct stop but he couldn't identify her or her clothing.'

Gully paused in case Goodhew needed to comment on the frustration of being hampered by witnesses who steadfastly refused to commit to confirming or denying a key event because they had strong instincts about not getting involved. Goodhew said nothing. 'Consequently no one is certain how far she made it – CCTV wasn't installed as standard on the buses then either. She was gone for eight days before her body bobbed up about a mile downstream from the Graduate.'

Gully's fingers tapped lightly on the folder. She was tempted to pull out the photographs but decided to wait a few minutes more. 'The body was spotted by a team from the university who were running a series of tests on water quality. They called it in then kept pace with the body as it drifted in the current. Remember Callum Watkins?'

Goodhew glanced away for just a second as he dredged his memory for the details. 'PC from Bedfordshire? Transferred here for about a year before he retired?'

'Yes, that's the one. He was first on the scene and helped to recover the body onto land. His report was pretty much as you'd expect but it's also clear that he was very upset afterwards and there are several notes in the file referring to his insistence that it had to be murder.'

'What did the autopsy conclude?'

'Monica had drowned and the water in her lungs was consistent with the water from the Cambridge section of the Cam. There were a few other bruises on her body but nothing to suggest a fight. The inquest settled for an open verdict. Afterwards her mother, Sylvia Davenport, said that she was unhappy with the outcome but accepted it. Monica's funeral went ahead eleven weeks after she'd gone missing. And then it takes an interesting turn. Do you want to take a guess?'

Goodhew studied her expression, keeping steady eye contact until she felt her cheeks begin to redden.

'Ah,' he said, 'you don't blush much any more, Sue, so I don't think I should let you off the hook too easily . . . I'm going to guess that there's a strong connection to the current case, you've unearthed details of it from Sheen . . .'

Gully felt a tell-tale deepening of the redness. Goodhew grinned. 'You went to him and pressed him for anything to do with facial mutilation, however tenuous and he came back with Monica. How did I do?'

'I hate you. How did you know about Sheen?'

'He mentioned you.'

'I take him a coffee and cake sometimes.'

'Good move, he loves Battenberg. Tell me about Monica.'

'A few days after the funeral we had a call from Mr Dimitri, the caretaker at the cemetery on Newmarket Road. It looked like an act of vandalism at first, there'd been a large number of bouquets and they were strewn across the grass. He spotted that much from the entrance at the other end, you know the size of that place?'

Goodhew nodded. 'Extensive.'

'It was only as he came closer that he saw that the earth which had covered the coffin had been removed.'

'It would have taken hours.'

'It would, although far easier to unearth the coffin when it's newly buried. The coffin was still in the ground but the lid had been opened and resealed and some of the earth pushed back into the hole.'

'Perhaps trying to fill it again then?'

'Maybe got disturbed or ran out of time. There were footprints, size eleven boots but nothing else.'

'But we reopened the coffin?'

Gully looked down at the folder then handed it to Goodhew. 'There are three photos, I've put them at the front.'

She watched him spread them across the desk. She watched his expression too, but it gave away nothing.

207

The first photo showed Monica alive, a cropped shot picking her out from her group of friends. It was time stamped at 20.14, a couple of hours before she'd vanished. The second came from the autopsy, a head and shoulders, the bloated features barely recognizable.

When Gully had seen the third photo she'd looked away, a reflex made her recoil, before slowly turning back to study it. Goodhew didn't flinch, instead he seemed to stare so deeply into the image that she wondered whether the mutilation to Monica's eyes was even in focus for him.

'This is different,' he said finally. 'Look at the damage to the socket, it's frenzied. Ratty and Lila's eyes were punctured with little more than a single blow to each eye.'

Gully pressed her lips together, holding back from insisting he was wrong before he'd even finished telling her that they weren't related cases.

'I can see why Kincaide isn't convinced that there's a connection, but I'm with you on this.'

'Really?'

'The death and the damage to the eyes might not be related to one another but this damage was inflicted on the body in an incredibly deliberate way. Her death should have been re-examined.'

'Funny you should say that. Mrs Davenport requested it but was told it had already been reviewed with no reason to reopen it. PC Callum Watkins made noises about it too but all that was investigated further was the incident in the cemetery.'

'And?'

'Nothing. One set of footprints, and not much else. I want to visit her mother, Watkins too, just to see if anything turns up.'

'Like what?'

'That's the thing, Gary, I don't know – I could be wasting your time and mine.'

'Same with the garages, Sue. Find out whether Mrs Davenport's around this afternoon. I can take an hour after your shift ends. If necessary Watkins and the garages can wait until I'm off duty. We need an address for him.'

'I already have it.'

'Then I'll see you at two. If I'm late, wait and I'll text you.'

'Thanks,' she felt as though there was more that she needed to say, something to sum up the mixture of relief and gratitude she felt at not having her idea dismissed out of hand. But sometimes when she opened her mouth she regretted it so, instead, she just nudged him out of her chair. 'You need to clear off, Gary, I have loads to do.'

# FORTY

Sylvia Davenport lived in a ground-floor maisonette in Histon. Her entrance was at the front, decorated with a shrub rose in a terracotta pot, a wooden folding chair and, next to it, a chipped mug containing half a dozen cigarette ends. When she opened the door cigarette-laden air slipped out to greet them and an already-lit one smouldered from between her fingers.

She was a couple of inches taller than Gully and at least two dress sizes thinner. She looked vaguely famliar and as they were now just a few streets from Gully's parents' home she wondered whether this was a woman she ought to recognize. Mrs Davenport didn't seem to see anything familiar in either her or Goodhew, though – apart from the obvious; that they were the police and wouldn't have anything new to offer her.

She'd already made a pot of coffee, overly strong and half cold. Still, any coffee was often better than none. Gully took a couple of sips while Goodhew introduced them both. Gully winced and added more sugar.

'What do you remember of the weekend Monica went missing, Mrs Davenport?'

She nodded. 'It had been her first weekend back in months. She worked for a family in North London, with a day and a half off each week. Mostly she'd go into central London with friends but decided to take a couple of extra days and come up here.'

'Arriving on the Friday?'

Mrs Davenport drew deeply on her cigarette and nodded. She exhaled slowly. 'Dropped their kids at school then caught the train. I'd taken the day off and met her. I'd been feeling low for a few weeks, she came to cheer me up.'

She caught the frown on Gully's face then, 'I'd had minor problems I suppose, gone over on the credit card, a fault with the washing machine, flat tyre, job uncertainty. I was on low-dose antidepressants like everyone else. Of course none of them are problems now and seem so trivial . . .'

Her words faded but she didn't need to explain the rest.

Gully knew how it easy it was to look back and understand how perceived problems hadn't been problems after all. How death could leave a footprint large enough to obliterate the petty irritations of everyday life.

Mrs Davenport tipped her next cigarette from the pack and lit it from the burning butt of the old one.

'Monica coming for the weekend was a high point. I'd booked us in at Browns on the Sunday; she liked it there and I can't think of the place without picturing her waiting for me at one of the tables.' She closed her eyes for a few seconds. 'We used to go a lot before she left home, you know, then she was coming back for one weekend and I was talking about it like it was the main event of the year.'

'How well did you know her group of friends?'

'Well enough, they're a useless bunch, out for laughs and not much else. I wish she'd stuck with them, though, but they all wander round at night like it's only ever going to happen to somebody else. The police are still certain none of them were involved, right?'

'Absolutely,' Goodhew nodded. 'I've read the case notes but I wanted to hear the background from you too. I'm involved in another investigation and there's a single, but potentially significant, similarity between the two cases.'

Gully realized that she and Mrs Davenport were both staring at him; Mrs Davenport undoubtedly wondering what he was about to say, Gully hoping he'd find a way that would minimize Monica's mother's distress.

'It's about the attack on Monica's grave,' his voice was even but clear, 'we have another murder victim who suffered similar injuries to the face . . .'

'Specifically the eyes?' she asked sharply.

'Yes. Straight after death in the other case, but nonetheless . . .'

'Do you want some insight from me on the motivation?'

'Do you have some?'

'No, but not for the want of trying. But I will show you how it's affected me . . . my memory of her . . .' Mrs Davenport left the room and returned a few seconds later with an unframed print, a close-up of Monica in a party dress. 'School prom. See how beautiful she looks.' Monica was wearing a black dress with spaghetti straps and a metallic sheen to the fabric. Her hair had been put up in a complex-looking plait and twist 'do'. Smoky eyes and pale lips. Gully wouldn't have known where to start with hair and make-up like that. 'Popular' girls all seemed born with the ability to pull off looking glamorous. 'And look at her eyes,' Mrs Davenport instructed.

Gully already had, they were a deep chocolate-brown, and, in the photo, bright with anticipation.

Mrs Davenport pressed her thumb across the upper half of Monica's face. 'And without them? That's what I see when I look at any photo of her now – a blank space where the eyes should be.' She moved her thumb again. 'I identified her body and she was a terrible mess. And that should have been enough for anyone to deal with . . . seeing their own child like that. What sort of person would dig up a body and do more damage? What he did to her eyes was so much worse.'

'He?'

She shrugged. 'I just assumed it was a man. When my mind turns it over it's always a man, a shadow behind her as she walks.' Her eyes drifted out of focus then back onto Goodhew. 'Every time I think of her or dream of her there is nothing where her eyes would be, even the dreams when she's a small child again . . . and when I see any photo of her.' She exhaled slowly. 'Of course I want to look at her, but that's why there are no pictures on the walls.'

Goodhew spoke quietly, picking his words, but didn't get far before she cut him short. 'If we could establish a link between your daughter's death . . .'

'Murder. And I know that's not the official line but the one thing that desecration convinced me of was that no one would go to those lengths and take that risk if they hadn't needed to cover something up.'

'Like what?'

'Don't you think I haven't tried to answer that?' She frowned, deep, well-practised lines appearing. 'She'd been buried for Christ's sake. Why would a killer think that they might be found out at that point? Shouldn't they be breathing a sigh of relief and putting distance between them and the victim? It's like they knew they had to cover up something when they should have been thinking they'd got away with it. But if I'd had her cremated I might have gone on thinking that she'd died as a result of her own carelessness.' Her voice tremored and her eyes filled. 'There's a blessing in there somewhere. It's just hard to see it.'


'What do you know about Callum Watkins?' Gully turned from the A428 onto the road that snaked through Lower Cambourne. 'He'd retired by the time I came to Parkside. I heard he was known for lunchtime drinks and afternoon naps.'

'There were a couple of times I suppose. Station myths mostly, Sue – he was famous for his temper though. On a bad day he'd shout before he'd speak. When his name cropped up my instant reaction was to wonder whether he'd still be alive. He'd yell at people and turn crimson; I was sure he was a heart attack risk.'

'But he's still with us.' Gully reached the next junction and turned right before pulling up outside of a double-fronted detached house. A white MGB GT stood on the drive on a patch of wet ground and a bottle of Mer car shampoo had been left on the doorstep. 'And enjoying his retirement.'

She paused to admire the interior as they approached the house. 'It's beautiful inside,' she commented.

'A car's a car, Sue. It either gets you from A to B or it doesn't.'

'You're kidding, right?'

The front door opened before he had time to reply and although he recognized former PC Callum Watkins at once he was startled by the dramatic change in the former police officer.

Watkins looked amused. 'Sober and awake, you look surprised. Come on in.'

He led them into the sitting room where patio doors faced into a small but colourful garden. 'Thanks for phoning by the way, I doubt I can add anything new but the Monica Davenport case is more meaningful to me than any other I can think of.'

Gully and Goodhew exchanged glances; he wasn't sure of what Watkins expected or where this was about to lead and, judging by Gully's expression, neither did she.

'I transferred to Cambridge to see out my last few years before retirement. That's what I told myself and my wife at the time, but in truth I didn't know how to let go of the career, such as it was. I'd become increasingly frustrated. Nothing goes on forever – good or bad – and Monica was my turning point.'

As he spoke Goodhew realized that the words had the surety of a frequently told anecdote. He nodded encouragement and Watkins continued, 'I picked up a call to investigate a possible body in the river. I'd been checking a complaint of minor vandalism and it only took me a couple of minutes to get there. A bunch of researchers had found her and I could see why they hadn't pulled her out. She was bloated and bodies look pretty grim in that state, but she was moving with the flow of the water and they'd been walking alongside the river so as not to lose sight of her.' He paused and ran the tip of his thumb across the tips of his fingers.

'I radioed it in and made the decision to enter the water and secure the body.' Quite abruptly his tone had switched and he now sounded as though he was reading from a notebook. 'She had been face down and slightly below the surface. I had been aware of a missing person's report from the previous week and realized at once that the missing woman's general appearance seemed to match that of the body.'

He drew a breath, released it slowly and, with it, the formality vanished. 'To be honest, I was acting on my wits, there was a bunch of people looking to me to take control of the situation and it made sense not to risk losing the body, but once I had hold of her I didn't know how to recover her to the bank without making a mess of any evidence. Assistance was on its way so I decided just to stand there holding her until it arrived. It was a hot day but the coldness of the water got to me pretty quick. And after just a few minutes my arms were aching and I was finding it hard to keep my footing with the current pushing at me, so I moved closer to the bank and . . .' he stopped and frowned at his arms which bent to ninety degrees at the elbows, with his forearms upwards and his hands cupped in front of him. 'Maybe it was an instinct thing, I really don't know, but somehow I turned her over so one arm was under her shoulders and the other behind her knees. And I looked at her face and her eyes were open. They were colourless, grey and blank, but she seemed to stare at me. And the water from the Cam trickled back out of her nose and mouth, and I guess it was that movement that gave the illusion . . .'

'That she was alive?' Gully frowned as she said it.

'No, of course not, decomposition was well on the way, but still . . .' again he drifted into silence.

Goodhew tried, 'That she could communicate something?'

'Or I could communicate with her perhaps, because I spoke to her, don't know what I said but I was fighting the tears when the next officers arrived and those researchers were looking at me with total pity. Did you read the transcript from the inquest?'

Goodhew and Gully both nodded. 'But not every document. We do know you felt it should have been investigated further.'

'Probably because I'd become *involved*. I was doing what friends and family do when they need a deeper reason than bad luck or bad judgement. I stood in the river holding her for the best part of an hour, though, and it had a profound effect on me. I could feel the weight of her in my arms and her eyes on me for weeks afterwards. That's the kind of reaction that leads to a lot of piss-taking – even if it's not to your face. Seemed like the nudge I needed because the other choice would have been to bury it under another layer of alcohol. So I took my early retirement and I have Monica to thank for it.'

Watkins may have reached the end of his story but Goodhew knew that there had to be more to Monica's.

'You asked about the inquest?'

'I described the scene and the recovery of the body. I've always been a steady witness but I became,' he paused and coughed, 'slightly emotional and said that I couldn't help wondering what she'd seen in her last moments. I suppose what I really needed was a release from the image of her staring at me. It was still going round in my head. I resigned the day after the inquest, and I do think that I wasn't entirely myself from then until I left.' He smiled. There was a little regret in his expression but mostly a peacefulness that told Goodhew that Watkins might be a man who'd been on the edge and knew what it was like to make it back to more solid ground.

'The papers reported a brief version of what I'd said, I felt it was too much of a coincidence that within days she'd been dug up and her eyes had been attacked.' He shook his head. 'Who would have done that except someone responsible for killing her? What I said at the inquest would have reminded them of the look on her face as she died. When they dug her up that's what they needed to destroy.'

They left Watkins chamois leather in hand and about to give the already pristine car some more TLC.

'What do you think?' Gully asked as they pulled away.

'He seems OK now but I wonder how reliable his recollections are. Sounds like he struggled with that one.'

'For his sake, I'm just glad he retired.'

'Me too.'

Gully drove them back towards Parkside and for the first half of the journey neither of them spoke. It seemed to Gully as though it was a pensive silence. They'd stayed with Mrs Davenport long enough for the cigarette smoke to leave Gully's eyes smarting through most of their visit with Callum Watkins. She'd left a lingering impression although the final twenty minutes with her had been fruitless. Goodhew had gone into more detail, tried to probe the family background looking for any connections that could have been made between Monica and Lila, or Monica and Ratty. There had been nothing.

'Interesting that Mrs Davenport never asked about our current case.' They hadn't been specific, hadn't even explained that they'd seen the same injuries on more than one other victim.

'Yes, I thought that too.'

Gully flashed back to the slight tremble in Monica's mother's eyes that showed up each time she held the spend cigarette against the new one as she lit it. 'Perhaps she has reached her limit – can't take more on board?'

'We'll see,' he mused. 'Might just take a while for her to process it. Perhaps she'll come back to us with a bunch of questions in a day or so. And the same might be true for us.'

'I don't think she added anything at all to what we already knew.' The lights ahead turned red and Gully had pulled up before continuing to speak. 'Except the part about the damage to the grave. Ever since she said that I've been asking myself what the killer might have wanted to cover up . . .'

'Covering up by making a new crime scene? No, I don't buy it. She's thinking about it from the wrong angle.'

'And the correct angle is what?' The lights turned green before Goodhew replied and she'd driven through the next set without any response. She glanced across at him but he just seemed to be studying the pedestrians and the shop fronts. She didn't repeat her question; he was too deep in thought.

They were in the car park at Parkside and she'd already opened the door when he finally spoke. 'I was thinking about Watkins.'

She smiled to herself; Goodhew never had been the best at quick-fire repartee. 'Exactly what he said at the inquest?'

'Yes.'

'I'll put the report on your desk.'

'Thanks. And I need to catch up with Dr Addis and continue to look at the garage situation.' He frowned. 'And, if it's the same killer—' he began.

She interrupted him immediately, 'Can we stop saying that for now?'

'OK. Until we know otherwise, you and I will assume it is. We need to work out what it was that made mutilating the eyes an afterthought in Monica's murder that made it imperative in the next two.'

'That makes sense,' she said slowly, thinking it through as she spoke. 'With Monica it was the step he'd missed, by the time he killed the others it had become a honed performance.'

'That's blunt, but yes. We all improve with practice; learn what we would or wouldn't do the next time. Textbook in terms of criminal

217

behaviour I suppose, but is it any different to the way we develop skills in life?'

'Cheery thought.'

'Yep.'

'And on that note I'm going inside, getting changed and going home.'

'Really?'

'Yes, Gary, it's called being off duty. It's when I go and have a private life.'

'Sue, I'm really not that bad.'

She smiled to herself and silently agreed with him. As they walked towards the rear entrance she saw the reflection of a familiar grey Volvo swinging into the car park. She glanced over her shoulder to check, then at Goodhew, 'And, with perfect timing, your next appointment is here, Detective.'

She left him on the back step to wait for Dr Addis. The double door had almost closed behind her when she heard it reopen, then Goodhew's voice. 'That gives us a new question, Sue. Lila's body was hidden, Ratty's was found immediately, how are those differences improvements on dumping a body in the river and letting the water destroy half the evidence? That will give you something to think about in case you're at a loose end this evening.'

'Thanks, Gary,' was all she replied. Part of the answer had come to her instantly and, if Monica's murder became officially linked, it would be in the thoughts of everyone connected with the case; it took more than three killings to end up with so much skill at murder.

# FORTY-ONE

Goodhew waited at the rear entrance of Parkside with the door propped open. By the time Dr Addis had opened the boot, taken out his case, checked the case, reclosed both and double-checked that the car doors had locked properly Goodhew could have been at his desk with coffees for both of them. He'd noticed in the past that Addis and Strickland, the pathologist, had a similarly particular and not-to-be-hurried style. And both had the same habit of becoming even more pedantic if anyone tried to rush them. Gully thought Addis was his next priority but Goodhew had already decided that a visit to DI Marks was more urgent. It was just the timing that made it easier to wait for Addis than catch him later.

He held the door long enough for Addis to step through.

'It's a quick question.'

'Good, I don't have long, I have a couple of new arrests down in the custody suite, I need to confirm that they're fit to be held.'

Goodhew nodded. 'Does the name Kyle Phipps mean anything?'

'Is he one of them?' There was no flash of recognition from Addis. Showing him a photo might be a better way to nudge his memory.

'No. Look, would you have a quick look at his photo, it will only take a couple of minutes?' He hoped it wouldn't take longer and led Addis to his desk. 'We have two related murders.'

Addis was already looking at Lila's photos on the board, 'That's the body in the garage then?'

219

'Yes. Lila Rasnikov.'

'And how can I help with this?'

Goodhew pointed to the photo three shots away from Ratty's. 'Kyle Phipps, he was brought in here on 29 July 2011 and you examined him.'

'I can't remember him.' Addis frowned and shook his head. 'I see a lot of people, Gary, do you have my report?'

'Sure.' It was already at the top of the pile of Goodhew's paperwork, he turned it to face Addis and slid it across the desk.

Addis read through it in his usual methodical way. Goodhew willed him to flick through it more quickly but quashed the urge to interrupt. Finally, as Addis turned to the penultimate page, Goodhew saw a quick rise of the doctor's eyebrows as the first flicker of a memory hit him.

'Yes, yes, the young man with the shaking hand.'

'I'm sorry?'

'His knuckle was skinned, he could have grazed it on something I suppose but I had the idea that he'd used it on another man's face. He was rowdy when he was brought into the station, had obviously been in some kind of fight, but none of it was serious so I patched him up, he calmed down and stayed in while he slept off the drink. But his hand shook the entire time.'

'And you were concerned?'

'I would have asked him whether it usually shook and compared both hands in case there was something untoward – neurologically that is – but he said that it wasn't a new problem and that he'd had treatment. This long afterwards it tends to be my notes that I rely on. If I didn't write it down, I didn't have any concerns – it's all about risk assessment and record-keeping these days. But I do remember that much.'

Goodhew stared across at Kyle's photo. 'I'd like to know who he'd fought with and anyone he'd been with that night. It's possible there's a link to Lila Rasnikov somewhere in all this.'

'Nothing yet?'

Addis stared at Kyle's photo too, then back at the report. 'Listen,' he said finally, 'I didn't write it down but he said that his mum would be angry, but she'd have forgiven him by now if he'd done it in the first place.' Addis pushed the file back towards Goodhew. 'Not the exact words but something of that sentiment, and I only remember that much because the shaking hand rang a bell.'

'It's always strange the way our memories work.' Goodhew smiled to himself. 'Not my area of course, but if something else does spring to mind.'

'As you say, memories can always surprise us,' Addis held out his hand to Goodhew, 'but I'm astonished that I could recall as much as I did.'

Goodhew headed towards Marks's office, thinking about Phipps. Neither Addis nor the paramedics' accounts hinted at any connection to Lila Rasnikov, but it was a long shot after so long and from witnesses whose jobs meant they'd seen hundreds of cases since. He didn't hear Marks walking behind him until he was almost at his boss's door.

'Paying me a visit, Gary?'

'I thought I should.'

They said nothing else until they were seated with the door closed.

'OK then, Gary, fire away.'

'I've come to ask for two things and apologize for one.'

'Go on.'

'I've carried on looking at the possibility of other lock-ups, I know you didn't feel it was relevant . . .'

'It might have been relevant along with many avenues of investigation,' Marks sighed. 'It's not about relevance, it's about resources.'

Goodhew silently spoke the last three words with him.

'I'm a DI, I do plenty that ought to be handled by someone more senior, and that filters all the way through until everyone has run out of time and energy and we lose officers because they're too spent, too jaded to carry on.'

'Well, despite you telling me otherwise, I've been compiling a list of garages.'

Marks raised his hand, stopping Goodhew mid-sentence. 'I know you opened sixteen garages in Mill End Road. By all means apologize but it won't change that situation. It has been logged as forced entry, the law isn't there to be broken by you . . .'

'I'm not apologizing about the garages, sir.'

'Gary, don't interrupt.'

'I wanted to be able to convince you to look further.'

Marks narrowed his eyes. 'You and I both looked at Ratty's body and knew we were seeing the work of an experienced killer. That is almost certainly the case with Lila Rasnikov's murder as well. I looked at the garage too, Gary. It was well prepared, nothing more.'

Goodhew started to speak but Marks silenced him with a glare.

'But I'm taking a chance on you with this one. DC Knight has begun compiling a list of garages using the local authority maintenance database, we have some data on those that are privately owned but some aren't even on planning documents. Any uniformed officers within sight of a lock-up will be making visual checks for obvious signs that the locks have been upgraded. It's a crude exercise but the most we can do without more proof. And anything you can add to that would be appreciated.'

Goodhew felt slightly stunned. 'Thank you, sir.'

Marks just frowned. 'And your apology?'

'Sue has asked me to look at a case with her, one that she feels may be linked. She already raised it with Kincaide and felt that he dismissed it out of hand. I know why she wouldn't want to drop it and she doesn't want to go over his head. I agreed to help her, but suddenly I can see the pitfalls – for her and the investigation.'

'And?'

'It was a glimpse of the case from your point of view. So I'm sorry for the times I should have come to you but didn't. I don't want to see Sue getting into a difficult situation just because she's undervalued and frustrated.'

'Undervalued?' Marks raised one eyebrow. 'Until recently that may have been the case, but I no longer underestimate her astuteness. Stop playing games and tell me which case.'

'Monica Davenport.'

Marks's first reaction was disappointment. 'We've checked, Gary, there's no reason to make a connection.' He frowned. 'Unless you're about to tell me you've found one?'

'We have no proof of anything,' Goodhew conceded, 'but both her mother and Constable Watkins who found the body . . .'

'Were swayed by circumstance.'

Gully had brought the idea to him, Goodhew thought to himself, she ought to have been present for this even if it didn't go as she hoped.

Marks continued to dismiss it. 'Mutilation after a burial and in a case that has also been ruled a non-suspicious death is a bizarre circumstance, but nothing more. It's an old case, it's closed, unless new evidence comes to light and I doubt that it will. It doesn't relate to our current investigation—'

'No.' The word was abrupt and stopped Marks mid-sentence. Goodhew pressed on without hesitation, 'Gully wants us to look at it the other way around, the killer found a reason to rupture the eyes, left it late the first time but didn't make the same mistake again.'

'There's still no link beyond the mutilation.'

Goodhew's voice grew more determined. 'If you see Monica Davenport as an early attempt you can also see how he's refined his process. It fits.'

'It fits because you are making it fit, probably nothing more,' his reply sounded dismissive but then, as though something across the room had snatched at his attention, he stared off in the direction of the furthest wall. 'And I suppose that looking into this case is your second request?' he said quietly.

'Yes it is. We've already visited Sylvia Davenport and Callum Watkins.'

'Where's the connection?' Marks sounded as though he was thinking aloud.

Goodhew didn't attempt a response, instead he just waited.

Finally Marks pulled his attention back to the two of them. 'Risk and compulsion.' He said it as though they were the only three words Goodhew needed. 'None of us understood the motivation for digging up Monica Davenport's body. There was so much risk of discovery, and for what? A seemingly motiveless crime? And Ratty's murder also seems motiveless right now.'

'It's not motiveless if the intention was to lead us to Lila's body.'

'Why not just leave the garage door open and wait for it all to kick off?'

'Because we might not have been led to Kyle Phipps. He might not have been identified at a contaminated scene.'

'We would still have had the name Aaron Rizzo and we would have tracked Ratty from that.'

Goodhew was suddenly reminded of a game he'd owned as a child. It had had interlocking cogs, each affecting the next. He had the feeling now that something was close to alignment. Goodhew had his elbows resting on the desk, his hands clasping at the back of his neck and he stared down at an inch-long ink squiggle that stained the desktop. 'But then Ratty would have been alive,' he said slowly, 'and maybe he would have been able to identify the killer.'

'And Phipps can't?'

'Can't or won't. I don't know.' Goodhew exhaled with slow frustration. 'According to Kyle's family, he cleared off before Lila's body was found. He was either forewarned of something or behind it.'

'I don't see him as the killer. Under pressure he's impulsive, not a planner.' Marks narrowed his eyes. 'More likely that he's bolted; the garage has been revealed and so has he.'

'Killing Ratty and giving up Lila's body was a ploy to flush out Phipps?' They both knew that it was just a theory, but as Goodhew thought about the fragmented nature of the case he could also see how the separate pieces had begun to assemble into a solid shape. 'And that means that the killer wants Phipps just as much as we do and we can't go public with his identity,' a shadow passed across Marks's face, and Goodhew sensed that they'd just had the same thought, 'unless it's already too late.'

Marks leant back in his chair, 'And we both know what that would mean.'

# FORTY-TWO

There was no daylight left by the time Gully arrived at her parents' house. She parked behind their rusting Nissan. It was seventeen years old with just over 200,000 miles on the clock and rust patches that seemed to be spreading upwards from the sills and wheel arches. Their philosophy was simple, *stick to what you know,* and so many of the parts had now been replaced that she guessed they knew the car pretty damn well.

She slapped her hand affectionately on the front wing as she passed it on the driveway. Yes, they really needed a new car but she would be as sad to see it go as they would; everything about this house was tired but comforting.

Only the upstairs landing light was lit. She let herself in through the side door and flicked the kitchen light switch. Her dad was probably working late; he drove for a removals firm and frequently arrived back in time for *News at Ten* or the *News at One* the following day if the job had taken him further afield. She guessed her mum was home but didn't call out to her, instead filled a clean glass with tap water and headed for the stairs.

The landing bulb cast a yellowed light onto the stairs, an old-style energy-saving bulb that *would be good for a few years yet.* She promised herself that she'd change it for an LED one the next time she cat-sat, and crossed the landing carefully.

She nudged open her parents' bedroom door. 'Mum,' she whispered, 'it's only me.'

He mum lay flat on her back, her head surrounded by a triangle of pillows. Her left hand was pressed across her eyes.

Gully crept to the bedside table and carefully placed the glass down so that it made absolutely no noise. Equally silently, she manoeuvred herself onto the bed next to her mum, closed her own eyes and waited. It took an indefinite period of stillness but then she felt her mum's hand reach for her and pat her leg.

'I pat your old Nissan like that, you know?'

'Must be love.' Her words were a little too spaced out but clear enough.

'When did it start?'

'About lunchtime.'

'And you've taken painkillers?'

'About double the prescription.'

'Mum!' Gully hissed, but wasn't surprised, she'd been unlucky enough to inherit migraines from her mum's side of the family too, though she wasn't yet affected quite as frequently. When one hit her she knew there wasn't much she could do but ride it out with enough painkillers to take the edge off it. 'I read an article the other week, there's been a new study into food triggers . . .' Her mum interjected with a muted grunt, Gully pushed on regardless. 'They concluded that the first signs of a migraine within the brain come up to three days before an attack. So, by the time you have that cheese or wine or whatever else you think triggers it, the migraine's actually already started.'

'Both of those trigger it, Sue.'

'Not according to this study. They reckon the change in brain activity leads to a food craving and the craving for that food is seen as the trigger for the migraine when really it's a symptom.'

'I know cheese triggers my migraines.'

'Maybe you should mention it to the doctor.'

'He says stress is my trigger. And that I can believe. Especially when your dad's away.'

Sue held her mum's hand, but didn't reply. There was no real need to worry when he worked overnight – no more than for any other person who lived on this slightly rough but still relatively safe street.

'I'm sorry, Sue, it just came out.'

'Instincts, Mum. None of us can help those. Sometimes I hear sounds, like footsteps on uncarpeted stairs or the slam of a door and my heart starts to race. Maybe when I'm older and it's deeper in my memory I won't notice, but I'll find myself laid out with a migraine too . . .'

'Bless you.'

'I brought you a glass of water. Can you sit up yet?'

'I'll wait a bit longer.' For the first time she uncovered her eyes, so far so good. 'How's your day been?'

'Usual – bike thefts and paperwork.'

'All mundane and safe.'

'Absolutely everything you want to hear. There's just one thing, though, that came up today. Gary went to visit a woman who lives near here and I wondered if you knew anything about her . . . in a local gossip kind of way.'

'Who?'

'A woman named Sylvia Davenport, she was the mother of . . .'

'Monica? Yes, I know who she is. Monica wouldn't have been much younger than you – three or four years I'd have thought. I don't know her to speak to but once something like that happens . . . it becomes big news in a small area like this.'

This warren of mid-century housing development wasn't small, but Sue knew exactly what her mum meant; the ill-fated and the notorious would be as recognizable as reality show contestants to many people round here. She loved her mum dearly but knew she was as nosey as the rest of the ladies she met for weekly coffee or a fortnightly darts match.

'What about her?'

'I suppose I was wondering whether there was a reason that it was her daughter. She was Monica's main connection to Cambridge, the reason Monica was here for the weekend.'

'Anyone can get pissed and fall in the river. Doesn't matter if you're a tourist or student or resident does it? Pissed is pissed.'

Gully smiled, 'You're right.' Her mum had a wonderful way of distilling a situation down to its core facts and, like every other member of the public, she had no way of knowing that Monica's death had a connection to anything current. 'I shouldn't have mentioned it. Don't bring it up, even with Dad.'

'Never would, Sue. You know that.'

'Sometimes I look too deeply – and I really don't have Gary's brain.'

'Who'd want it, eh?' Her mum pulled herself into a sitting position, groaning only slightly as she moved her head and waited for her balance to readjust accordingly. She took the glass of water from Sue. 'If someone broke in here tonight and attacked me,' Sue began to protest but her mum waved her silent, 'if they did, would that mean that my instincts all these years had really been a premonition? No, of course not.'

'Mum?'

'No, let me finish. Most likely it will never happen but would that mean that I've been stupid to react the way I do? No, I do my best but, in the end, I can't help how I feel. Right?'

Sue nodded and shrugged. 'I guess.'

'You could drive yourself crazy looking at the before and afterwards of anything and trying to see what it all means. So don't, just leave it, Sue.'

'Sorry.'

'You're not.' She rested her head on Sue's shoulder for a moment. 'My migraine prescription stopped being strong enough when you joined the force, please don't do anything to trigger them getting worse, Sue.'

She wrapped her arms around her mum and hugged her. 'Is Dad back tonight?'

'Due back at ten, but there's a mess of traffic on the M4. Early hours I reckon.'

'Does he know how you've been today?'

'Sue, you understand migraines but I don't burden you with them unless I need to. Some things you don't dump on your nearest and dearest. Do you share it all with me?'

'Of course I do,' she joked. But just then she thought of the one thing she never would; Kelly Wilkes dead on the ground.

The image was pushed aside by the silent throb of her mobile. It lay face down beside her on the bed, she flipped it over and saw Ted Moorey's name flash up on the screen. 'That's odd,' she muttered in the moment before she answered. 'Ted?'

At the other end the young constable coughed nervously. 'I know you're off duty . . .'

'It's fine, Ted, what's up?'

'DI Marks has asked everyone to keep their eyes open for lock-ups with extra security, you know, extra locks like the one where Lila's body was found.'

The news came as a surprise but she just muttered, 'So?'

'When I started at Parkside I did six weeks working with the Crime Prevention Team. Neighbourhood Watch visits mostly, and I'm sure I saw a lock set-up like that.'

'Where?'

'That's the thing, I remember the areas we visited but not the specifics. Even if I could get hold of the CP records tonight, it wouldn't help.'

'I'm not sure what you want me to do.'

'Do you think I should tell Marks what I just told you . . .' His sentence trailed into nothing with no sign of a full stop at the end of it. But she could guess the rest.

As much as she wanted to stay here, she remembered the fear of looking foolish in front of colleagues and didn't wish it on Ted either. She sighed. 'Do you want me to come in and help you look?' She ended the call then bent to kiss her mum. 'I'm sorry, but I need to go.'

# FORTY-THREE

Julie Phipps moved around the pub, dropping beer mats onto any tables without them. 'Yep,' she said, still moving and her voice fading out each time she turned her back to Goodhew, 'I've worked here for about eight years. This place could have disappeared like all the other pubs. It had a couple of near misses, but it always seems to bounce back when it needs to.'

Her fierce loyalty to the Haymakers sounded like a comment about her own outlook. Or perhaps he just imagined it.

'We need to speak to Kyle urgently, Mrs Phipps.'

'Nothing's changed, I still can't help you.'

'We're becoming concerned for his safety.'

She paused for a moment, the next beer mat just a few inches from the table. 'What's that code for?' She dropped it then turned to study Goodhew. 'You know what, the whole time he was in Afghanistan I was,' she made quote signs with her fingers, '"concerned for his safety". He didn't come back then, thanks to me, and he won't this time either.' She turned back to the tables, this time straightening the chairs until she'd been around them all in tight-lipped silence.

'I'm not bluffing, Mrs Phipps. We are investigating a series of crimes and we have reason to believe that your son may be targeted next.'

'I'm not going to help you lot fit him up, you know. Nice try.'

Goodhew followed her across the room. 'Mrs Phipps, please, this is a murder investigation. We don't want Kyle to be in danger.'

'I know why you want him and he didn't hurt that girl,' she stared at Goodhew coldly, 'but, if I hear from him, I'll pass him your message.'

He knew she wouldn't budge, but thanked her anyway. 'I have another question.'

'You don't know when to give up, do you?'

'Mrs Phipps, it's obvious you love your kids. Why wouldn't you help?' He kept talking, 'We've been over statements relating to an incident that occurred on 29 July 2011. Your son was involved in a fight, but didn't name the other participant.'

She smirked, 'Participant? Is that what the term is?'

'Do you know who Kyle hit?'

'I know who hit Kyle and I dealt with it.' She folded her arms and did her best to act like she had it all covered. 'There's nothing there for you to follow up.'

Goodhew picked the nearest seat, a chair which stood across the corner of a rectangular table, and sat down. He placed his phone and notebook in front of him and did his best impression of a man in no hurry to go anywhere. 'I need to make up my own mind on that one. That night might be the link between Kyle and Lila Rasnikov.'

'It's not.'

'I can't take your word for it.' Goodhew knew the chance of Lila being there that night was slim but learning anything at all about Kyle would feel like progress. 'That person needs to speak up, if you are really sure Kyle's not involved . . .'

'Of course I'm sure.' Julie Phipps dropped into the seat opposite. She studied Goodhew for a long minute before she spoke again. 'Kyle could kill. I reckon he has, even though he's never told me as much. Some events change you. I knew the first time he had sex – not because he told me or anything weird like that, but he just *seemed* different, more sure of himself and a bit too cocky even. This army thing was the opposite, it put him somewhere dark. Oh fuck.' She slapped her palm down on the table-top. 'I'm saying exactly the opposite of what I'm meaning. Kyle could kill in a combat situation. I wouldn't be surprised if he could kill because he lost control, but never something planned and,' she jabbed the air with the tip of her index finger, 'not twisted, not like that.'

'So Mrs Phipps, who did he fight?'

She sighed and gave in. 'Dennis Bell. We had this on-off thing for a couple of years. Kyle felt that Den was treating my place like a doss-house – turning up when he wanted and hanging round between jobs. I had it sorted. I thought Kyle was just doing that territory thing, I told him to butt out, but it all spilled over into a scrap. Turned out it wasn't the first time Dennis had taken his hand to my kids and I kicked him into touch right away.'

'Will he back up that story then?'

'Doesn't matter what he says. That's how it happened.'

'I'll need an address for him.'

'Give it ten minutes and he'll be in. The first pint pulled is usually his.'

Dennis Bell was a squat man with pudgy fingers and square palms that he flashed upwards whenever he spoke. The more he spoke the more his hands juggled the air. And from the first sentence onwards he made it clear that the world had it in for him. 'I was good for that family and what did I get for it?' Julie Phipps had left them alone in the bar but it seemed that Bell was of the opinion that she would be eavesdropping every word. 'I loved her no matter what Kyle says.'

'The night you and Kyle fought . . .'

'I was in town with workmates and he turned up. First thing I knew was him in my face, shouting me out.'

'And was he alone?'

'I didn't see anyone. A few people were standing round, you know, rubbernecking, but it seemed like he was alone. Just as well my mates broke it up, Kyle was off his face. I'm not an aggressive man but I needed to defend myself, didn't I?'

'Off his face?'

'Drugs, drink . . . I dunno.' He paused for a moment. 'Just booze, I suppose, or the army would have kicked him out. Whatever. He was the one bleeding his mother dry, not me, always scraping around for cash, but he had enough of it to get hammered when he wanted to. Think about that.'

232

'Do you mean that he spent too much or was actually in debt?'

'Same difference.' Bell shrugged. 'He'd wanted five hundred off me the week before, said he was in the shit.'

'Did you give it to him?'

'Did I fuck. Told him to sort his own shit out, most likely that's the real reason he went for me.'

'Do you know why he needed the money?'

'Why all the questions? Is he trying to press charges or something?'

'Not at all. It's in connection with another enquiry.'

Dennis Bell pondered this for a moment or two, then, like Julie Phipps less than an hour earlier, decided to become a little more talkative. 'Hannah, that bloody girlfriend of his, she spends money like water and, back then, Kyle would always look for quick money over grafting for it. What's this other enquiry you're interested in?'

His last couple of words were interrupted by Goodhew's mobile; he took it from his pocket and glanced at the screen. Gully's name flashed up. She was off duty and he'd be free to ring her back shortly; he declined the call. But the timing had been good enough for him to ignore Bell's question. 'Was the night of the fight your last contact with Kyle?'

'Yeah, absolutely. I saw her a few weeks later though,' Bell stopped mid-sentence as Goodhew's phone buzzed with an incoming text.

'Hannah?'

'Yeah.' Goodhew slid the phone towards him as Bell continued. 'She was all cocky about how they'd now got more than they needed. Said I could take my money and fuck off.'

'Money from where?'

Bell shrugged. 'How would I know?' Then he leant back in his chair and bellowed in the direction of the cellar door, 'Julie!'

'What?' she shouted back before coming into view.

'Straight after that fight, Hannah and Kyle got a load of money, where did it come from?'

Julie Phipps shook her head. 'No idea what you're on about, Den. Never saw them with any money.' She glanced at Goodhew in a way that implied it was all nonsense.

'It's fine,' he said, 'I'll ask her directly.'

'Don't bother going now, Leah's babysitting again and Hannah's gone out having "Hannah time".'

Goodhew nodded. They would need to speak to Hannah Davey again but later would do. Finally, he switched his full attention to his phone. The text was also from Gully and read, 'With Ted Moorey, we've found a garage. Blinco Grove.'

# FORTY-FOUR

When Goodhew joined Gully at the entrance to the small block of garages tucked behind the houses at the Hills Road side of Blinco Grove she'd been sitting on a low fence staring at the face of her mobile phone. He'd seen her out of uniform plenty of times before but right then she'd seemed different, perhaps it jarred only because she was off duty and this was still work. She was wearing black jeans and a long-sleeved grey T-shirt. The night was clear and the temperature had dropped dramatically, but if she felt cold she showed no sign of it.

Her hair hung loose and she didn't bother to push it away from her face as she spoke, 'I never took much notice before.' She handed him the phone, her camera roll was up on the screen. 'I've been photograph-ing garage blocks for over an hour. It really is another side to the city, they're all buildings but not documented in the way other buildings are.'

'We can find out who owns them.'

'Of course, but how much does that mean when they can be let and sublet and stand unopened for years? And there are so many of them, Gary.' She'd made the same point that he'd made to Kincaide earlier, but she said it better. Her eyes shone and he could see an energy that he knew very well from his own early cases, a hunger to push further.

He'd clearly arrived well after the first response from Parkside. From where they stood the garages were obscured by houses and garden

235

fences, but the white glow of floodlights and the blue pulsing lights advertised their presence.

'And how did you and Moorey find this one?' he asked.

'Ted did a stint with Crime Prevention when he first arrived and thought he'd seen a garage with similar locks to the one in Mill End Road. All the sites they had visited were in the same area so we checked them until we found it.'

'What happened to "off duty", Sue?'

'He didn't want to create something over nothing so asked if I'd drive around with him and take a look.' She smiled. 'I didn't mind and I think he was worried about making a fool of himself.' She stood and he followed her towards the lights.

The garages had been cordoned off and the area was being treated as a potential crime scene even before the door had been opened. Moorey stood near a group of four figures; all but Moorey wore white coveralls and he hung back as if he was worried about contaminating them.

'They haven't opened it yet?'

'No, they're still examining the outside.'

'And Marks?'

'He's on his way.'

He couldn't see much detail from where they stood, and moved closer. Gully seemed to know what he was looking for. 'All the locks, hinges and padlocks are identical to the ones at the first site,' she told him.

He nodded and blew out a long slow breath as the moment they'd found Lila replayed in his mind.

'What's the latest?' The voice came from behind them and Goodhew turned to find Marks approaching.

'It's unlocked now, sir. Looks like they'll be entering shortly.'

He tipped his head towards the lock-up. 'It's privately owned and rented out to a D. Gordon. He left a mobile number only and that directs to a voicemail. The phone's a throwaway and unregistered.'

Those details alone weren't enough to be suspicious but Goodhew still felt a growing sense of unease at what they might uncover.

'Does the owner have a description of Mr Gordon?'

'He's been renting it for several years,' Marks continued. 'We'll try to pin down more details, but the owner says she only saw him once or twice at the start. A very polite young man, apparently.' Marks's eyes didn't roll but they may as well have done. 'On top of that there are eighty-one "D. Gordons" listed locally. We need to see what's in there first.'

A rasping sound scraped through the air and, as one, everybody turned towards the lock-up. The door had been opened a few inches and a white suit shaped like DC Worthington dropped to the floor. He shone his torch inside then scrambled to his feet and gave the thumbs up to his colleagues. From there the door swung noiselessly upwards. Marks moved forwards. 'Time to find out what we've actually got,' he said.

DS Kincaide was white-suited and in the thick of it. Goodhew felt a childish pang of envy, followed by an even more childish pang of satisfaction when he saw that Kincaide was shivering. He pushed it all aside when they reached the open door. Both he and Sue stopped in their tracks when they saw the interior, bleakly bright under the floodlights and eerily familiar. The sectional construction, the concrete floor, the patch of carpet and the chest freezer, all as before. The same cleanliness, the same symmetry and the same sick feeling in the pit of Goodhew's stomach.

Marks stepped closer to the entrance. 'What do we have, Michael?'

Kincaide coughed to clear his throat. 'This is as far as we've progressed, sir. I thought you might like to take stock.' He looked uncertain. 'To be honest I wasn't sure whether it might be better to move the freezer with the contents in situ.'

'First tell me what the contents are, and then I'll decide.'

Moments ago just the sight of Kincaide had irritated Goodhew, but now he felt nothing but sympathy as Kincaide approached the freezer in his awkward crime-scene suit, gloved hand outstretched, clasping a smaller version of a tyre lever.

'I'm glad that's not my job,' Gully whispered.

Goodhew didn't answer at first, names of missing people were scrolling through his head. Kincaide eased the tip of the lever into the seal and popped the lid. 'It's empty,' Goodhew whispered back to her, just a couple of seconds before Kincaide looked over to Marks's head and shouted the same.

'How did you know?' she asked.

He turned so they faced away from the scene. 'The other lid had been weighted down – a decomposing body would have released gases and forced it open.'

'So this is what? A freezer prepared just in case?'

'Not just in case, Sue. Ready for the right moment.'

'There will be more sites like this.' She shivered then. 'I can feel it.'

'So can I.' It was Marks who'd spoken. He stood just behind them and Goodhew guessed that neither of them had heard him approach. 'But how will we ever know that we've found them all?'

Goodhew stared at the freezer.

*No body this time within the freezer . . .*

*Within the garage . . .*

His Venn diagram flashed in and out of his thoughts, the overlap of the interlocking circles suddenly filling with an extra detail.

*A. Rizzo.*

*D. Gordon.*

Goodhew turned towards Marks. 'Do you know Gordy, sir?'

Marks shook his head slowly. 'I don't think so.'

The name out of context wouldn't mean much to anyone. 'You might have seen him,' he began, but stopped when Gully drew a sharp breath.

'The Scottish guy,' she said. 'Other times they call him Dougal?'

'Bingo.'

Marks continued to shake his head. 'A clue would be good.'

'He's another rough sleeper.'

'Like Ratty,' Gully added.

Marks considered it for a moment. 'Someone's using the identities of homeless people, real identities from people who don't use them themselves?' Marks thought through what he'd just said. 'That's a new one.'

'Not so much the identities, just using their names.' Goodhew replied.

'And smarter than using details of the deceased.'

'Especially, in the case of Ratty,' Gully mused. 'Not so many people even knew his real name.'

Marks smiled humourlessly. 'Our killer did.'

# PART THREE

# FORTY-FIVE

*I had a moment of solitude, of clarity. I realized that I had been pre-sented with a unique opportunity. Writers are told 'write what you know'. No one wakes up as an expert in any field, it takes research or practice or dedication, but I woke up one day and saw that the mangled existence I'd been living had given as well as taken away. The choices she had made for me had taken me down a path I never would have chosen. She had stolen from me, but as I stood looking back at where I'd come from and turned to face ahead, I knew my future wouldn't be about another attempt at love, or marriage, or family.*

*She had opened an entirely different path for me. And it was Sylvia Davenport who led me to it. By chance I suppose, though perhaps I was just ready to see things in a new light.*

*And when I went home that night I used the evening to consider my idea. I scribbled notes, brainstorming on page after page of my note-pad. Then I slept, and woke in the morning with my ideas undimmed by the full light of day.*

*I would write what I knew; grief.*

*I could research and observe with subjects who wouldn't even real-ize that their shock and trauma and anger and on-going struggles were contributing to something far more significant.*

*I would call it 'One Hundred Years of Grief'; as a title it worked beautifully.*

# FORTY-SIX

'How did you do it, Kyle? The police already searched through this house, and ours. They went through our loft and I actually wondered if they'd find you up there.'

He knelt on the floor, close to Leah but watching his son. 'I've slept in people's garages.'

'You broke in?'

'Old habits,' he said quietly, 'and, when it was safe, I slipped in and out of both our houses.' After a few seconds Harry brought two of his Duplo figures over and pressed them into Kyle's hand. 'Find me the cat, Harry. Where's the cat?'

Harry turned back to his pile of bricks and Kyle turned his full attention to Leah.

'A few years ago I saw a man go into that garage in Cherry Hinton. I recognized him . . .'

'Who is it?'

He shook his head. 'It doesn't matter. I don't want you to know more than you need to.'

'So why are you telling me any of it?'

'Leah, listen, it's important you know enough. I want you to be clear about what I'm telling you, just in case,' he hesitated, 'just in case you hear other versions later. So let me say it, all right?'

'All right.'

'I used to open garages all the time, check out what was in them, lift bits that I didn't think would get missed. I'd never seen this guy round here before but I recognized him, and he looked,' Kyle frowned as he tried to find the right word, 'he looked out of place.'

'Like he didn't belong at a garage?' she tilted her head and looked sceptical.

'Like he didn't belong there and was in a hurry to get away. He didn't see me but *I* clocked *him*, and later on it was still bothering me so I went back and opened it.' He bit on his lower lip, suddenly unsure about how much he could tell her.

'Kyle?'

'There was nothing inside but a freezer. I opened it and found the body. Lila's body, that girl the police are asking about.'

'So why didn't you go to the police when you found her?' Leah was the mature one but she looked at him now with an almost childlike naivety – an expectation that somehow he wasn't about to shatter the respect she had for him.

Ironically he hadn't been concerned about protecting her from the grisly details of the discovery of the body as much as from the revelation that he'd done the wrong thing. And continued to do so. His heart sank a little, but what the hell. 'I decided to blackmail him instead. I knew who he was and he hadn't seen me, the garages aren't too near our house and Hannah and I needed the money.'

There was a moment when she looked hurt, then Leah's gaze hardened. 'And Mum's brought us up to steer clear of the police, right?'

'Exactly.'

'That works both ways, Kyle, don't dob others in and don't get yourself in the shit either. But she meant it for small stuff, not murder.'

'My head wasn't straight. No, that just sounds like an excuse.' Leah moved as if to stand but Kyle shook his head urgently. 'Leah, don't, just listen.'

She sat back and glared at him. 'OK Kyle, I'm listening.'

'I contacted him anonymously, I found out where he lived and posted it there, telling him to contact me via a fake email I'd set up.'

'Posted what exactly?'

'A photo of the body. I told him I wanted £2,000, not much to keep that quiet, but enough to get us out of debt . . . He replied from his own fake email that he wouldn't pay, that he'd left no forensic evidence at the garage and the only traces would be mine.' Kyle shut his eyes for a moment and recalled the exact wording, 'He said, "I don't know who you are, but you've broken into a garage and tried blackmail. Hardly a credible witness are you?" I knew then that I was completely out of my depth.'

'But you could have gone to the police and said you'd just found it.'

'He said that as soon as the police became involved he'd be able to find me. And then he would kill me.'

Leah studied him, her eyes welled with tears. She let them subside then reached across and touched his face. 'He actually said he'd kill your family, didn't he?'

'He said he'd kill us all, Leah, and I saw what he'd done to that body. I stopped right there. Then I went overseas again and tried to put it out of my head. But it was the wrong place to be if I didn't want to think about people dying. Shit, Leah.'

He grabbed on to her then and whispered the rest that he needed to say, 'Harry made me see straight, like I had another chance, but I'd lied to Hannah, told her he'd paid, and said nothing about the threats. That was fine for a while but then she went after more money. And now he's coming for us.' He knew he was trembling but he could feel her shaking too.

'Kyle?'

'It's started, somehow he made sure the police opened the garage and he was right about the forensics. That's why they're after me, that's why I don't want you and Harry in this house. I need you in one place so I can watch you.'

'That doesn't make sense, it doesn't solve it. Tell the police you haven't done anything.'

'I've told you, it won't work. I need to protect you and Harry. I know what I'm doing; Hannah's had an email from him, I've read it and she's going to meet him tomorrow. He hasn't worked out who we are yet, otherwise he would have been here. But he'll know when he finally meets Hannah and I'm going to be there to sort it out.'

'I don't like this. It's all wrong.'

'Just trust me.'

'I do but . . .'

'I'm not making excuses, and I don't blame anyone but myself, and that's why I *will* sort this out.'

# FORTY-SEVEN

It was 10.30 p.m. when Marks took Goodhew back to Parkside, and they sat at facing desks in the incident room rather than in Marks's office.

Goodhew spent the journey making a mental list, and as soon as he was at his desk he grabbed a pen and wrote it out. It was a list of the present and past rough sleepers that he could remember encountering. 'Here are all the names I can think of.'

Many, like Sam and Mooch, were nicknames, and the pets added as nothing more than an aide memoire to help identify them later. In other cases they were known by their surnames or abbreviations of, names like Greenie and Clarksy and Barnsy, perhaps remnants of being bellowed out across the playground. Spanner, Small and Curly would be trickier. 'We need to speak to Sheen.'

Marks nodded. 'I've rung him already. His wife said it's his bowls night but she'll get him to come in as soon as he's home. Usually about eleven.'

'No mobile?'

'He only switches it on when he needs to make a call.' Marks caught Goodhew's smirk. 'It is Sheen after all, he only dabbles with this century.'

Marks opened his notebook and took out two other sheets of paper, 'I sent Gully home for the night, but here's her list of homeless people.'

He looked down it for the first time since seeing Goodhew's. 'Most of the names repeat but there are a few new ones here too, and this,' he handed Goodhew the second sheet, 'is my list of missing people, don't follow anything on this unless it jumps out at you.'

Goodhew scanned each piece of paper. Gully's had a few names he didn't recognize. Marks's list of missing people was almost identical to his own, and he recognized the extra two names Marks had written down, Aimee Palmer and Lucy Stirling.

'You went back further than I did, sir,' and as he said it, he realized why. 'I started in the year Lila vanished, you went back as far as Monica.'

Marks shrugged. 'Your logic made sense. I added these two today, after your visit to Monica Davenport's mother. Of course, I still hope your theory's wrong.'

He understood that comment; uncovering a truth that revealed people's missing relatives as murder victims was bad enough, having to tell them what the body had subsequently suffered, right down to its abandonment in a lock-up, would be a trauma of its own. Some missing people did turn up again having lived years of an alternative life, but on this list of nine it wouldn't be all of them.

He looked up again as Marks spoke. 'If they have all been hidden like this, how many unsuspecting people have lived within yards of murder victims?'

'How many will continue doing so until we find them all?' It would be a difficult search but, painful or not, there was no point in anything but the truth.

'I will see as much of this through as I can before I leave. I don't know whether or not this case will postpone my retirement, but the day it happens I want to talk to you.'

'About what exactly?'

'An unsolved case that still bothers me.'

'Only one?'

'No, but that more than any other.'

Goodhew knew that if Marks had wanted to share more he would have done so already, but that didn't stop Gary from pushing him, 'Which case are we talking about?'

'It doesn't matter right now.'

'Was it before my time?'

Marks stood and began gathering his phone and papers. 'Very much during your time if you must know. Forget it right now.' He shook his head. 'I was just thinking ahead. For now just focus on this. I'll have my phone if you need me.'

Goodhew watched him go then gathered up his own papers and, for the first time, noticed an extra file lying on top of his in tray. He flipped open the front cover and, as Gully had promised, found that she had dropped off Monica Davenport's inquest file. He gathered it with his other papers and headed upstairs, assuming that the best place to see Sheen was always when Sheen sat at his own desk ensconced in his cave of information.

The corridors were lit by the same bulbs as during the day, but switched to low wattage overnight. It made the hallways seem longer and narrower, and the whole building more deserted. He crossed paths with no one. Then Goodhew realized that it *was* more deserted; all the available officers were now working on this with little need to return to the station during their shift. Petty criminals could get away with even more right now – if only they knew.

Goodhew placed the three lists on top of Sergeant Sheen's desk. The lists of the rough sleepers were woefully incomplete. Gully had included names that had been mentioned by other homeless people, names that could have been people passing through in the space of days or muddled versions of names they already knew. And of course the only names they ever heard were the ones that came up in conversation with the police; it didn't mean that they'd been troublesome, but the ones who had truly kept a low profile wouldn't be on the list at all.

Sheen came up behind Goodhew and startled him when he spoke. 'Ratty would have known the most names.'

'I didn't hear you come in.'

'Wanted to catch you raiding my files. I just spoke to Marks on the phone, he explained it all to me. I don't understand how you'll take a list of homeless people and find out which of them rented lock-ups; most garages are rented privately so, without some big publicity campaign, we'll never know.'

'We realize that's a problem. Marks wants to start with the city council rentals, but both of those we've opened up were privately rented. If they all are, then we'll be no closer.'

Sheen reached up to the shelf over his desk and began to pull files out, dumping them on the table-top. Sheen then sat at his desk, the three lists between them but facing towards Goodhew. Sheen scooted the third towards him, spinning it round as he did so. 'Missing persons? We might do better with this. If they were originally treated as unrelated cases we might find something.'

'They were cross-referenced initially but no connections were found.' Goodhew stared at the upside-down list. Lila's name was missing from it just as Ratty's was missing from the lists of homeless and former homeless people. Goodhew mentally resurrected his original diagram that put Ratty and Lila on the same page. 'We think that the purpose of Ratty's death was to lead to the garage being opened.' He didn't know how much Sheen already knew. 'Killing Ratty gave us the garage, which gave us Lila Rasnikov. It seems as though we were supposed to find her, but not any others, it was more luck than anything that led us to this latest garage. What we don't know is of any relationship between Lila Rasnikov and Monica Davenport. Or anyone else on that list of missing persons for that matter.'

'Monica Davenport,' Sheen echoed her name, 'she left a mark on a lot of people.'

'I was around back then, I don't remember much.'

'That's because uniform dealt with most of it. She was a missing person, then an accidental death. It wasn't until she was dug up that it went further, and it never was a murder investigation, Gary. It hit Watkins hard, but he wasn't the only one.'

Goodhew picked up the inquest file but Sheen broke off mid-sentence as Goodhew's mobile began to ring. It was Gully.

'Where are you, Gary?'

'At Sheen's desk.'

'Seriously? And he's there?'

'Right across from me. What's up?'

'Nothing, I'll be right up.'

Goodhew hung up then pointed to the phone. 'Sue's in the building. On her way up now.'

249

She came through the door less than a minute later. She wore the same clothes as earlier with no hint that she'd spent several hours at a potential crime scene. She looked at Goodhew first then across to Sheen.

'It's about the current investigation,' Sheen told her. Goodhew thought he caught a slight inflection on the word 'current' but didn't comment.

'Yes,' Gully seemed distracted for a moment but regained her focus very quickly. She took the file from Goodhew, 'Did you read it?'

It was more than the inquest report alone, the file included photocopies of witness reports from when Monica's body had first been found and photographs from the cemetery. Goodhew had unclipped the pages and for the first five minutes the three of them had sat in a silence that was broken only by the occasional muttered observation.

Goodhew found Watkins's statement. The constable had outlined the call that had sent him to the river then begun with a factual but overly detailed account of the recovery of the body. Goodhew could tell from the transcript that Watkins was there to provide background and context alone because nothing he had had to say would have affected the coroner's ultimate verdict. But Watkins had missed this, he'd been determined to argue that Monica Davenport's death had to have been more than an accident, that the trauma of recovering her had damaged his health.

Goodhew realized that Sheen was looking over the top of his glasses, at the same pages. 'He was the boy that cried wolf.'

'Watkins?'

'He came with a reputation for wringing everything he could out of situations. He'd had long periods of sick leave before he arrived here, then turned up and was claiming emotional trauma. No one took much notice.'

'But it was genuine?'

'Yes, in the end I thought so. Maybe he wasn't as strong-stomached as some but he certainly struggled after that.'

'You said earlier, though, that Watkins wasn't the only one?'

'Kev Holden had it worse.'

Gully looked up sharply. It was the first indication that she'd been paying any attention to their conversation. Her gaze met Goodhew's, 'Holden again?' They turned to Sheen.

'Again?' he asked.

'When Kyle was arrested and brought back to Parkside he took a swing at an officer – it was Holden,' she replied.

'But supposedly it was random,' Goodhew continued.

'And Holden reckons he doesn't even remember it,' Gully finished.

Sheen's attention had switched back and forth between them. 'Holden was only a few minutes away from the cemetery when the call came in, he was first on the scene, arriving in the middle of a torrential rain storm. The site was already awash and he decided to capture as much evidence as possible. Two ground workers held a tarpaulin over the body and Holden rushed to document and photograph anything that might be lost before the SOCOs arrived.'

'It would have been a good opportunity to wreck evidence too,' Gully commented.

Goodhew took the photos from the file. 'Holden took these?' There were at least twenty shots and now he realized that while some had all the hallmarks of crime-scene photos – the markers, scale rule and precise focus – others were less well composed and taken with a lower-quality camera. 'He used his mobile,' he added.

The first showed the positioning of the body, its advanced decomposition, the way the undertakers had done their best to dress the corpse and how rain and the juices of decay had discoloured the pale floral cotton. Holden had moved in closer, snapping a shot of her bloated waxy face, the rivulets of rain making narrow paths into her hair and the entrails of the eyes hanging in dirty tracts. Goodhew moved to the next shot and, for a moment, thought it was a duplicate, then realized there were miniscule differences in the focus and angle. The same with the next. And the next. And the next.

'Gary, Holden's not a killer,' Sheen said quietly.

Goodhew looked across at Gully. The paperwork in her hand was becoming crushed, her voice urgent. 'Kyle swung at him. That wasn't for nothing.'

'You don't understand,' Sheen began, 'Holden's marriage broke down, he was erratic and confrontational . . .'

251

'Unstable then?' Goodhew reached for the phone. 'I'm calling Marks.'

Marks appeared in Sheen's doorway within minutes and glared at the three of them. 'Where's the proof, Gary?' he asked.

'I'm telling you as much as I've found, as I've found it.' Goodhew sounded calm when he began the sentence but she could hear the tension rising in his voice. 'You wanted to be informed, sir.'

Gully had rarely seen Marks or Goodhew look so angry. She shot a glance at Sheen who was making a point of staring at nothing but the documents on the desk.

'What you've told me is not grounds for arrest, Gary.'

'It's grounds for caution and Kyle Phipps is in danger, sir.'

'Kyle Phipps is missing,' Marks shot back, 'and Gary, Holden has been in the middle of things many times in the past. It doesn't make him a suspect.'

'He never declared any knowledge of Kyle. He never came forward with any possible case connected to the eye mutilation, and yet he took these photographs?' Goodhew held the prints in front of Marks.

There was a long pause before Marks spoke and when he did his voice was dangerously hushed. 'I have asked him to come in right away, and I will be asking him to explain anything which I feel needs clarification. And I do not appreciate the implication that I would do otherwise.'

'I never meant to suggest that you wouldn't, sir, and I am sorry that I have made you angry. But, deliberately or not, he's held back and I will be glad when he's here, in the building.'

The two of them calmed then although, at least to Gully, the air remained taut. As Marks was about to leave she felt a fingertip gently prod her forearm and looked across at Sheen. He cast his eyes downwards and she followed his gaze onto a page of the report she hadn't seen before. It was a list of names: the research scientists who had spotted Monica Davenport's body in the water. She scanned down the column, then, two names from the end, saw Dougal Gordon and, beneath it, Samantha Lockwood. She gave the smallest shake of her head and neither of them spoke until Marks had gone.

'That went well,' she said.

'Holden's probably not our man,' Goodhew muttered. 'But there's something he hasn't told us.'

'And here's something too,' Gully echoed.

'We just spotted this, but we didn't think Marks needed any more diversions.' Sheen pushed the page at him. 'Dougal Gordon was there when Monica Davenport's body was found, and look who was with him.'

Gully noted Goodhew's fleeting expression of surprise. 'Sam?' he breathed. 'I didn't know she'd even been in Cambridge then.'

'So, someone else who hasn't told us everything,' Sheen added pointedly.

They drove the short distance to the night shelter in two separate cars, expecting to head out from there in different directions as they searched for Sam. But the volunteer who had opened the door had immediately ushered them inside and asked them to wait. Now they sat side by side on two low chairs.

'Does Marks want you to keep him posted or not?' Gully asked.

Goodhew shrugged. 'He's known Holden a long time, it was an instinctive reaction, a loyalty thing.' He really didn't sound put out but Gully wasn't convinced.

'Be honest, you didn't want to tell him about Sam any more than Sheen or I did.'

They heard approaching footsteps and the clack of dog claws on vinyl, then he smiled. 'Let's see if there's anything to tell.'

Sam sank into the furthest chair and Mooch scrambled into her lap. Sam's skin was broken with a crop of spots and there were dark shadows under her eyes. 'I started feeling ill,' she said, 'I wouldn't come in without Mooch though,' her words were addled with tiredness. 'They bent some rules.'

'Sam, do you remember seeing a body pulled out of the Cam?'

'Last summer I saw a dead calf in the river on Stourbridge Common.'

'No Sam, a person? A woman?' Gully sat forward a little, reached out to Mooch and let the dog sniff her hand, 'It's a while back now Sam. Several years.'

Sam's gaze flicked to Gully then back to Goodhew. 'Before I knew Ratty?'

'Possibly,' Goodhew replied. 'Before you came to Cambridge this time.'

'Sure I do,' Sam nodded. 'She floated like the calf, they blow up big in the water.'

'Do you remember who you were there with?'

'Yeah, Gordy. Before I knew what an arsehole he is.' She waved the comment away, 'We're all arseholes to someone.'

'That's true,' Gully smiled. 'Do you know anything about the woman in the water?'

'No.'

'Could Ratty have known her?'

'I don't know. Ratty knew loads of people.'

It was a fair point. Ratty had frequently claimed to know about people when he didn't, then, at other times, had far more contacts than Goodhew had expected.

It was Gully who spoke next. 'Can you tell me what happened that day, by the river?'

'Gordy had been drinking and I had some weed,' she shrugged. 'Old news, right?'

'Absolutely.'

'I saw these people dipping jars in the water and making notes as they came along towards us. But then I sort of missed what was happening at first because suddenly they were excited about something just along from our bench. So we went to look. And that was the body. She was floating, but under the water too, always near the surface, like someone under glass.'

She stopped to stroke Mooch, and it occurred to Goodhew how different she seemed. Between Monday and today, it was just four days but the smart answers and defiance had all but gone.

'A few of us followed her along in the water until one of yours came. He got in with her and held on to her the best he could. To keep a grip on her he had to lift her slightly and then her face broke the water,' Sam closed her eyes as she remembered. 'Of course I was half stoned, but she looked like an un-dead. He looked at her face and looked away

254

again but then I saw him keep looking back at her, like he didn't dare not to. And by the time they got the two of them out of the river he was sobbing. And Gordy asked him who he saw in her eyes, because he's a superstitious bastard and said that the policeman should have been able to see the last thing that she'd seen.'

'Did he say anything?'

'Not then. But Gordy and me were called as witnesses at the inquest.'

'Really?'

'Yes, Gordy didn't show and I sat outside for a couple of hours then cleared off when no one seemed interested. But I saw your policeman. Watkins, right?'

For a moment neither replied, then answered simultaneously, 'Yes.'

'I saw him go in, then when he came back out he had that same look that I'd seen at the river. I thought the way he'd held on to her was brave. It might not sound it, but most people would have let her go. I told him too but he was all over the place,' she circled her index finger beside her temple. 'But that doctor was there.'

'Doctor?'

'One that works at Parkside. He's got rectangular glasses.'

'Dr Addis?'

She shrugged. 'Maybe. He calmed him down and I just slipped out of there, then right out of Cambridge.'


They phoned ahead, Goodhew relaying the briefest details to Marks, then returned to Parkside in their respective cars. It was gone half twelve and Gully's next shift was due to start in just a few hours but he knew that it was too late for her to get any sleep now. In fact, she didn't look close to flagging.

'Now what?' she asked.

'We see Marks and explain it in detail. Monica Davenport is the connection to Dougal Gordon; it proves the link to Lila's murder.'

'And what about Holden, Watkins and Addis?'

'He'll tell us that there's no evidence that there's any internal connection . . .' Goodhew paused then frowned. 'Apart from the obvious,' he said, 'that only someone with inside information could have been sure of finding out Kyle's identity from his fingerprints.'

'Holden could have done that quietly.'

'But not Addis, or Watkins once he'd left.'

They'd stopped on the stairwell, halfway between the ground and first floors. They spoke quietly and it had been natural for them to move closer so that their words were no more than a murmur, and when she suddenly touched his arm she barely seemed to move, even though the result was to pull them closer still. 'Do you remember when we saw Monica's mother? She said she was taking antidepressants *before* Monica died. Addis treated Ratty and Kyle Phipps, what if he's Mrs Davenport's doctor too?'

They both looked to the top of the next flight as they heard Sheen's voice, 'Marks has gone.'

'Where?'

'Dr Addis's house,' Sheen shook his head. 'You said enough, they rang Sylvia Davenport and Nina Rasnikov. Addis is Mrs Davenport's doctor, and Nikolas Rasnikov's too. You watch, all hell will be let loose now.'

'He wouldn't have shown up in the victims' backgrounds,' Gully protested.

'No,' Sheen replied, 'and he was one doctor in a team, they weren't even registered to him, but chose him because he "looked after them". But all hell will break loose and, as Marks says, it's about resources.'

# FORTY-EIGHT

Sometimes the minutes between calling 'last orders' and kicking-out time passed so fast that Julie wondered whether the habitual drinkers had had the time to down the final pint. Most days lately the time dragged, the nagging doubts about Kyle kept her mind drifting towards home, and tonight the last man at the bar was Dennis. He'd stayed later than usual tonight, waiting for the inevitable conversation that she'd be happiest to avoid. She tapped his elbow and he lifted his arms and pint from the bar so she could wipe it down.

'I'll be locking up in a minute, Den.'

'I wanted to have a word, you know?'

'Yeah. I guessed you did.'

'Did you give the Old Bill my name?' He knew the answer by glancing at her. 'Yeah, I thought so.'

'And what did you tell them?'

'I told them Kyle went for me and I defended myself. I said it was something over nothing and I'd given him a bit of a hiding, but he'd gone for me first.'

She spent an extra few unnecessary seconds wiping down the pumps. Did it really matter who hit who first, or that Dennis had actually come off far worse than Kyle? Six of one and all that. What difference did any of the details matter now? 'Did he ask you anything else?'

'He wanted to know whether Kyle had been alone, or whether I

thought he'd been with anyone before the fight. He showed me a picture of some girl.'

'And?'

'There was no one with him but as far as recognizing someone from
four years back? No chance.'

'Thanks. Now you need to get off, Den. I have to lock up.'

'That visit got me thinking though . . .'

'Don't even go there.'

'We were good together for a while.'

She smiled just enough to be friendly and keep the atmosphere light.
'For about five minutes, but you crossed the line when I found out you'd
slapped my kids.'

He rocked back on his bar stool. 'It was nothing, just a bit of discipline when they needed it.'

'Yeah, we've done this conversation, Den.' She kept moving, turning stools and chairs onto tables. 'You have your good points, but I'm
not getting into anything more than being on one side of the bar while
you're on the other.'

He shrugged and pushed the remaining half of his pint away from
him. He smiled ruefully and she knew then that he'd leave without any
further fuss. 'Worth a shot,' he muttered partly to himself.

If he'd been their dad then maybe he would have had some kind of
right to pull Kyle and Leah into line like that, but not some boyfriend,
any boyfriend. She'd seen it too many times, over the years; almost
strangers acting as stand-in dads for a while and making the kids pay
too heavily for minor mistakes or sometimes for nothing at all.

# FORTY-NINE

Marks and Holden travelled in silence, racing through Cambridge and then north, straight up the A10 into Ely. The scenery coming out here had changed quickly and, by the time they came within sight of the cathedral, it felt as though they had driven more than just fifteen miles through the flat, dark countryside.

Marks turned on the interior light; he had the bare facts about the property on a short printout. It had been bought at auction seven years earlier. House prices had been high and climbing then and the purchase price seemed low. He had a basic floor plan retrieved from old sale details and the auctioneer's description, which included the phrases 'cash sale only' and 'plenty of potential'. The photos he'd been handed dated back to around the same time and showed a dilapidated single-storey extending out from a tiny two-storey cottage. There were marks on the external brickwork that showed the ghost of a fireplace from when there had once been an adjoining property.

It wasn't what or where he'd expected it to be. The last he'd known, Addis had been married with children and living somewhere on the north side of Cambridge. He would have guessed at a modest but well-kept house. Neat. Reserved. Not like this.

Holden glanced across, then back at the road. 'Are those pictures up to date?'

'No, about eight years old. It's the only address we have for him so he has been living in it.'

'We'll be there in a couple of minutes now.'

Marks nodded, he knew how much further. He had lived in Ely for a year when he and his wife had first married. They'd rented a flat just off the High Street, and once or twice a year they still stopped there for a coffee and a change of scene. He knew the layout of the city and the location of the closest villages, but he hadn't known until today that Dr Addis also called it home. But now Marks thought about it he wasn't sure he knew much about Addis at all even though, in a professional capacity, they'd crossed paths on many occasions.

'It's at the end on the left,' Marks told Holden.

Holden leant across the steering wheel so that his face was closer to the glass. 'And Addis lives in that?' he muttered.

'Apparently so.' The house stood in darkness, the driveway empty. They stepped from their vehicle and Marks ran his torch over the front and side of the house, then knocked at the front door and called through the letterbox. He only waited a few seconds for a reply. 'Stay here, I'm going to check round the back.'

He left Holden near the front of the house. Ivy wrapped the side gate and he had to push against the weight of it. He had no view of the rear of the property until he'd squeezed beyond it. His torch made a quick sweep. The rear door was as weather-beaten as the rest of the property, rotten at the bottom where the paint had spent years flaking away. It also appeared to provide access to the two-storey section of the house. He moved close to the window and shone his torch through the pane into the kitchen.

The room was small and square, part-renovated with an old cooker on a concrete floor alongside new cupboards and a recently retiled wall. He rattled the door handle then returned to Holden, 'I'm going to look inside.'

'Not waiting for the search warrant?'

Marks shook his head. 'It's up to you if you want to report it.'

Holden just shrugged. 'I can't see the back of the property from here anyway.'

'I'll be as quick as I can,' Marks replied, and was inside the house within a couple of minutes. He started downstairs, where each room was small and cluttered, like the early years of a hoarding obsession with piles of boxes topped with piles of books and papers. He lifted random sheets and found nothing but junk mail and old post. There were no personal items on the walls, no homely touches. Just storage. He headed for the stairs, and as he ascended could see that there were only two rooms leading from the yard-square landing.

One to the left and one to the right.

He shone his torch into each; the first, a bedroom, was sparsely furnished and clear of junk. A MacBook lay on the bedside table, its charging light was green and he guessed it was just on standby but he knew better than to touch it. He flashed his torch into the second, slightly smaller room. A desk and chair faced a large bookshelf packed with journals, books and loose sheets of paper. He intended to look without disturbing anything but he'd only shone his torch onto the first few of the handwritten sheets before he took a pile from the shelf and sank into the chair.

*Sylvia Davenport came to see me. She was a regular, a tightly wound woman with a list of insignificant worries and the need to be nurtured. I drifted out of the range of her monologue for a moment, and then back in again. She was worried. She'd always been worried, her life could be summarized by a steady trickle of minor complaints and low-dose antidepressants.*

*That day she hadn't wanted to bother me – she really hadn't – but her mood was poor and she couldn't shake the headaches. Probably stress-related, she'd said, as though my opinion was only valid if it took hers into account. She wittered on about her lack of purpose, of motivation, and her general lethargy.*

*'What could I do about it?' she wanted to know.*

*That's when my concentration drifted, I heard myself give a couple of non-committal 'hmm-mms', but inside I wondered what had ever happened to her that could even begin to compare to everything I had suffered.*

*She hadn't suffered loss. Her worst was up there with my happier days. And I realized that I knew about grief and despair. I had become an expert.*

261

*I pressed my lips into a gentle smile and made myself listen as she told me the only thing she had to look forward to; her daughter's visit. How even that would be over too soon. 'What to do then?' she asked.*

*A seed landed and instantly germinated.*

*'Come back next week; make an appointment for Tuesday or Wednesday.'*

*'Really?'*

*I don't know why she seemed surprised when she'd made her whole pitch about needing support and having no one to talk to.*

*'Sometimes people feel low for a day or two,' I told her, 'I'll be interested to see whether your mood picks up by then.'*

*That was when I made my first plans.*

*Sylvia Davenport told me all I needed to know about Monica's visit home – more than I needed – and she probably didn't remember that she'd said a word of it. We hadn't, after all, been discussing Monica. It had all been about Sylvia. And I had found the cure for her lack of purpose and her lethargy. I would give her minor complaints greater context and in doing so would document her every visit.*

*Killing Monica was one step in a project.*

*It made sense of what my wife had done and gave me the direction I'd lacked. It was never something I planned to continue forever, but long enough to make it a meaningful study of grief.*

*Setbacks. Every project has them; it's how they're dealt with that counts. My setbacks both came with the first subject – 01MD. I'd decided that ten subjects would provide the data I needed, and, if I studied the grief response in their closest relative for ten years, I would have one hundred years of grief.*

*01MD – Monica Davenport – was an easy target. I'd had her as a patient in her early teens. She'd had a couple to drink and she recognized me. Like I said, it was easy. The days between dumping her body and it being recovered from the Cam were not at all. I barely slept, kept awake by the fear that I'd left too much evidence on the body. That the sedative might show in the toxicology analysis, or there might be grip marks where I held her boots at the ankle as I drowned her. And then there were fears that were not related to the evidence, but equally important. The prime one of these: what if Sylvia Davenport decided to start again somewhere else?*

*The mistake had been to let the body be found. If 01MD had simply been missing then the arc of Sylvia Davenport's grief would have been slower and more unique. How many parents would move away when it would be tantamount to abandoning their lost child?*

*The solution was for the others to be undiscovered for the duration, until the time I'd compiled my one hundred years.*

*The second setback was less predictable and harder to resolve. I spoke to Callum Watkins after he'd found 01MD's body. I steered the conversation but I knew he wouldn't suspect anything more than professional interest. 'Her eyes were open and all the colour had gone, they just stared. Is that because of the water?'*

*It was, and I think he knew it was too, he was just speaking out and trying to shake the image from his mind. I think he succeeded because from then on I saw her staring at me, night or day. And I had no one to tell, no one to pass it on to.*

*I was – I am – a man of science but I couldn't just dismiss what I saw. I fought it. I tried to rationalize it as the natural steps of decomposition but she still stared at me whenever my mind wasn't focused elsewhere.*

*I was scared I might lose my sanity.*

*By the time I dug her up, I was almost mad with the lack of sleep and the endless oppression of seeing the image of her eyes. What I did that night was a risk, but afterwards my sleep was restful and my waking thoughts became clear. Setbacks only served to move me forwards; none of them would stare at me again.*

*A few days later a man made an appointment. He was worried about his job and the recurring pain in his lower back. I asked about his family and he told me about his wife and three teenage children.*

Marks was only a few lines in when he contacted Parkside. He spoke but at the same time he kept reading, unable to detach himself from the narrative unfolding on the page. He bagged the pages that he'd seen and gripped them tightly as he retreated from Addis's house and returned to Holden.

'Yes,' he told Holden. 'He's the one.'

'I guessed,' Holden replied. 'Knight and Worthington are on the way.'

'Brains and brawn?'

'Something like that. Don't worry, I do know how to be thorough.' Holden passed him the car keys. 'Your boy Goodhew's been busy.'

Marks nodded. 'Addis will have a list of victims – even if it's disguised, it will be there.'

# FIFTY

Julie locked up half an hour later than usual; hardly unheard of either, but her conversation with Dennis and thinking it through afterwards had left her feeling strangely proud. She had no illusions; she wasn't demonstrative with her love for her children the way that some mums were, but she really had picked them over a bloke back then, and tonight she realized that she always would. Her maternal instinct was more switched on than she had known. Her thoughts were still on Kyle and Leah as she pulled up in front of Kyle's house. She knocked and waited for a full couple of minutes, but the house was silent and the only light was upstairs. When Leah babysat, she always planted herself on the settee and watched TV or poked around on the Internet, or both. Julie could usually see the light from the screen dancing behind the curtains, but not tonight.

Julie returned to her car and called Leah's mobile. After ringing for about ten seconds it diverted to voicemail.

'It's me. I'm here to pick you up but I can't get an answer. I'm going to ours now, but if you're not there phone me.' She could hear that her message was in danger of rambling after the first couple of sentences. She took a breath and added, 'Just don't walk home, it's too late.'

She pressed 'End Call' and drove the couple of minutes back to her own house, expecting the call to be returned at any moment. She pulled up to the kerb and studied the frontage. It was as though her house had

265

settled down for the evening when she'd left to go to work, and the fact that the door hadn't opened since was somehow evident from its stillness. She sensed immediately that Leah wasn't here either.

She pulled the keys from the ignition and, as she walked up her garden path, her fingers automatically turned the bunch over and found the front door key. Despite the familiarity, though, she still fumbled, steadying the key on the scratch plate before dropping the bunch to the ground. 'Come on,' she muttered, then successfully opened her door at the second attempt.

'Leah?' she called and ignored the thought that answered. *She never came back.* She pushed open the door to the sitting room and glanced at the sockets where the TV was plugged in, both 'off', something Leah never remembered to do. Julie went upstairs next but Leah's bed was empty and unmade. It seemed perpetually unmade. She managed to smile at it as the image of Leah lying there listening through her headphones flashed through her mind. It was chased away by the same thought; *she never came back*, and she felt her smile hang around for several seconds after it had died.

She rang Leah's mobile again. Then Hannah's. Both rang out, both diverted to voicemail, and in both cases she listened as each of them said 'hi', introduced themselves and invited her to leave a message. Both times she just asked them to call, trying to sound casual but hearing the tension in her own voice as the words came out clipped and a little too abrupt.

She told herself to wait for a reply before doing anything, but found herself heading back to her car in any case and driving back to Kyle and Hannah's house. She stood on their doorstep next and tried Hannah's phone. After a few seconds more, she heard the faint sound of its bleating ringtone from inside.

She kept her ear close to the open letterbox and decided to call Leah's mobile for the final time. She heard nothing and wondered whether it was switched to silent or somewhere else with Leah, but as she did so, her gaze wandered further along the footpath that led towards her home. She saw a bright rectangle of light on the pavement, spotting it just as it faded. She moved towards it and pressed redial on her own phone. Obediently it lit up again as she reached it. She heard herself give a yelp, half gasp, half tumble of words. Leah's phone lay on the path in front of her. She sank to her knees and huddled over it, her shaking fingers searching the case. Slipped inside was a £10 note and Leah's bank card. Julie fumbled with her own phone and pulled out the number of the only person she thought she could trust.

# FIFTY-ONE

Within minutes, Parkside transformed. The phones started first, quickly followed by officers who cut short other activities to return to the station. The objective was simple: find Dr Addis, find Kyle Phipps.

Goodhew and Gully left for Kyle's house, a second patrol car to his mother's. Gully drove, using the blue light but no siren. 'Kyle's not there,' she pointed out.

'Addis doesn't know that. He doesn't know that the whole game is up.'

'He'll have nothing to lose then.'

'He's dangerous either way.'

They fell silent then but it was cut short as Goodhew's phone began to ring. He glanced at the screen and didn't recognize the number, but in the half-second gap between pressing to accept the call and giving his name he picked up the urgency in the caller's breathing.

'This is Julie Phipps. Leah's gone. I don't know who else I can call.'

'Where are you?'

'At Kyle's. Leah's not at my house either.'

'We're already on our way.'

'I found her phone,' Julie Phipps was breathing heavily now and concentrating on speaking to him seemed the only thing holding her back from full-blown hysteria. 'I found her phone lying on the path.'

'Where?'

'Just along from Kyle's house, on the way to mine. Like she'd started walking home.'

'We'll be just a few minutes. Is anyone with you?'

'No. It doesn't matter. There was a message from Hannah and it doesn't make sense.'

'Read it to me.'

'"Exchange by 2 a.m. The place you said before." '

'That's it?'

'What does it mean?'

Gully accelerated onto Newmarket Road, jumping the lights at the first two junctions. The message was from Hannah's phone but not from Hannah. And it wasn't meant for Julie, or for Leah. It was meant for Kyle.

Goodhew knew he needed to keep Julie Phipps calm and on the line.

'What does it mean?' she shouted again. 'Where's my daughter?'

'Stay where you are, Mrs Phipps.' He gritted his teeth and Gully drove faster. He didn't know how to answer her question. Gully shot him a worried glance; they both knew, no matter what, Addis's plan was for Kyle to die.

# FIFTY-TWO

Kyle had slept heavily. He had imagined that soldiers' sleep would be fitful the night before conflict, and for the first nights of his overseas posting that had been the case. Afghanistan hadn't been just a different setting with his unit transplanted into the middle of it. The air had been unfamiliar, hot and heavy with dust and the smell of engine oil. He'd left England in the autumn when the air had turned damp and rich. Daddy-long-legs had danced on the front wall of the house. He noticed them as he turned to say goodbye and over there, in the heat, he imagined them drying out and disintegrating. So he slept poorly at first but soon learnt that rest, any rest, was a valuable escape.

He had stirred when he heard Hannah come home, then the brief, muttered conversation between her and Leah. Hannah closed the door when Leah had gone and seemed to be alone. He didn't hear her speak or check on Harry. That was all now until morning and he allowed himself to fall deeper, detached enough from the real world to not really care when she reopened the front door again. So what if man after man came back for the night? After tomorrow he wouldn't need to stand guard any longer and she could do what the hell she liked. He was relieved that he could be so close to her having sex with another man and feel so little for her that it might just have been two strangers shagging in the next room at a party.

270

And at that point his truly heavy sleep began. The kind of sleep that hits you when you finally give in to exhaustion. A dreamless lights-out. It should have been the sleep that carried him to mid-morning, until the hum of post rush-hour traffic reached him through the eaves. Instead it was Harry. If Harry was within earshot he could wake Kyle from anything. Kyle lay still, listening for any movement from Hannah, but only a moment elapsed before other sounds reached him too. Distant banging. Someone shouting Hannah's name. And for Leah.

Kyle had sat bolt upright then. It was his mum's voice, outside because it sounded muffled, but raised and urgent in a way he hadn't heard since . . . He threw himself towards the loft-hatch . . . since his father had collapsed and died. He pulled back the cover and swung himself down to the landing below, hitting the carpet heavily and stumbling back against the door frame. He blinked as he realized that only this area was lit; it was still night-time and apart from the one overhead bulb the house was in darkness.

Harry had wailed from his cot. Kyle stepped into his room and turned on the night light. Harry was standing at the cot bars, and reached up when he saw his dad. 'Settle down, buddy,' Kyle whispered and kissed his son's head, breathing in the smell of his hair. 'Go to sleep.'

Now he turned to the stairs, creeping down one step at a time while the crying behind him increased in intensity. His mum was banging on the door and shouting. He could see her silhouette in the frosted panel at the top of the door and, in the distance, the first flashes of an approaching blue light.

Hannah's phone rang again and he felt his way in the blackness, following the sound as it led him towards their front room. He spotted it lying face-down beside the sofa, the call ending and the screen dying just as he reached it. He turned it over and unlocked it. Six missed calls. Four new voicemails, all from Leah or his mum. One unread text.

From outside the lights had stopped flashing, he could hear the voice of a man who was talking to his mum. He needed to get out right now but pressed the unread message in any case.

'Exchange by 2 a.m.' He read the first few words and felt himself sway. He recognized the sender's number. The text had come from this phone, the one he was holding, sent just minutes ago by someone who'd been in the room with the phone in their hands. He stuffed it into his pocket and fumbled for the light. If he was still here they could do this now. Kyle backed up to the wall and flicked the switch.

Hannah faced him. She sat on the floor, propped up between the coffee table and the wall, her head tilted back just a little so that she would have been looking directly at the open doorway, if she hadn't been dead. If her eyes hadn't been obliterated.

Above him Harry wailed.

Outside his mum kept calling for Leah.

In his head he knew what he needed to do. And damn the consequences. Harry mattered, Leah mattered, and so far he'd screwed it up.

Kyle ran through the house, slammed open the back door and began to run.

# FIFTY-THREE

Someone was inside; Goodhew saw a shadow pass behind the front door and a few seconds later the glow of an interior light escaping through a small gap at the top of the front-room curtains. Julie Phipps stood with her forehead pressed to the door and her fingers clasping the knocker. She was sobbing and calling to Hannah and Leah. Mostly to Leah. Between her sobs he could hear a toddler's scream.

'I'm going round the back,' he told Gully and ran to the rear of the building. 'Stay there,' he shouted over his shoulder as he realized Julie Phipps was attempting to follow him. He kicked through the flimsy side gate and was almost at the back door when it was flung wide and a dark shadow of a man propelled himself into the garden. He hit Goodhew with his full weight, sending him sprawling onto his back.

Julie Phipps stopped just short of falling onto him, held back by Gully who finally had a firm grasp on the woman. He scrambled to his feet in time to see the figure scaling the rear fence. Julie shouted out and the man yelled back, 'Get Harry.'

Goodhew didn't make the decision, his instincts chose and he was up and over the fence before she'd gathered herself enough to shout, 'Kyle!'

Ahead of him he could see Kyle more clearly now; he'd come out onto Peverel Road with about a hundred yards to go until the road turned and Kyle would be out of view. In the shrinking distance behind

273

him he could hear Julie Phipps shouting to Gully. Goodhew pushed forward, determined to close the gap as much as possible. He didn't reach for his phone, knowing that every stride gained would be vital.

Up ahead, Kyle turned the corner. Goodhew reckoned there was less than fifty yards between them now. As long as he could keep Kyle in sight he guessed he had the stamina to run for as long as Kyle could. He pushed the pace harder and closed the gap again. Kyle had crossed Barnwell Road and they were heading in the direction of Coldhams Lane, criss-crossing the estate, and the options would be limited, reduced by the inaccessible sections of railway line.

Kyle took the slip road that led into an industrial area on Coldhams Road. Goodhew slowed as he knew the other side of the units were surrounded by high fences. He had no intention of losing sight of the entrance but no intention of letting Kyle slip away either. 'Kyle,' he shouted, 'I know you didn't kill Lila or Ratty.' Goodhew slow-circled a skip piled high with broken pallets. 'Leah's in danger. She needs our help.'

Beyond the skip stood a trailer unit from an articulated lorry. Goodhew ducked and squinted underneath but the security lights in the yard didn't reach that far and he saw only shadows. 'You're the only one who can help us find her.' He straightened and turned in time to see a length of two-by-two slice at the side of his head. He swung his arm up in time to deflect the worst of it and send it flying from Kyle's hands.

'Kyle,' he managed to grunt before the fist connected with his stomach. Goodhew hit back fast, landing a solid blow to Kyle's jaw before a second blow from Kyle sent him staggering backwards. 'I can help you,' he grunted through the taste of blood. Kyle lashed out with a final kick that connected with Goodhew's ribs and sent him onto the concrete.

'Why would you when he's one of yours?' Kyle spat, then turned to flee. Goodhew flung himself forwards, grabbing clumsily at Kyle's ankle, finding himself unable to grip anything but his trouser leg – but it was enough.

Kyle managed a stagger forward but then lost his footing and fell.

'We know it's Addis, Kyle. We just found out.'

If he'd fought against Goodhew then he could have broken away, but he stayed down. 'He's got Leah,' he breathed. 'And it's my fault.'

# FIFTY-FOUR

It was 1.45 a.m. and Kyle Phipps waited alone in the car park of the football stadium. The very place that he had chosen all those months ago. His reasons for picking it were hazy now. He remembered that its familiarity had appealed, it had made him feel safer. And it's location on Newmarket Road had made it seem possible to escape in any direction.

It was cold enough to see his own breath but he could feel the heat of adrenaline that pumped through his body and the sweat on his back. He kicked at the ground, small chips of old tarmac breaking away and scattering like tiny chunks of coal. And, somewhere nearby, Goodhew waited. And further afield he knew that there were other, faceless officers, and more still converging on them.

Goodhew's instructions had been clear; if Addis came by car, Kyle was not to get in. If Addis came on foot then Kyle was not to go with him.

'What about Leah?' Kyle had demanded.

Goodhew had spoken firmly then, more calmly than Kyle remembered how to feel. 'Kyle, Leah may be dead already.'

Kyle had tried to pull away but Goodhew had gripped his arm with a surprising amount of strength. 'He'll take me to her.'

'No, Kyle, he won't. He will kill you both and you know it.' Goodhew's voice had been an angry whisper then, his face close to Kyle's, 'It's over for Addis, taking him in is the *only* hope for Leah.'

The old Kyle would have lashed out then, but the old Kyle wasn't so smart.

So, instead, this Kyle stood in the cold and waited, knowing that the police wouldn't be letting Addis leave, knowing that not all the plans could be theirs.

The cluster of buildings across the road from Cambridge United football ground looked as though it had once been a house and mill; it backed onto Coldhams Brook and the larger building still showed evidence in the roofline of the door that would have been opened for sacks to pass through. Goodhew didn't need daylight to remember this, he'd grown up seeing the buildings fall into neglect, then, eventually, spring back to life in their current guise as flats and restaurants and a betting shop.

Goodhew and Marks were positioned inside the China Chef, both thankful for restaurant owners who lived on site. They'd pulled two chairs into a clear space and sat a few feet behind one of the darkened windows. 'I hope Addis shows,' Goodhew muttered.

'He wants Kyle and he told him to come here.' Marks leant forwards slightly and checked Newmarket Road in both directions. 'It's an easy location for Addis, easy for him to spot anyone else approaching too. Phipps chose a good meeting point.'

'Apart from the railway track and the river.' River was an exaggeration. Goodhew knew the length of Coldhams Brook, from the point it appeared at Barnwell Road to the tree-tunnelled ditch that carried it into the Cam. It was overgrown in places and usually shallow enough to wade through, but it also gave another route out and another hazard. Beyond the brook was the railway line, the main line to Ely and north from there.

'Do you think one of them is going to run?'

'No, but I think Kyle will kill him if he gets the chance.' Goodhew leant forwards so that he had the same view as Marks. 'And I think he has a weapon in his pocket. It wasn't there when I searched him, but watch him now, he keeps touching his jacket to make sure it's still there.'

'We'll be moving fast as soon as Addis shows.'

*What about Leah?* Kyle's question was on Goodhew's lips but he said nothing. He knew that Leah would be on Marks's mind, and he didn't want to hear any false assurances like the ones he'd been unprepared to offer Kyle. 'What did you find at Addis's house?'

Marks continued staring from the window. 'He's writing a book. A fucking book. A research project where he watches families through the stages of grief.' He glanced at Goodhew, then away again. 'That's why he kills them; to create grief.' Marks had no need to whisper but he spat the words low and hard, 'That man has been in and out of Parkside for years. Helping us, while all the time knowing that he's committed crimes that don't even exist on our books.'

Goodhew looked away too. 'I'm sorry, sir,' he said, although he didn't know quite why.

'I'm sorry, Gary. The moment this is over—' he began, but Goodhew cut him short.

'Hang on,' Goodhew said, and adjusted his earpiece, listened, then looked along the road in the direction of the centre of Cambridge. 'He's driving and he's about half a mile away.'

Across the road Kyle Phipps stood near the centre of the car park; an exposed figure standing deliberately in a pool of lamplight. The Volvo appeared over the hump where Newmarket Road crossed the railway line. Kyle must have caught sight of it then because Goodhew saw him straighten and his hands slip out of his jacket pockets. He remained motionless as the car began to turn. Goodhew drew a sharp breath, but the car slowed and Kyle stepped back.

Goodhew spoke into the radio, 'Addis is through the gate.'

Marks stared out at the car park, his head tilted to one side and his expression back to its impenetrable norm. 'We wait until Phipps gets him out of that car.'

# FIFTY-FIVE

It had been a dreamless sleep and as Leah Phipps woke she was aware that her consciousness was returning in waves. It was dark for any night, pitch-black unless her eyes were still adjusting. She let her eyelids droop for a moment, listening to the unyielding silence. Her mouth felt weird.

Then she felt the throbbing in her arms and wrists and remembered his hands grabbing at her, her phone tumbling to the pavement and the way he'd knocked the wind out of her as though she was made of paper.

He'd scrunched her up and tossed her into the boot of his car, then leant in and stuck her with a syringe. 'Sedative,' he'd muttered, she could remember that much at least. Then he'd slammed it shut and she'd heard him move away. It wasn't like films: no prolonged fight, no underdog moment, no quick-thinking anything. The syringe was overkill, a single blow had been enough and it must have been over in seconds. Perhaps the longest time had been spent slipping into a stupor. If that had been her moment to cry for help then she had missed it and, even now, if her mouth hadn't been gagged, she suspected that silence was still all she could manage.

Her ankles and knees were tied too. She fought the urge to struggle.

*You're the sensible one.*

How many times had she heard that from Kyle? From her mother?

*Keep it together. I must be the sensible one.*

She held still and tried to work out where she was. Not in the boot of the car, that had smelt oily and faintly of exhaust fumes. This smelt faintly of mould. She was lying on her side, and although her face was close to a corner and her back pressed against something solid, she knew that this was less cramped than the car, too. Maybe some sort of narrow cupboard then.

She moved her legs a little, stretching them out to see whether they would knock against a door or partition wall, or anything else that might give a clue. A dead metallic sound bounced back at her. That, and the total blackness, were enough for her to know, but she still slid her bound hands forward a little, extending her fingers and stroking them along the panel in front of her, and recognizing the gently stippled texture and the glass-smooth finish.

*I'm in a freezer. A fucking freezer.*

Then it was as though he'd struck her again, she gasped and sucked in air and, despite the gag and the absolute silence, imagined that she was shouting out, flailing with her tethered arms, swamping herself in enough panic to numb everything.

She twisted her neck, moving her face away from the panel, then slammed it back again so that her forehead smacked hard against it. She repeated it twice more, then stopped. She lay still again. There was no panic now, just her and the blackness.

*Think.*

She needed air.

And, at some point he would come back, expecting to find her dead. If she was still alive, he would kill her anyway. But if she was already dead his coming back wouldn't matter.

She needed air. She needed freedom.

She twisted herself into a half-sitting position, then reached up, praying it wasn't locked. She pushed against the lid and for a moment she thought she felt it give. She was wrong.

And then she knew she wasn't getting out.

DC Sandra Knight sat at Addis's computer, Worthington and Holden were going through the bookshelves.

'Perhaps he never wrote a list,' Worthington grunted.

'He will have,' Holden replied, as he gathered another pile of hand-written notes. 'He's documented everything. Sandy, have you searched the computer for the name Rasnikov?'

'Of course I bloody have.'

'It was just a question.'

'You two split up a long time ago,' Worthington snapped. 'Just shut up and get on with it.' He opened and shut several notebooks then rammed them back onto the shelf. 'Blank.'

Holden scanned the top sheet then flicked through the sheaf, break-ing it open at random points. 'What's "01MD"?'

Worthington leant across, 'Can I see?'

Holden handed him the top half of the pile, then began scanning his new top page. 'I have "02AP" as well.'

'They're people,' he pointed at the page. 'He talks about "01MD's mother". That'll be Monica Davenport.'

Knight was studying the monitor, 'It's in over two hundred files and counting. One of them will have what we want.'

'No,' Worthington shook his head, 'Monica Davenport wasn't in a garage, was she? Go with 02AP.'

Knight's fingers moved swiftly on the keys. 'Aimee Palmer,' she said, 'I was on that case.' She paused as the search results began to compile, 'Oh shit, loads of files.'

Suddenly Holden dumped his papers on the desk. 'Search Mill End Road.'

Sandra smiled, 'Or, better still, Blinco Grove.' Her smile faded as the search returned nothing.

'Or,' Worthington said, as he squatted on the floor next to her chair, 'you could do it his way, search MER or BG?'

She hit return and within a few seconds it listed a single file. She clicked it open, then looked at the other two. 'Bingo,' she grinned.

There were nine garages on the list, seven of which had been unknown until now, four of those with alpha-numeric codes against them, and another three where the descriptions were blank. From the darkened interior of the China Chef Marks had kept constant radio contact and ordered cars to be despatched to each location.

PC Ted Moorey had been sent to Humphreys Road with a house number and a postcode. It felt like Russian roulette, four garages likely to contain bodies, three that might not. One that might hold Leah Phipps.

He'd driven quickly using his blue light even though the streets were deserted. He didn't mind that he was alone, he doubted that he would have felt any less terrified at the prospect of opening the garage. He'd been there when they'd swung open the up-and over door at Blinco Grove and the tension had passed like a virus amongst them all. He pulled up close to the garage door and recognized the one lock, two padlock setup. He had bolt cutters this time, and a set of master keys for this type of lock. And a drill if that failed. Locksmiths would be with them all as quickly as possible. Cutting equipment was on its way. Humphreys Road and the two other potentially empty garages had priority; the logic was simple enough, Leah would be where Addis could safely hide her.

Moorey knew that he had to do as much as possible before they arrived.

He stood his lamp on the ground and went for the padlocks first. The bolt cutters barely scratched them so he set to work on the spot where the brackets had been screwed to the door frame, prising them away with a tyre lever and a hammer. He'd worked as quickly as possible but, as he rushed through the selection of master keys, he was only conscious of the minutes that had dragged by and the help that was yet to arrive.

At the sixth or seventh attempt the lock released and the key turned smoothly. He took a breath, steadied himself, then swung the door up, over his head.

The lamplight trickled inside, too diluted to show all the detail. Strong enough for him to see the rectangle of burgundy carpet, the freezer that stood on it, both positioned symmetrically in the centre of the back wall. This freezer was larger, at least two metres wide. A row of cardboard boxes had been lined up across the lid.

He snatched up the lamp and shot forwards, his gaze drawn to the deeper shadow at one end of the freezer's lid. The light wobbled across it as he moved but the shape was clear.

Fingers.

They protruded from inside, the thumb and three fingers curled around the smallest, the palm just in view.

He dumped the torch on the floor and began heaving the boxes on to the concrete. He spoke into his radio, his words rapid but calm. His objective was to open the lid, not think about the unmoving hand.

Or its livid colour.

Or the body he was sure he was about to find.

# FIFTY-SIX

Kyle Phipps stepped back and waited for the Volvo to stop. He closed his small knife and slipped it from his jacket pocket, palming it then moving it to his back pocket, just as he'd done when Goodhew had hurriedly searched him. Addis pulled alongside and lowered his window to about halfway. He wasn't a big man, twice Kyle's age, with pale skin and a clammy sheen to his face. He didn't look unfit but had that indoor, cossetted, office-bound look; nothing about his physical appearance should have intimidated Kyle, but everything did.

'Where's my sister?'

'I'll take you to her.' When Addis spoke, only his lips moved but the unease was there on his face, too.

Kyle shook his head, the police wanted Addis out of the car, and so did he. 'How do I know she's alive?'

'Do you think she is? Or are you just scared to die?'

'I don't want to die without saving her.'

Addis snorted with brief amusement, 'You're dead either way, and I need to end this tonight. You've pulled me away from my work.'

'What work?'

'My project, my contribution to medicine. I'm only halfway through.' Addis began to raise the window, then lowered it again. 'I'm not getting out of the car, Phipps, but I am driving away now.' Addis released the boot and it swung open. 'Get in. It's why you came.'

The engine was idling but the car was out of gear. He'd bet that the doors were locked too, but the window still had that arm-sized gap.

'And you won't hurt my son?'

Addis began to reply and Kyle pounced, snatching the key from the ignition and retracting his hand, stumbling back from the vehicle. He held the keys aloft and reached towards his back pocket with his free hand, retrieved the knife and broke it open.

The driver's door flew wide and Addis scrambled out, his face white with rage.

It was the moment that the police had wanted, the signal for unmarked cars to move and officers to break cover. Kyle grabbed Addis first, spun him round and locked the crook of his arm around the man's throat. Dragging Addis back against his own car, he pressed the knife up under Addis's ribs and bellowed in his ear, 'Is she dead?'

Addis tried to turn his head; his eyes stared wildly around the car park.

'Is she?' Kyle repeated, prodding against the skin.

'Kyle?' The voice came from his left, from the centre of the car park that had been empty just moments before. Kyle turned slowly towards Goodhew to find him just a few feet away. 'However he answers, I know you'll want to kill him.'

Goodhew was right. 'He shouldn't live,' he shouted. Kyle's hands were sweating now but his fingers gripped tightly around the handle of the knife.

'But *you* need to be OK. Harry needs you.'

'Harry needs Mum and Leah.'

Goodhew shook his head. 'And he might not have you or Leah unless we question him.'

Kyle thought he had seen the answer in Dr Addis's face, a sadistic flicker to the lips, an air of victory, of unassailability; Kyle was almost certain that she was dead. Goodhew watched him, his gaze steady. Was Goodhew just ready to say whatever it took to make him let Addis go? Asking him to throw everything onto a single grain of doubt.

*Probably.*

*But how could he risk it?*

He pushed Addis away and dropped the knife to the ground. The police rushed in from all sides, restraining both of them. It was Addis who spoke first, 'Everyone's a liar, my work was collecting the truth.'

Marks approached them, 'Dr Malcolm Addis, I am arresting you for murder . . .'

'You've lied to him,' Addis shouted, butting his head first towards Marks, then Goodhew. 'And Goodhew's a liar, Phipps, your sister's gone.'

He was pulled away then, towards the nearest police car, Marks doggedly continuing with the remainder of the caution.

No one had arrested Kyle as yet but he was still being held, one officer gripping each arm. He glared at Goodhew. 'Why lie to me?'

'Your sister has been rescued, Kyle. If I told you she was safe, I think you would have killed him.'

'Safe?'

'Injured, shocked. He shut her in a freezer and she crushed her hand getting air. But she will be OK, especially when she knows you are. She's at Addenbrooke's with your mum and Harry.'

Gently they released their grip on him. The ground was uneven but he stood more firmly than he'd thought possible. 'Can I see them?'

'Someone will take you,' Goodhew nodded. 'Then we will need a statement. It won't be quick.'

'But not as long as it might have been.' Kyle even managed a smile then, 'And you're right, I would have killed him, but I'm already glad I didn't.'

# FIFTY-SEVEN

Sue Gully pulled up to the pavement outside the China Chef. She watched Addis being loaded into a police car and driven away in the direction of Parkside. Marks watched it go, then spotted her car as he turned. He opened the passenger door. 'Do you mind?'

She shook her head and he got in next to her. 'That was tough,' she said.

'You look a mess.'

'Thank you, sir.'

She leant back against the headrest and watched the activity in the car park opposite. Marks seemed to be doing the same – as though they both needed these few minutes to take stock. Gary sat on the wall of the car park, just yards away but with his back to them. He didn't seem in any hurry to leave.

Marks broke the silence. 'Goodhew and I were waiting for Addis to show up earlier and I decided that I had to tell him tonight about his grandfather. Then Addis told Goodhew that I lied to him. You were right, he should have known all along.'

'It's better now than later.'

Marks nodded, 'I know.'

He closed the door behind him and she watched him cross the road. She saw Gary turn, then stand and shake his boss's hand.

'Shit,' she muttered. She pressed the horn once and they both looked across. She hurried after Marks then, and found herself standing on the pavement. Wordless at first.

286

'Sue?' Gary sounded different already; something had changed.

She spoke to Marks, 'I'm sorry, sir,' she steadied her breathing. 'This needs to be me.' Suddenly there was a lump in her throat. 'It really does.'

Marks studied her face for a moment, then gave the smallest of nods. She gave Gary the keys. 'Take us somewhere where we can talk.'

They sat in and he started the ignition, then killed it again. 'Here will be fine, Sue.'

'OK.' She took a breath, wondering how to begin. He watched her closely. 'I don't want to hurt you, Gary . . .'

'You won't, just tell me.'

'I found some old files in the archives. From July 1992.' He looked past her then, a shadow passing across his face. She reached out and clasped his hand. 'Gary, do you know what I'm about to tell you?'

He started the engine again then. 'Not here.'

July 1992 only meant one thing.

Goodhew had no thoughts about where they were going, he just knew that he needed to be somewhere else, but he soon found that he was headed for home. It was inevitable, it contained the most memories of his grandfather.

Now they sat in his grandfather's study.

She'd always been direct with him, her gaze rarely wavered, and it didn't now.

'He was murdered. It's unsolved.'

The words hit him, he understood them, of course he did, but he felt distant from them. He knew he was shocked but couldn't feel it. He studied her face. 'Are you sure?'

She didn't need to answer; somewhere, deep down, he'd known all along. He sensed that immediately, even though he remembered nothing and had suspected nothing. 'How long have you known?'

'A month. Just over.'

He asked her for the details then and she told him all that she could remember.

'Who else knows?' he asked eventually.

'Your grandmother, Marks, Sheen . . . whoever was there. I don't

287

know why they kept it from you.' She bit her lip. 'They must have had a reason.'

Those words hit him too, harder this time, twisting in the pit of his stomach. 'So that's what Addis would have meant when he said that Marks had lied?'

'I guess so. When I first came to Parkside, Kincaide told me that you'd be a problem. That Marks kept a file on you and it was this thick,' she held her finger and thumb about two inches apart to demonstrate. 'So one night, when no one was around, I had a look for it.'

'And?'

'I found it, but Marks came back before I'd had a chance to open it. The file said "Goodhew" on the spine but I thought about it afterwards and never understood why it would be that size when you'd only been at Parkside for about a year longer than me.' She pushed her hair away from her face. 'Then recently, when I found out about your grandfather, I went to look for it again. Marks had it locked in the bucket drawer of his desk, and it's not your file, it's your grandfather's, filled with notes that Marks has kept about the case. I guess he hoped to make progress with it.'

'You're usually good at loyalty, Sue. You should have told me.'

'You're usually good at gathering the facts before you judge.'

Goodhew thought about that. Sue hadn't let anyone down but it was a fact that his grandmother had kept the information from him every day. And another that Marks had known for the whole time Goodhew had worked at Parkside. Sue had been in a difficult position. He looked across at the Cambridge map spread across the nearest wall. There had been bodies hidden in those streets and now the city seemed altered, distorted from the image he'd grown up with.

It would be light soon. The new day would look different too, he could already feel the shock of the news beginning to shift. Many things would feel raw then: murder, deceit and trying to understand how he'd lied to himself as effectively as they'd lied to him.

'I need to visit my grandmother.' The things he'd wanted to say to Sue needed to wait now. She reached for her jacket but he stopped her, 'Will you stay until I'm back?'

She smiled, tired and sad and relieved rolled into one. 'Absolutely.'

# FIFTY-EIGHT

**Three days later**

Two half-drunk mugs of coffee stood beside Marks. He pushed the last sheets of Addis's draft manuscript across to Goodhew. They'd read all the previous pages in two hours of heavy silence.

'He intended this to be separate from the rest,' Marks told him. 'To be used like a press release. The prosecution will love it. Unfortunately, so will the defence.'

One hundred years of grief. My methods will cause revulsion, I do understand that. But, by the time I have competed a ten-year study of my last subject's family – I estimate that it will be twelve years from now – I will be sixty-one. Not old, but without a career in front of me.

I won't have remarried or re-established contact with my children. Even if my daughters came to find me I would turn them away.

I will reveal the locations of the bodies at some point during that year, or perhaps the following year, in any case, as soon as my full notes have been written up, my research analysed. And then there will be the revulsion, the outcry and my arrest.

But ask yourself this; what can they really do to me? What can they take from me that will be less than I will have gained by doing this?

I do not approve of capital punishment but I'll admit this may be one of the rare cases where it might have acted as a deterrent; living to see the outcome was always more important to me than my freedom. One day I would have had to reveal myself in order to achieve publication and being alive to see my work flourish has always been in my plans. Part of my motivation has been in knowing that eventually the horror of what I've done will subside in some more educated scientific circles. There have been other studies of grief and families of the missing, but mine alone will have been taking place as the events unfold. It won't be a mere retrospective like the others.

10 families x 10 years. No other research of the subject can possibly be as unique and insightful. That could only happen if someone adopted my methods and expanded them, and how will that happen until they've been published?

Once I am put on trial my findings will appear as evidence, parts of them as public record.

And even after I am sentenced I know that it will also be in public record that my wife drove me down this road. She will feel guilt, she will be free but not unpunished and, yes, I do relish the thought. And the thought that she might one day contact me and apologize. I won't accept her apology any more than I would apologize to those families, because my research is more important, more influential to the understanding of all our grief.

And once it's written and I'm incarcerated, when then?

There will be some quiet months, longer possibly, where my brain will stagnate and the files lie unread. But I know they'll never go unread forever – can you imagine them sitting idly in a box somewhere just gathering dust when so much human life has been invested in every page?

Can you?

No, I don't think so either.


Goodhew set it to one side but he knew that some of the words would stay with him. And, after that, there was only a single sheet, deliberately formatted to make them stand out on the title page.

*No one understands grief as I do.*
*I have learnt how to control it, then magnify and prolong it.*
*Now it thrills me to be able to share my findings.*
*I dedicate my work to Teresa, whose choices made all this possible.*

'We found her and her children living under an assumed name. They also have enough to fill a book.' Marks drained his coffee cup. 'This is the kind of investigation where it feels good to be bowing out.'

'And then will you talk to me about my grandfather?'

'Of course. I know you need all the details, Gary, but now isn't the time.'

'I know.' Goodhew felt strangely at peace with the idea of waiting another week or two. He was already writing down notes about his grandfather's final days – small memories that were at risk of being lost or overwritten once other people began to talk. 'Will you miss being here, sir?'

'We spend our lives saying goodbye to people and places. This is a bigger jump and I do have mixed feelings, Gary, but I know it's the right time.'

They looked up as the door opened. Gully stepped inside and drew it closed behind her. 'A message from Kincaide, sir, the family has formally identified the final body.'

Marks stood wearily, 'There's never a final body, Sue, just the last one and the next one. Once you work that out you know it's time to leave.'

# EPILOGUE

**Two weeks later**

Ratty's funeral had been at 10 a.m. Early in the day, but Ratty wouldn't have cared, Goodhew was sure about that. Matthew Rizzo had given a short eulogy and Sam sat at the back with Mooch.

She'd waited outside for Goodhew. 'Remember what Ratty said about choices, how we always have them, even if they're crap.'

'Hobson's choice, this or none?'

'I've been offered accommodation, it's not crap and they take dogs. I don't want to end up like Ratty.'

There had been too much death and too many funerals in recent weeks. He and Sue had stopped long enough to drink a toast to Ratty, now they were in his grandfather's study and he was glad of her company. She was curled on the sofa, Goodhew sat on the floor, his back against his jukebox. The sound was turned down low and the valves in the BAL-AMi quietly hummed.

She was looking through his grandparents' photographs. He watched her turn the pages, stopping to study the white-edged snapshots from Hawaii to England.

'Someone can be right in front of you,' he began, 'might have been there for years. Then, suddenly, for no particular reason, the angle shifts and you see them differently. It's so clear that you wonder how it hadn't been obvious all along.'

'Your grandfather?'

'It's just an observation.'

'Well, it's the same picture, Gary, you're just seeing more of it.'

Goodhew had written down everything he could remember of the day his grandfather died, and in the last two weeks had found fragments of forgotten memories returning. He had enough to tell her now.

'I was called out of class and I knew something had to be wrong. I'd had a bad feeling that whole afternoon.' He looked at his hands, one already gripping the other.

'It was the last Thursday before the schools broke up for the summer. End of year tests were over and we weren't learning much, so I slipped out at morning break. It was easy then, not like now with locked gates and proper vigilance . . .' He closed his eyes and could smell the mown grass and hear the playground fading into the distance. 'I decided to visit my grandfather, he was always the best company . . . he had a library full of furniture; bookcases mainly and a bureau and desk with these incredibly deep drawers.' He smiled at the memory. 'I could look through those and find some random item or another, maybe just a pen or a matchbook, or something more obscure, like a shot glass or a playing card.' He unclenched his hands and held his left one flat, palm upwards. 'They were usually small enough to hold,' he said, 'and I'd ask him about it and he'd tell me a story.'

'What kind of story?'

'Usually a mystery of some kind, a missing person or an unsolved theft. He used to tell me they were all true. I was beyond the age of believing that but I loved hearing them anyway.'

Goodhew paused, his throat tightened and he took a few seconds before he spoke again. 'He was funny, used to say he'd done some outrageous things and never told me off if I skipped out of school now and then.'

'And that particular day?'

'I'd found a cufflink inside a cigar box. It was a very plain design. But it was gold and looked expensive, damaged too – something had left deep scrapes in the flat surface and the post was bent at a sharp angle. I handed it to him and he stared at it for a while with this smile

293

slowly spreading across his face. I really don't know if he was remembering it or making it up.

'"This cufflink vanished in a theft from a Mayfair mansion in 1948. Sixteen years later it turned up in a burnt-out car in Detroit. But it hadn't been the only thing stolen."'

His grandfather's stories often began with a dramatic opener. Until this last week he'd assumed they'd been the inspiration for his own need to uncover the details.

'Then part way through telling it we were interrupted by the phone, and when he answered I saw him look at me and frown. For one second I thought it was my mum, or the school, that I'd been rumbled. But almost instantly I could tell it was more than that. The front doorbell sounded as he hung up. He told me to be quiet. We were on the second floor but suddenly he didn't want me to say a word and he led me down to the floor below and pointed for me to hide under the bed.

'"Promise to stay there," he whispered.

'"Why?" I tried to make him answer me but he pressed his fingers to his lips and shook his head.

'"No matter what happens, do not come out."

'The bell rang again, buzzing more insistently. "Wait until they're both upstairs then go quietly back to school and say nothing. No matter what." He pushed me underneath. "It's the only way, you have to forget you were ever here."

'He shut the door behind him but within seconds of him letting them in downstairs they seemed to be throwing open every door in the house. There were two of them and I saw their shoes as they stood close to the bed. I pressed my face to the floor and covered my head so I wouldn't be tempted to look again. And when they reached the second floor I did what he said.'

Goodhew pressed his face into his hands, and blinked away the tears that burnt in his eyes. He opened the window to draw fresh air from Parker's Piece, then sat beside her on the settee.

'The last words I said to him were "I promise". And the last thing he said to me was that he loved me.'

'You're smiling.'

'It's a good memory and I'm glad to have it back.' Her eyes were bright, her gaze unwavering. 'Besides, I remembered something else he said.' Goodhew stroked her cheek, then pulled her closer and kissed her on the lips, softly at first, then more deeply as her arms wrapped around him.

# ACKNOWLEDGEMENTS

Firstly, a huge thank you to my ever supportive agent Broo Doherty and all at the DHH Literary Agency.

And to Krystyna Green, Grace Vincent, Amanda Keats and my copy-editor Charlotte Cole for their commitment to both Gary Goodhew and *The Promise*.

This book contains two very special cameos: Jean-Paul Hewlett appears in support of Gillian Foreman's fundraising for Marie Curie Cancer Care. And Tina Cooney, proof of the fun of serendipity.

Thank you to the following who have all helped: Lisa Sanford, Stella Etheredge, Kelly Kelday, James Linsell-Clark, Richard Reynolds, Genevieve Pease, Charlotte Hockin, John Mayes, Jenna Hawkins, Lisa Hall, Milo Rambles, Geo Edwards, Toppings of Ely and Ian (Happy-to-Help-but-Anonymity-is-Better). To the Royal Literary Fund for their continued support. To Dr William Holstein for his ever informative (and often entertaining) specialist advice. And, as always, to Christine Bartram and Claire Tombs who, for quite different reasons, deserve a permanent place in my acknowledgements.

Thanks to all the loyal readers who have waited a little longer for this one. Sometimes events overtake us in life but I really appreciate all the communication we've had about the Goodhew books over the last year. I'm on Twitter @Alison_Bruce.

Finally, and most importantly, I have to say a big thank you to my very supportive husband Jacen, Natalie, and (our own Team Bartowski) Lana and Dean who make our home a happy and creative place to be. xxxx

# The Soundtrack for *The Promise*

A picture may paint a thousand words but the power of music is equally potent. These are the songs I played and used as inspiration as I wrote *The Promise*. I have spent many hours with this playlist now and these songs will, to me at least, always be the soundtrack to this book. I hope you enjoy them.

The Angels Listened In – The Crests
Come What May – Clyde McPhatter
Crash – The Primitives
Gentle on My Mind – Dean Martin
I Fought the Law – The Bobby Fuller Four
I Wanna Be Sedated – The Ramones
King for Tonight – Billy Fury
Midnighter – The Champs
On My Own – Vince Vincent and the Villains
The Pall-Bearer's Song – The City Shakers
Short Shirt, Long Jacket (Instrumental) – Cake
The Worrying Kind – Tommy Sands

For more information please visit www.alisonbruce.com.